Devil's Chew Toy

Devil's Chew Toy

A Novel

ROB OSLER

CROOKED
LANE

NEW YORK

Published in the United States by Crooked Lane Books, an imprint of The Quick Brown Fox & Company LLC.

Crooked Lane Books and its logo are trademarks of The Quick Brown Fox & Company LLC.

Library of Congress Catalog-in-Publication data available upon request.

ISBN (hardcover): 978-1-64385-943-9
ISBN (ebook): 978-1-64385-944-6

Cover design by Meghan Deist

Printed in the United States.

www.crookedlanebooks.com

Crooked Lane Books
34 West 27th St., 10th Floor
New York, NY 10001

First Edition: February 2022

10 9 8 7 6 5 4 3 2 1

To Brian and all best friends,
who celebrate our best,
withstand our worst,
and are there for the in-between.

Chapter One
Man Down

Half opening my good eye, I squinted up at the fluorescent tube dangling from the stained popcorn ceiling. The club's manager had suggested the storeroom as a place for me to chill until my nose stopped bleeding. I appreciated the gesture. The idea was a win-win. It saved me from the pointing and whispers of the crowd, and getting me off the dance floor restored the party atmosphere typical of a weekend night at Hunters.

Despite the damage done to my face, the worst of the experience had been me being the center of attention for all the wrong reasons—embarrassing for most, excruciating for yours truly. Everyone who knew me would say I was quiet and reserved—perhaps to a fault. My latest ex had joked that my tolerance for thrill-seeking maxed out on the teacups ride at Disneyland. I'd brushed off the comment with a laugh, but in truth, the remark had stung. Being five foot four (rounding up) and weighing 125 (again, rounding up) makes one sensitive to such jabs. Add in the fact that I'm freckled and possess a shock of red-orange hair that that same ex had pegged as being the color of a Cheetos bag, and you understand why I might take offense.

"Damn, dude, you're going to have a nasty shiner. Does it hurt?"

The voice startled me. I hadn't heard anyone enter the storeroom.

"Yeah, a bit. Though it probably looks worse than it feels," I replied, trying to come off as tougher than I was.

The guy stepped closer to my impromptu bed of liquor crates. It was the dancer. *The* dancer who had accidentally kicked me in the face. He leaned over me, momentarily blocking the harsh light, made a soft whistle.

"Ugly."

"You really know how to flatter a guy," I said, propping myself up on my elbows. He laughed, reached down a hand with the letters *X.O.X.O.* inked across the knuckles. "I'm Camilo."

"Hayden. Good to meet you, Camilo."

I had only ever seen Camilo up on stage. Now at ground level, he appeared to be taller than me by a good eight inches. I'd say he was about six feet.

"Be back in a minute," he said. "Just need to tell Hank I'm headed out for the night."

Camilo's sneakers thumped across the concrete floor. Earlier, I'd noticed his shoes had no laces; the tongues of his shiny red high-tops had flapped wildly as he'd bounced across the plywood-covered pool table. Tonight wouldn't be the first night I went home alone feeling sorry for myself. Though I had elevated my game considerably: I'd be returning to my apartment bruised and bloodied. Still, I could use the evening's main event as material for a new post for *Mates on Dates*, where I took on topics related to the perplexing and often disheartening world of gay dating. I'd been toying with the notion of a humorous piece, and if I couldn't squeeze a laugh out of this, then I should hang up my blog. Suddenly a moment of inspiration struck with the title "Go-go Boy Misfire."

Camilo burst back into the storeroom. "Feel good enough to stand?"

"Yeah, we have achieved coagulation." I flashed an enthusiastic thumbs-up.

"Say what?"

"I'm good."

Camilo gripped my arm and pulled me upright. The sudden action made me feel as though a dimmer switch in my head had been lowered.

"You okay?" Camilo had noticed the flickering of my eyelids. "You look a little pale, and for you, that's saying something." He grinned to ensure I knew he was joking.

"Thanks, yeah. I just need a second or two."

"Take as long as you need. Don't need you down for the count a second time."

I nodded, then slowly tried getting up again. Feeling all right, I swung my legs over a crate of Cuervo and made a little hop down to the ground.

Camilo shook his head. "Nothing like that has ever happened before. I mean, not even close."

"Believe it or not, that was the first time I'd ever tipped a dancer." Realizing the inaccuracy in my recounting, I added, "Or tried to."

"Seriously? Talk about bad luck."

"Bad timing."

"Yeah, well, still my bad."

I liked this Camilo. It's not every day you meet a guy who is both superhot and genuinely nice. From the moment he had taken the stage, I'd been mesmerized. Sure, he was out of my league, but still, a guy can dream. Tall but not too tall, muscled, brown skin. His few tats here and there—a pretty, long-haired Latina woman on his shoulder; the word *Familia* in an elaborate script running down his rib cage—were enough to convey a certain edge without being too much of a statement.

"So, my place?" Camilo asked, reaching for his gym bag.

"Sorry? What?" Had he just invited me over? It wasn't that I totally lacked confidence in my looks. There were guys out there who went for my type: clean-cut, fit, with a straight-off-the-tractor look. I just didn't think Camilo was one of them. And let's be honest, there are different levels of good-looking. On a good day, just after a haircut and wearing my favorite Nadal-style sleeveless shirt, I would give myself a 7.3—the three-tenths thanks to my mother's insistence on braces when I was in junior high. On the other hand, Camilo, sweaty and spent from three hours on top of a pool table (and illuminated by the least flattering light possible), was still a solid 9.2.

Camilo wrestled on a pair of baggy gray sweatpants over his red high-tops, up his defined quads, and over a red jockstrap. Registering my nonreply, he looked up. "Is there a problem? You don't want to come over?"

"No, no," I sputtered. "It's just that I wasn't expecting—"

"How old are you, anyway? If you don't mind me asking."

The question caught me off guard. Yes, I looked young for my age—I reflexively reached for my ID whenever approaching the person working a club's front door or buying a six-pack of lager at the store. Still, it was an odd thing to ask, and I had to wonder for a moment if there was a right and a wrong answer.

"I mean, you're legal, right?"

"I'm twenty-five," I replied with a curt tone, before considering what message that might send.

"Hey, me too," Camilo said, smiling as if someone had just slipped a twenty under his elastic waistband. "Taurus."

It took me a moment, but then I replied, "Cancer."

"Ahhhh." Camilo's drawn-out reply said interesting information had been conveyed, though, as I didn't follow zodiac signs, I hadn't a clue what that might be.

"You want to ride with me? Or follow in your car?" He hoisted his backpack over a shoulder, which drew my attention to the charcoal-like etching of the Latina, her long black hair wrapping around his lump of bicep.

"I'll take the ride, since you're offering."

We walked side by side to the back door of the club. The cool evening breeze slid through the doorway and soothed my swollen eye.

"Sweet, isn't she?" Camilo pointed toward the parking space next to the dumpsters. The large pickup truck was easy to spot—its color was a close match to his jockstrap and high-tops. The apparent fact that red was Camilo's favorite color boded well, me being a ginger and all.

Camilo tipped back his head and breathed in deeply through his nose. "Nice night! I love summer." He draped a lazy arm around me in a casual bro sort of way. "Again, buddy, sorry about what happened in there. Glad you're all right, though. And hey, the night is young. We'll see what we can do to make it up to you." He added a mischievous wink.

My experience with hot guys—usually limited to ogling them from across the room—was that they inevitably turned out to be a-holes. That disappointing observation had been the subject of a blog post titled "Why Are Some Guys Too Hot to Deny?" in which I'd laid the blame at the feet of their followers, who seemed to give them a blank check for having bad attitudes. Now, admiring Camilo from the corner of my eye, I realized my criticism had been too comprehensive.

"You don't have a car here?" Camilo asked.

"Out front. But I'd just as soon ride with you, if you're cool with that."

Camilo shrugged. "Works for me."

The car I'd driven to the club was backed into a parking space at the farthest and darkest end of the lot. I didn't want anyone inside Hunters—or anywhere else, for that matter—to associate me with the white Prius, adorned with no less than a dozen bumper stickers proclaiming the fervent evangelical beliefs of its owner. The most cringeworthy of the decals being *Cometh the rapture, this car will be driverless*. While my Fiesta was in the shop, and having no other way to get from my apartment in West Seattle to my job teaching eighth-grade social studies in Federal Way, I'd accepted the offer to borrow my aunt Sally's car while she was visiting my grandparents in Palm Springs.

As we approached Camilo's truck, he surprised me by walking to the passenger side and opening the door for me. Whether he did so because of my somewhat shaky state or his natural inclination to be gentlemanly, I didn't care. I felt like the homecoming queen being whisked away to a private outlook by the captain of the football team.

The cab's interior was immaculately clean and smelled so new I was surprised the F-150 already had plates. I logged the finding of cleanliness with pleasure. While I could deal with another guy being messy—clothes on the floor, an unmade bed, a cluttered desk—a tub that hadn't been scrubbed for weeks was a deal-breaker.

Camilo fired up the engine, switched on the stereo, and started singing along to a twangy male voice spilling from the speakers.

"The easiest thing for me is falling hard for you."

Camilo's dancing talent and looks hadn't prepared me for his lack of vocal ability. The guy was a horrible singer. He wasn't just flat; he was so far off hitting the notes that I thought he was screwing around. But his genuine enthusiasm told the truth: he was utterly tone-deaf. I twisted my grimace into a smile just as he looked over at me.

"You like this song?" he asked. "Stanley Kellogg. His new album's dope."

"Sorry, I don't follow country."

"No? Like, not at all?"

"Pretty much, yeah."

"What do you listen to then?"

"Podcasts mostly." As soon as the words left my lips, I wanted to reel them back. I wanted Camilo to like me, and so far, I knew he was an amazing dancer and that nothing on his "likes" list—red, high-tops, trucks, and country music—suggested "podcast enthusiast."

"Right, those can be cool, I guess." His tone was less than convincing.

I shuffled topics in my head, hunting for possible common interests. Before I could shift the conversation, he said, "So . . . like what sort of podcasts?"

Deciding to be vague in the hope he'd lose interest, I said, "Oh, you know, NPR programs. That sort of thing."

"NPR? Oh, right! National Pro Rodeo." Camilo looked over, his eyes bright with delight. "I wouldn't have guessed you were into that."

My mind raced. The last thing I wanted was to blow the moment, and I most definitely didn't want Camilo to feel stupid, but really, what could I say?

Camilo erupted into laughter. "Oh my God, Hayden, if you could see your face! I'm just messing with you, man. I know what NPR is." He produced a gigantic grin. "I may dance on a pool table and drive a truck, but that doesn't mean I'm a clueless hick."

Busted. "Um. Sorry, I didn't mean—"

"Seriously, no worries, man. I lured you into that one."

Again trying for a safe topic, I said, "So you live in Columbia City?"

"Yeah. It's convenient for school and the club. I'm just renting, of course. This area used to be one of the more affordable neighborhoods in Seattle, but not anymore. I'm saving up. One day I hope to buy something. I need space, though. A big yard. Even better, several acres." He steered the truck into the driveway of a modest one-story bungalow. "But for now, this is it. Home sweet home."

Camilo's place was nicer than I had imagined for a part-time dancer/student. The exterior of the small house was in good shape and painted a pleasing shade of green. A porch light spilled golden light across a row of red geraniums, which filled two window boxes on either side of the arched wooden door. I followed Camilo up the short sidewalk to the front steps, my nose registering the unmistakable fresh-cut-grass smell—a minor miracle given all the dried blood clogging my nasal passages.

Camilo pulled open the screen door, which welcomed us with a sustained high-pitched squeak. Swiveling his head back to me, he said, "Oh, meant to tell you: I've got a roomie, but he's harmless. Mostly."

My heart sank. I was nervous enough without the added awkwardness of being introduced as "a friend," one with a black eye and blood on his shirt.

The home's interior, though sparsely furnished, was in keeping with the exterior: clean and orderly. A standing coatrack held various jackets, ball caps, and a sleek red bike helmet; a few black-and-white photographs of nature scenes featuring expansive vistas hung on the white walls. Somebody had arranged a half dozen textbooks on the coffee table in two neat stacks. Taking a cue from the lineup of trainers, boots, and sandals that hugged the baseboard just inside the door, I kicked off my white sneakers.

From the hallway, a medium-size dog bolted into the living room, his toenails making a series of rapid-fire clicks on the hardwood floor as he raced across the room, bound straight for Camilo.

"Commander! Hey, buddy, did you miss me?" Camilo scooped up the dog and allowed the mutt to get in a few licks to his chin before returning him to the floor. "Hope you don't mind dogs. I did you warn you, though."

Reading the confusion on my face, he explained, "Commander's my roommate."

The truth was, I did like dogs. But at that moment, I'd never loved a dog more. I knelt and gave Commander a scratch behind his black pointed ears, the only parts of him that weren't white. "What kind is he?" I asked, noting the unusual collar around Commander's thick neck: a miniature version of the traditional collars worn by Saint Bernards—the type featuring a brandy barrel.

"He's a bull terrier."

"Not your everyday breed."

"I know, right? My friend says he has swag. I fell for him the moment I saw him."

"How long have you had him?"

"Just over a year. Commander thinks he owns the place."

I nodded. "Hence the name."

"Exactly." Camilo clapped me on the back. "Anyway, have a seat, Hayden. Make yourself comfortable." He nodded toward a low, dark-green sofa that faced a large television. "Get you anything? Water? Red Bull? OJ?"

"Just water, thanks. I won't say no to some ibuprofen either, if you've got it."

"Between CrossFit and working at the club, I practically live on the stuff. Anyway, pretty sure I've got an ice pack in the fridge, too, if you want it."

"Sounds good, thanks."

Camilo returned from the kitchen balancing two glasses, a pill bottle, and a blue rubber ice pack. "Would you believe this is like the third time this week that a date started with these same supplies?"

I sputtered a laugh before wondering if he might be even a little bit serious.

Instead of joining me on the sofa, Camilo tilted his head toward the hallway. "I'm beat. You coming?"

My knees quivered as I got to my feet. Despite my desire to sprint into the bedroom, I measured my steps, not wanting to appear too eager, too desperate. The speakers on the dresser sounded the soft return of Stanley Kellogg: *Because the easiest thing I've done is falling hard for you.*

Camilo started singing along. Commander cocked his head, whimpered. I gave the dog a commiserating glance as Camilo slipped off his sweats and tank top. He swiped his phone, set it on the nightstand. Doing my part, I yanked off my T-shirt and cargo shorts with such excitement I nearly lost my balance.

As Camilo mercifully stopped singing and pulled me onto the bed, the improbable night delivered one last surprise.

"There is something you should know," Camilo said as he propped himself up on an elbow, his expression suddenly serious. "So you don't get the wrong idea . . ."

My throat went dry. I'd heard this same preamble before—the last time it had ended in the word *girlfriend*.

Camilo grinned. "I generally just cuddle on a first date. I hope you're okay with that."

And with those words, what I thought I'd wanted most was replaced by something altogether better.

Chapter Two
Morning After

I awoke to the low rhythmic hum of snoring. I blinked and pried my eyes open as my brain tumbled over the past several hours, searching for an answer to where I was and what had brought me to these unfamiliar surroundings. In the next instant, everything snapped into place. Impossible as it seemed, I was in Camilo's bed, my legs tangled in a sheet. As I turned my head, a pain shot up my neck, the result of sleeping on a too-soft pillow.

Commander lay curled in a ball at the foot of the bed, snoring peacefully. I blinked. Blinked again. Sat up. Camilo wasn't there. Listening carefully, I tried to detect any sounds coming from other parts of the house. There were none. Had Camilo moved to the sofa? I didn't think I snored, and hogging the covers was hardly an issue in the middle of summer. Perhaps he was just an early riser and had slipped out of bed, not wanting to wake me?

After unwinding myself from the bedsheet, I found my shorts on the floor and stepped into the hallway. The unsettling silence seemed to ask for slow, cautious movement. The bathroom was vacant; the open door suggested as much. Surprising, however, was the empty living room. That left one possibility. An uneasy feeling wriggled up my spine as I stepped into the kitchen. There was no sign of Camilo.

Yap!

I jumped and spun around. Commander had quietly followed me and now stood before his food bowl.

Yap!

"Seriously, boy. You scared the crap out of me." I knelt and gave him a scratch behind the ears. "What? Is it time for your breakfast?"

Yap!

"Stupid question, I know. But I think your owner should tend to that. The only problem is, I don't know where he is. Do you, boy? Any idea where Camilo has gone?"

Suddenly there was pounding on the front door. I jumped and turned toward the living room. Despite it being just after eight o'clock on a Saturday morning, whoever was on the other side of the door wasn't worried about waking anyone up.

I pressed my good eye to the peephole. *What the—?*

There was another knock, louder, insistent.

I unbolted the door and cracked it open a few inches, revealing a narrow sliver of my face to the two police officers standing on the front porch. "Hello," I croaked.

The female cop said, "Good morning, sir. Are you Camilo Rodriguez?"

"Um. No. I'm a . . . I'm just a friend." As disturbed as I was by the presence of Seattle's Finest, her question threw me. I looked as much like a Camilo Rodriquez as I did a LeBron James.

"And you are?"

"Sorry?"

"Who are you? What's your name, sir?"

"Hayden McCall."

"Would you mind asking Mr. Rodriguez to come to the door, please?"

"Mr. Rodriguez?" My nerves turned the answer into a question of its own.

The female cop sighed. "Yes, Mr. Rodriguez. We'd like to talk to him. Now, if you don't mind."

I looked back over my shoulder, hoping that by some miracle Camilo had suddenly materialized. Seeing only Commander pouting at the kitchen doorway, I turned to the officers. "I'm sorry, but Camilo doesn't seem to be home at the moment."

The male cop entered the conversation. "He doesn't *seem* to be? Or he isn't?" I didn't appreciate his snarky tone. I decided he was a bully or a jerk. Quite possibly both.

I swallowed hard, my mouth dry as a sauna. "I'm afraid Camilo isn't here."

"Do you know where he is?" The female cop's voice had a hint of irritation, as if she'd had to ask the same question too many times.

"I don't know," I replied, trying my best to come across as casual and unruffled when in fact the combination of Camilo's absence and the police's visit had me freaked out.

"When did he leave?" she asked.

"I don't know."

"When did you last see him?"

"Um . . . I think we fell asleep around two."

The male cop shifted his weight, stood taller. "We?"

Oh boy. I felt my knees starting to shake. "Yes, that's right. Camilo and me."

The female cop continued, "So you went to sleep around two o'clock this morning and haven't seen Camilo since, and you have no idea of his whereabouts? Do I have that right?"

I nodded. "Uh-huh."

The male cop opened the screen door. "Mind if we step inside, sir?"

"I, uh . . . yeah, sure, okay. Mind telling me what this is about?"

"How about we do that inside, sir?" he said.

I swung the door wide. They stepped inside. The look on the female cop's face changed, signaling something amiss. She glanced at her partner, then turned back to me. "You might want to put on a shirt, sir?"

I looked down, remembered I had on only my cargo shorts. "Oh, sorry. I'll be right back." Leaving the two cops standing in the living room, I felt their eyes roll as they watched me jog toward the hallway. In the bedroom mirror, I checked my hair, which was disheveled under the best of circumstances. *Ay caramba!* My stomach dropped. My black eye. No wonder they'd given me those weird looks. I scrambled for my shirt on the floor. My shorts were fine, but I couldn't stroll into the living room wearing a bloodstained shirt. I traded mine for Camilo's red tank top.

Back in the living room, I tried hard to smooth the quiver in my voice. "So, Officers—"

The woman cop cut me off. "May we sit, sir?"

"Yes, yes, of course, please." I made a grand sweep of my arm toward the furniture before realizing the gesture was overdone.

The two cops settled on the green sofa. I lowered myself onto the room's single armchair, a simple straight-backed design that imposed upright posture, suitable for the moment.

The male cop reached inside the back pocket of his navy-blue trousers, retrieved a small notebook, and flipped it open. "When did you first notice that Mr. Rodriguez wasn't here?" He pulled a pen from his shirt pocket, clicked its end. "What time?" The pen hovered in anticipation above an empty white page.

"Just now. I woke up. Camilo wasn't in bed. I looked in the other rooms, but he isn't here. Then you knocked on the door."

"You were saying you're a houseguest of Camilo's?" the female cop said.

"Any idea where we might find him?" the male cop added.

"I don't know . . . I don't know him well enough to know where he might be."

"No idea at all?" The male cop's tone was incredulous. "But you slept here last night, and now here you are, alone in his house?"

The female cop jumped in. "How well do you know Camilo?"

The blood drained from my face. "Not well. We just met last night."

"Let me get this straight." The male cop lowered his note-book to his knee as if it were in the way of him making himself clear. "You met Camilo last night, you came home with him, woke up, and"—he snapped his fingers—"just like that, he's gone. No idea when he left? Or where he went? Or why he might have left?"

"Yes, that's right."

"What's that?"

"Yes, that's right," I said, louder than intended.

The female cop, steady as ever, said, "Camilo left you alone in his house, but you had only just met. You are more or less strangers to one another. So why would he do that, do you think? Leave a stranger alone in his house?"

"I don't know." I dropped my head and drew a deep breath. "None of this makes any sense."

"Where did you meet Camilo?" the female cop asked.

"At Hunters. The dance club on Capitol Hill. Camilo works there. He's a go-go boy."

The male cop looked up from his notebook. "*Go-go boy?*"

I nodded. "It's from the French, *à gogo*, meaning in abundance." (Thanks here to Mrs. Gasquet, my high school French teacher.)

He scowled. "I was asking about the boy part."

"Some gay bars pay hot guys to dance. They're usually shirtless and wear tiny shorts or jockstraps. They're called go-go boys."

I shifted in my seat, seeking an escape that would come only if the chair had a trapdoor. There was no way to avoid the truth: Camilo had seemed like a decent guy, but what did I know about him?

After taking another deep breath, I told the cops just that. When I'd finished, the two officers glanced at each other, sharing the type of look I had seen on countless crime shows: *can this guy really be so stupid?* Had they asked me to weigh in with an opinion, I'd have done myself no favors.

The female cop leaned forward, signaling that her next question was of utmost importance. "You're sure that's all we might want to know? Think carefully, sir. There is nothing else relevant here? Nothing else happened last night between you and Camilo?"

I looked at the female cop, searching her face for a clue. Finding only a stoic stare, I shifted to the male cop, who winked, providing the hint I needed.

"Oh . . ." Like a comedian laughing at his own bad joke, I chuckled. "You're probably wondering about my eye."

"You fought with Camilo?" The female cop nodded her head to suggest she already knew the truth and wouldn't it be easier if I just agreed with her. "Why don't you tell us about that?"

I absolutely, positively did not want to tell them about that. Explaining the reason for my being in Camilo's home was embarrassing enough. But so far I'd told the truth, and because of that, I hoped the cops would believe me. Besides, young people meeting at a club was hardly an unprecedented event. But explaining how I'd gotten the black eye was a story even I found hard to believe. Still, it was the truth. And so I began.

"Like I was saying, Camilo dances at Hunters. I thought he was hot, so I decided I would, you know, tip him."

The male cop looked mildly disgusted. "Tip him?"

"Yeah, like a stripper. Just that go-go boys don't strip, you know, all the way. They don't get naked. They just dance. But you tip them just the same by slipping bills in their under-wear." I paused to make sure the officers were following the story so far. When the female cop nodded, I continued. "So I was right up next to the pool table as Camilo was heading in my direction. Just as he reached the end of the stage where I was standing, the music suddenly stopped. Camilo dropped to a squatting position right in front of my face. I reached toward him. Then *bam!* The music was back on. Gaga at top volume. Camilo sprang into the air but lost his balance. He fell backward. His right leg shot out from under him, and—"

"You can't be serious." The female cop dropped her just-the-facts demeanor.

"Size twelve, right in the face," I said. "It all happened so fast; I had no time to get out of the way."

The smirk on the male cop's face had grown to a wide grin. He started to shake, holding back laughter. The female cop, meanwhile, stared at me wide-eyed. "I take it people would have seen this? Just as you describe it?"

I sighed. "More than I care to think about. Dozens at least. Camilo felt bad about the whole thing. It was the freakest of freak accidents. Anyway, afterward, he invited me here. But I already told you that part. Then, as I say, when I woke up, just minutes before you knocked on the door, I realized he wasn't here. And honest to God, that's all I know. So what's happened? Why are you here? Is Camilo all right?"

The male cop took over. He was no longer amused. "Earlier this morning, we received a report of an unoccupied vehicle, its motor running and a door open, in an empty parking lot. That vehicle was a new-model Ford F-150 pickup truck registered to Camilo Rodriguez at this address. When we arrived, the truck was there as reported, but there was no sign of Mr. Rodriguez."

Yap!

"Not now, Commander," I scolded.

Yap!

"You mind doing something about your dog?" The male cop scowled.

"He's not mine. He's Camilo's."

Yap!

"Then do you mind doing something about *Camilo's* dog?"

"Sorry, Officer, I think it's time to feed him."

Yap!

"Commander, no!" I shouted.

The male officer curtly waved a hand in the air. "Then go feed him, will you? And be quick about it."

I looked at the female cop. She gave an abrupt tilt of her head toward the kitchen. I hurried from the room and found a bin of kibble by the back door. With a trembling hand, I scooped breakfast into Commander's bowl and whispered, "Your master has a lot of explaining to do. I mean, a lot."

The cops switched gears and peppered me with questions about myself. My answers in order were *West Seattle apartment, live alone, eighth-grade social studies teacher, Federal Way Unified,* and *only Aunt Sally, who lives in Ballard but is currently visiting my grandparents in California.* Satisfied that I wasn't a squatter who'd broken in, they shifted back to Camilo, specifically to the topic of his temperament: how had he seemed? Had he been agitated or frightened? Happy or sad? Sticking with the truth, I told them that he'd been upbeat and had given no signs whatsoever of being bothered by anything. They asked about relatives, but of course I knew nothing about his family. Did I have his phone number? You'd have thought I would, but an exchange of digits commonly happened just before two people parted ways; when one of them quietly slips out of bed and disappears into the night, you kind of miss your chance. (I winced, realizing this awkward event had happened to me once before, though the bed partner and circumstances—a closeted Mormon boy who'd sneaked out of his parents' house—couldn't have been more different.) My physical description of Camilo was the only information I provided that seemed to satisfy the police.

As there was no reason to believe Camilo was in danger or a danger to himself, they weren't yet treating his disappearance as a missing-person case. They assured me that Camilo would turn up on his own. As for Camilo's truck, the police had impounded it.

With that, the female cop handed me a card with her name, Anoushka Anand, and a number to call. She followed her partner out the door; their heavy black boots clomped down the steps. As the officers opened the doors to their patrol car, I shouted the question that had been thrumming in my brain throughout their visit: "What happens if Camilo doesn't come home?"

Officer Anand shouted back, "Let's just hope it doesn't come to that."

Chapter Three
A Nice Find

Pulling my phone from the pocket of my cargo shorts, I checked the time: 11:25 AM. Still no sign of Camilo. I peered through the living room window, desperate to see him walking up the sidewalk, but my Spidey sense told me he wasn't coming back anytime soon. Terrible crimes were reported each day in the news, but it was easy to tune them out when they happened to strangers. But this wasn't other people. I was the last person to have seen Camilo before he went missing. There could be no shrugging off his disappearance. My life was now entangled with his.

In the bedroom, I traded the XL tank for my T-shirt. Returning to the living room, I heard an odd trickling, like a tap had been left running. Following the source of the sound, my eyes landed on Commander, his back leg lifted, pissing into the shoes I had left by the front door.

"No!" I leaped toward the dog.

Commander stood his ground, finishing his business. Despite my anger, I realized the dog hadn't been let outside for several hours and couldn't hold it forever. But in my shoes? I mean, c'mon, that was just spite.

As I scrubbed my sneakers in the kitchen sink, I pondered what to do with the dog. As long as Camilo returned, there would be no issue. But if he didn't, who would care for him? Once again, I considered how little I knew about the go-go boy from Hunters. I didn't know any of his friends or if he had any family to contact. Without any names or numbers, I was stuck. Surely there must be some scrap of paper, random document, something lying around that might suggest someone to call.

Twenty minutes of searching produced nothing. Well, almost nothing. I did find a photograph of a teenage Camilo and three people who I guessed were his sister and parents. Had it been that long since the family had taken a photo together?

I came to appreciate that Camilo ran a tight ship. Nothing other than the bedding was out of place. All evidence conveyed discipline, from the neatly arranged kitchen cabinets to the clothing precisely hung in the closet, each hanger facing the same direction. A quick perusal of the chest of drawers revealed the same attention to order: T-shirts folded, socks paired, and red briefs carefully stacked.

Knowing of no one to contact, I fell back on the hope, albeit increasingly unlikely, that Camilo would soon show up. As I laced up my wet sneakers, I noticed Commander staring longingly at the leash looped over the coatrack. There'd be no convincing me that he had to go out for number one, but number two? Seeing he had my attention, he whimpered and performed an excited pirouette in front of the door.

"All right, all right. But be quick about it, will you?"

The dog and I roamed slowly around the tiny backyard. A small black portable grill was sitting between two worn wooden Adirondack chairs, and leaning against the back fence was a bicycle. Since I remembered the bike helmet hanging inside the house, discovering a bike shouldn't have been a surprise. But the helmet had suggested a particular type of bicycle: something swift—a sleek frame with thin tires and a dozen speeds. What rested against the fence had a woven wicker basket and rainbow streamers hanging from the handle grips. It was a small red girl's bike. I squeezed the fat white-wall tires. I'd planned to walk back to Hunters, where I'd left my aunt's car, but the bike would cut the travel time considerably.

With Commander back inside the house, I left a note for Camilo with my cell number and a message saying it was urgent that he call me and the police the second he got home. I placed the note alongside Officer Anand's card on the kitchen table next to his laptop. After wheeling the bicycle through the backyard gate and out to the street, I sat my butt down on the sparkly red-flecked banana seat. The brisk morning air was invigorating, and as I pedaled faster, the bike's streamers fluttered in the breeze. I felt more optimistic. Maybe the situation wasn't as bad as it seemed. Perhaps I had fallen into my default setting of assuming the worst. Maybe, just maybe, everything would turn out all right.

Chapter Four

Upside Down

Noon and still no word from Camilo. Could he have made it home and not phoned me? There was only one way to know, and I was too worried to sit around, do nothing. I needed to return the bicycle anyway. And there was the issue of Commander. I had two options, neither of which I liked. I could either take him to an animal shelter or bring him home to my small West Seattle studio apartment. I hated the idea of a shelter, caging the already frightened dog in a strange place filled with a cacophony of barking. But my lease didn't allow pets; I couldn't risk eviction, no matter how much the dog tugged at my heart.

Falling back on my bed, I stared at the ceiling and dragged my thoughts across the past eighteen hours that had culminated in this totally effed situation.

What had started as a typical night out had changed the moment I stood in line at the bar and exchanged the ten in my wallet for singles to tip the dancer. For some guys, slipping a bill beneath a stranger's waistband took no more thought than ordering a drink. But that was not me. By tipping the dancer, I knew, I would call attention to myself, not only from him but from the surrounding crowd. Ridiculous? One thousand percent. Who cared? Absolutely no one. And still. What was wrong with me? I wasn't so embarrassingly timid in all situations. Standing in front of my classroom, I felt confident. Granted, they were junior high school students, so I had the advantage of age and positional authority, but they could be cruel jerks at times, and yet I managed to hold it together. Dates were another situation in which I felt more or less comfortable—depending on the other guy, of course.

Perhaps there was something about gaining the attention of a crowd of strangers that weirded me out.

Before my mom got sick, she'd taken me to a comedy show. It had been my sixteenth birthday, and she'd thought it would be "a fun change of pace." My mom loved a good change of pace. She had sprung for two first-row tickets, and when one of the comedians reached the audience-participation bit of his set, he plucked me from the audience. The comic asked me to read scripted lines on note cards to play the part of his wife. Standing up on stage, reading lines written for a woman, was humiliating. To be fair, the guy couldn't have known I was smack-dab in the middle of coming to terms with being gay. I was an emotional mess—hence my mom's idea for a night of comedy. After delivering a line about my new dress that drew the biggest laugh of the night, I reacted the only way I could. I ran off the stage.

Had the experience scarred me? I couldn't clap along at a concert without feeling a crippling self-consciousness, so I suppose there's the answer.

Thirty minutes later I pulled into the empty driveway at Camilo's rental house. After shutting off the engine, I sat for a moment in silence. Each minute that passed reduced the odds that Camilo was okay and this would turn out to be some crazy, harmless event. I mean, really—he had slipped out of bed in the wee hours of the morning and driven to some empty parking lot. Unless he'd been the victim of a random act of violence, he was mixed up in some bad business. I'd already been interviewed by the police. What did that say? I had no business getting involved—well, further involved. I should turn the car around and not look back. I could follow events as they unfolded on social media or the local news.

There was only one problem with that plan: Camilo's dog was inside the house.

Despite my better judgment, I pushed open the front door.

"Oh my God!" My head snapped right, then left, then back again. Someone had torn the living room apart. Cushions had been ripped from the sofa, releasing swollen chunks of foam rubber. A lamp lay broken, its bulbs shattered, and books were scattered across the carpet.

I ran into the adjoining kitchen and flipped on the overhead light. Cupboards hung open. Boxes of cereal and energy bars and plastic jars of peanut butter and vitamin supplements littered the countertop and floor. The refrigerator door cast its dim light on tipped cartons of chocolate milk and orange juice, their contents dripping from shelf to shelf and forming a sticky pool on the bright-yellow linoleum. Only the kitchen table was free of debris: a clear space the size of a place mat was bookended by a computer charger and a Keith Haring mouse pad. The laptop that had been there earlier was gone.

I moved to the bedroom, tripped on a pair of cowboy boots, and stumbled forward onto a bike shoe. Like the rest of the house, the room was a total disaster. Whoever was responsible had pillaged the closet and yanked drawers from the dresser. Clothes were strewn across the floor. I stood in the middle of the mess, holding the sides of my head, trying hard not to freak out. Then it hit me: Commander. Where was the dog? Given the number someone had done on the house, the noise would have scared him to death.

"Commander! Come here, boy! It's okay. You can come out. Commander? C'mon, boy."

Something made a sound under the bed. I lay flat on my stomach and peered into the low, dark cavern beneath the box spring. Two small circles met my eyes. Commander had tucked himself beneath the center of the bed and against the wall that met the headboard.

"Hey, buddy." I tried my most soothing voice. "It's okay. You can come out. I won't hurt you."

Commander blinked but otherwise didn't budge. I attempted coaxing the dog out for another few minutes before realizing I needed a different strategy. Remembering Commander's persistent protest for food earlier in the day, I went to the kitchen, filled the dog bowl with kibble, and returned to my position beside the bed. I shook the contents of the bowl, making a rattling sound. "C'mon, Commander. Mmm. Come and get it."

Again my efforts were met only with blinking eyes. I left the bowl sitting there and went to the kitchen. There could be no putting off what I had to do next.

"Officer Anand," she said, answering the call.

"Hello, Officer, this is Hayden McCall."

"Yes, Mr. McCall. If you're wondering about your friend, I'm sorry, but there is no new information."

"Um, yeah, well, that's why I'm calling."

Chapter Five
Good Cop, Bad Cop, Hot Cop

As the day slipped from afternoon to evening, the temperature started to back off from the day's high, eighty-eight degrees, which was warmer than average for a Seattle day in July. Officer Anand had told me to touch nothing and leave the house immediately. I was to wait in my car until the police arrived. When I'd asked when that might be, the answer had been abrupt: "Wait in your car. And don't leave."

An hour later, my apprehension had turned to impatience. My thoughts about Commander and whether he might need to pee had proven the power of suggestion. Given the way events had gone so far, I didn't dare go back inside to use the bathroom—the minute I did, the cops were likely to show up. And yet, when the police did finally arrive, they weren't likely to let me back inside the house. I had to act; nature was calling loudly.

Scanning the backyard for a private spot, I ruled out a too thinly branched azalea, opting for the backside of a large cedar tree. I unzipped and aimed into a nearby shrub, feeling an immense flood of relief. My gaze strayed right, then left, examining the surrounding ferns, the tips of their fronds browned by the indiscriminate summer sun. My eyes landed on an unusual cluster of stones beneath the largest fern. Had I not been looking so closely at that precise spot, I would never have seen the small formation that appeared to mark the burial place of a once-loved pet. Had the animal belonged to some previous renter or to Camilo? I hoped the latter was the case, not because I wished Camilo any loss but because the care shown in the display reflected well on whoever had created the peaceful resting place.

The sudden arrival of loud voices refocused my attention. Unless the neighbors had thrown together an impromptu block party, the cops had just arrived. I zipped up and hurried across the backyard toward the gate leading to the front of the house.

Officer Anand stood in the middle of the sidewalk. She must have heard me open the gate, as she was staring right at me. Her partner, Officer Charm, shouted from where he stood on the front porch, "You were told to wait in the car."

"I thought I heard something back there," I lied. As ridiculous a worry as it was, I didn't want the cops thinking I was the sort of person who took whizzes in other people's yards.

"I explicitly told you to wait in the car," Officer Anand said, as if I hadn't heard her partner.

I raised my hands in mock surrender. "I came outside right after we talked on the phone. I haven't been inside since." As a schoolteacher, I was well acquainted with the ploy of redirecting attention from the thing you'd done wrong to the thing you'd done right—my eighth-grade students attempted this trick countless times daily.

"And?" the male cop said. His aggressive tone startled me; I didn't understand the question. I looked at Officer Anand for help.

"And?" she echoed. "Did you see anything in the backyard or not?"

"Oh, it was nothing." I gave the air a casual wave. "Just two cranky cats in a neighborhood dispute."

Officer Anand shook her head. "Wait out here."

She followed her partner into the house. They were back outside in less than five minutes. The male cop marched to the patrol car, snatched up the radio, and started a conversation with someone on the other end of the line. Officer Anand barreled across the lawn in my direction. I could tell by her expression that she had a fresh set of questions.

I explained when I'd left the house after the earlier visit by her and her partner, why and when I'd returned, where I had been inside, what I'd touched, and for how long I'd been inside. I pointed out that Commander was still likely to be hiding under the bed and told her that, since Camilo was still missing, I'd like to take him home with me. I didn't want the headache of caring for a dog, and yet I was relieved to hear her say she didn't think that would be a problem—though, with or without Commander, it would be a while before I'd be going anywhere. Office Anand had summoned detectives, and they wanted to talk to me.

* * *

Thanks to the leading-man looks of one of the detectives, the experience of being questioned yet again was hardly torturous. He introduced himself as Detective Zane. At first,

I wasn't sure if that was his first or his last name. Attaching a rank to a first name seemed casual, even for a police department that prided itself on progressiveness. Only when his partner, the frumpy and in-need-of-a-shave Detective Yamaguchi, referred to Detective Zane as "James" was the question resolved.

Detective Zane was in his forties, tall, and fit. I was wary of his Stormtrooper haircut, which along with his other Aryan features made me wonder if he didn't enjoy a bit of off-duty goose-stepping. My suspicion alone should have made him entirely unattractive, and yet I was helpless against my prurient interests. I could not stop admiring him.

I had been lucky and mostly well behaved in my adult years, so my experience with law enforcement had until today been limited to a stern talking-to by cops called to a college party and a speeding ticket in the park—twenty in a fifteen. Beyond those minor transgressions, I had only television crime shows to help set my expectations for an encounter with the law. It turned out, police dramas pushed the drama envelope. The moments I'd half expected—"Turn around and put your hands behind your back," or, "We know you did this, McCall; you can talk now or later, but in the end, you will talk!"—never came. Instead, I answered the same questions over and over with the same seemingly unsatisfying answers.

The break-in had convinced the police that Camilo should now be considered a missing person. That his disappearance was being taken seriously by the cops was a relief. However, I hadn't expected Detective Yamaguchi's instruction that I not leave the city. "Expect us to follow up soon," were his departing words.

Chapter Six
The Beat Goes On

It turned out Commander loved to ride in the car. So much so that when it came time for him to get out, he wouldn't budge. As I wrestled the sixty or so pounds of stubbornness out from the back seat of the Prius, my next-door neighbor, Sarah Lee—yes, that is her real name, poor thing—descended upon us with a zeal for interrogation that rivaled that of the police. I realized my error in not having thought through a story to explain the dog. Sarah Lee quickly pointed out that Orca Arms (an absurd name for anatomical reasons) had a strict no-pets policy. At first, I was polite, wrongly thinking that a good dose of friendliness would win her silence about me taking in Commander for a short while, but her response to my charm offensive was a pursed-lips, hands-on-hips insistence that I remove the dog from the property at once. When I tried to cut the encounter short, Sarah Lee marshaled her girth to block the staircase to my second-floor unit.

For what happened next, I blame an unfortunate mix of exhaustion and exasperation: I roared, "Get the hell out of my way and bugger off, Sarah Lee!"

I shouldn't have said it. No one, not even Sarah Lee—and despite her comeback, "Screw you, you weirdo carrot-topped midget!"—deserved to be talked to so rudely. But honestly, she had picked the wrong moment to needle me. Still no excuse; not my finest hour.

With that neighborly exchange behind me, I tugged an obstinate bull terrier into my studio apartment. Commander found the foot of my bed, not hard to do in a space just a step above a dorm room. I kicked off my shoes and lay down next to him. He sighed loudly, stretched out his legs, closed his eyes.

"We've had quite the day, my friend. Let's hope your dad shows up tomorrow."

The dog appeared to have already fallen asleep. As much as I could do with a nap, I wasn't about to nod off. Too much worry swirled in my head. Would Camilo reappear anytime soon? Was he even alive? I needed to believe he was. He was out there somewhere, and I intended to find him.

* * *

Camilo kissed me hungrily, his weight pressed upon me. My groin throbbing, I rolled onto my back. His wet tongue slathered my lips.

Yap!

My eyes sprang open. Commander had been licking my face as I napped. "Eeew." I shoved him away. He jumped from the bed and ran to the door. *Yap!*

"All right, all right. I get the message." The clock above the sink read nine thirty. The sun was setting, spilling light through the window and onto an orange plastic bottle of dishwashing liquid, creating a pleasing stained-glass effect on the wall.

Outside in the building's courtyard, the temperature had dropped to a comfortable seventy degrees. Commander sniffed at some dandelions and rolled in the grass, eventually lifting his leg against the slender trunk of a young maple. As he watered the tree, I noticed Sarah Lee peering down at us through the yellow lace curtains in her living room. Her scowl was worrisome. She'd rat me out the first chance she got. Losing my apartment was a risk I couldn't afford. I'd looked for months to find a place that was decent, didn't bust my budget, and promised a commute of less than an hour to my school. When Ruthie Weiser—the old lady who owned Orca Arms—returned from her pilgrimage to Sedona, the dog had better be gone. Feeling Sarah Lee's stare drilling into me, I figured the sooner the better.

Back inside, before changing my clothes, I made sure Commander had some food in his bowl and changed out his water. Although it was a Saturday night, I didn't feel like going out. My usual motivators—to dance, to drink, or maybe get lucky—were missing in action. But still, I had to muster the energy. Tonight I was on a mission to find Camilo. And in the meantime, I needed to find a friend of his who would take the dog.

A half hour later, I swung open the door to Hunters. The place was packed. More than one hundred women and men filled a space the size of a school lunchroom—complying with the fire code didn't appear to be a concern.

Boom-boom . . . boom-boom . . . Six large speakers suspended from the ceiling by thick steel chains delivered tiny thumps to my chest. Reigning above the sea of gyrating bodies was a go-go boy. He pumped his outstretched arms above his head while thrusting his hips and shoulders from side to side. As he danced, his muscles flexed seductively. My God, Camilo? No. Impossible. The kaleidoscope of fast-swirling lights was playing tricks on my eyes.

Pushing my way deeper into the crowd, I found myself wedged in by four sweaty bears wearing grass-stained baseball uniforms. "Excuse me, guys. Excuse me, guys." One of the bearded ballplayers raised his pint, winked, and turned slightly, creating a narrow lane for my escape. Leaning in, shoulder first, I squeezed between their potbellies. My face brushed across a thick, hairy shoulder, which left a film of sweat on my cheeks.

As I neared the stage, the go-go boy revealed himself to be Eastern Indian, not Latino. He wore gold lamé as opposed to red and didn't have half Camilo's mesmerizing rhythm. Rather than dancing, the boy shuffled back and forth, side to side, while awkwardly punching the air. Despite that shortcoming, the crowd had rewarded him with clumps of singles, fives, and tens, no doubt owing to the impressive bulge of his jockstrap.

The only staff present besides the DJ were three bartenders. Joining the line for the bald, forty-something drink slinger wearing a tank top that said *Power Middle*, I hoped a sense of humor would translate into a willingness to talk to a stranger about a fellow employee. When my turn to order finally arrived, I said, "Hello, my name is Hayden. I was here last night. I was the guy who got kicked in the face by Camilo."

"What?" The bartender cupped a hand around his ear. A gold wedding band squeezed a hairy-knuckled finger.

"I was here last night! I was the guy Camilo kicked in the face!"

"And?"

"I need to talk to you. Something has happened to Camilo."

He pointed toward the storeroom. "Meet you over there. I'll come as soon as I can."

Turning to the wall of bodies, I worked my way back across the club. Last night I'd been too fixated on Camilo to appreciate the diversity of the crowd. At Hunters it was come one, come all. Every letter of LGBTQ partied together.

Ten minutes later, the bartender shuffled up in worn brown sandals. He hid his meaty legs beneath too-snug tan khakis. Curly black hair sprouted from his chest and shoulders. About Camilo's height—six two—he carried a good fifty pounds more than he probably preferred.

"Hank. I'm the manager," he said. Tiny red splotches of burst capillaries marked his cheeks and bulbous nose. He leaned his pie-shaped, unshaven face uncomfortably close to my mine to examine my eye better. "Hurt much?" he asked, expelling breath tinged with beer and cigarettes.

I took a half step back—enough to reestablish a comfortable distance but not so far as to risk offending him. "Throbbing stopped a while ago, thanks. As long as I remember not to scrunch up my face, I'm aces."

Hank seemed to chew on this report longer than necessary. "Saw you leave with Camilo last night, so your night wasn't all bad." He smiled wickedly.

"Yeah, he's a nice guy."

Another lascivious smile. "I prefer not-so-nice, if you get my meaning."

Hank seemed to have a one-track mind; I couldn't get off the train fast enough. "So listen, Hank . . ." I gave the manager a shortened version of events since Camilo and I had left the club the night before. When I finished, Hank decided on a smug look.

"That's gotta be a blow to the ego."

"Sorry?" I said.

"It's bad enough having a guy slip out on you while you're still asleep, but from his own bed? That's a first."

Hank had entirely missed the point. I tried to focus the conversation on his employee's disappearance. "So, any idea where Camilo might have gone?"

"Not a clue. We don't see each other outside the bar, not that I wouldn't like to. I invited him over to my place a few times; he always had plans. I could tell he wanted to, though."

Yes, of course, just like NASA wanted me for the astronaut program but I had midterm papers to grade.

"You try calling him?" Hank asked.

At last, the correct topic. "I don't know Camilo's number. Do—"

Hank was dialing before I finished asking.

C'mon, pick up, pick up. Too many rings; it was going to voice mail.

"Hey, sexy, it's Hank. I got a guy here—" He covered the phone with his hand. "Sorry, what did you say your name was again?"

"Hayden."

"Hayden. He's the guy you, you know, took home last night. Bit of a surprise, I have to say. Though I still wouldn't mind watching the video." Hank hadn't stopped staring at me since the start of the call. "Anyway, the guy says you split in the middle of the night. Bad form, if you ask me. But hey, I wasn't there. You probably had your reasons. Anyway, Hayward—"

"It's Hayden."

Hank brushed off my correction. "As I was saying, the guy wants to get a hold of you, buddy, so—"

"Tell him someone broke into his house."

Hank's eyes bugged; he turned the phone away from his mouth. "Say what? You didn't tell me that."

"Yeah, well, a lot has happened. Camilo should be careful. He needs to go to the police. I left a card from one of the cops on his kitchen table."

Hank narrowed his eyes at me before returning to his voice mail. He repeated what I'd said before closing with, "Okay, you take care, sexy. Get in touch as soon as you can."

I asked for Camilo's number. Hank scribbled digits on the back of a paper drink coaster, pressed it into my palm. "The second number's mine. Me and my husband play together or separate. Groups too. Whatever you're into."

Shouting *None of the above!*—while accurate—would not have kept Hank talking, a prospect I pursued with trepidation. "How long has Camilo worked here? I'm guessing he is one of your best employees."

"Been here longest of any of the dancers, three years or so. Camilo's a good guy. Reliable. Never flakes. The younger guys these days, they don't take the job seriously. They often don't show up at all. Sometimes they come in high, which is a huge pain. I send them home, of course. If I like looking at them, I'll give them a pass the first time, or maybe a second, but that has its limits. I don't need the aggravation. A month doesn't go by without some young stud showing up from Oklahoma or Wisconsin or wherever. All bright-eyed and bushy-tailed but dumb as rocks. The job's not building rockets, so if the jockstrap fits."

Once again, Hank had worked his way to a different topic. I needed him to refocus. "Sounds like you could use more guys like Camilo. I don't suppose he ever came in high or anything like that?"

Hank looked personally offended. "We are talking about Camilo."

When it became apparent that that was the extent of his answer, I asked, "Any idea what might have happened to him?"

"Not a clue. A lot of other guys, I'd suspect drugs. But Camilo doesn't even drink. Not a sip. Once I got up the nerve to ask if he had a problem with alcohol—you know, drinking too much—but he said he just didn't like what it did to people."

"Like a vegetarian working at a cattle ranch."

"Come again?"

"Never mind."

"I think it had to do with his body. Body as a temple, that sort of thing." Hank grinned. "Plenty of guys worshiped him, present company included."

"Has he been in any arguments lately? I saw his place; whoever tore it up wasn't messing around."

"As I say, Camilo is a straight arrow. No one I know dislikes him. Whatever happened sounds random to me. I sure as hell hope he shows up. He always draws a good crowd. Now, I need to get back."

"Sorry, just one more question—"

"Seriously, Hayward, I need to get going." Hank turned and started toward the bar.

I followed two steps behind. "Is there anyone else who knows Camilo well? Maybe a friend of his?"

Hank half turned his head. "No one knows Camilo better than Burley."

"Sorry, say again?"

Either Hank hadn't heard me or I had exhausted his patience for being questioned by a stranger. He hustled through the crowd, ducked beneath the counter, and retook his station behind the bar.

Since I wasn't the pushy sort, my instinct was to leave Hank alone, figure out who Burley was and where to find him some other way. But hardly was the situation normal. The guy I'd just spent the night with was missing. I had a name, and I wasn't letting it go so easily.

Again I waited in line at the bar, and when my turn to step up finally came, Hank was surprised to see me—and not in a good way.

"Seriously? I'm working here, Haywood."

"You said Burley, right? Is Burley here tonight?"

"Would be most nights. But she's throwing her girlfriend a birthday party." Hank pointed to the corner of the room occupied by a cluster of pinball machines. "Hollister and Mysti. They said they were heading to the party. You might catch a ride with them."

Chapter Seven
Hello, Ladies

I thanked Hank, left a five for a tip on the bar, and plowed a path across the dance floor, passing the pool table—now being worked by a tall, lean white boy in teal trunks and silver cowboy boots—and skirted the crowd by taking a shortcut behind the karaoke machine. I reached the two women I presumed to be Hollister and Mysti just as they stood from a pair of barstools. Both women were in their midthirties, but any similarity stopped there. The woman wearing a black T-shirt, black jeans, and black boots had the imposing stature of Serena Williams: tall, broad shouldered, and very curvy, both front and back. However, Serena, last time I checked, didn't have a six-inch mohawk. The petite woman—Korean American, I thought—wore a crisp, pink silk blouse, tan pants, and shiny high heels. Her long straight hair had lovely auburn highlights that screamed downtown salon. She made me think of television commercials for Asian airlines that featured gorgeous women with perfectly applied makeup, dressed in perfectly tailored flight attendant uniforms.

"Hello, ladies," I said. "My name is Hayden. Hank at the bar said you might be headed to Burley's party. If that's the case, I was wondering if I might catch a ride with you."

The Black woman said, "You a friend of Burley's?"

I shook my head. "I'm a friend of Camilo's. I was hoping I might meet up with him there." While this was unlikely, it wasn't a complete lie.

"We were just heading out. I'm Hollister, by the way. This is my girl, Mysti." She placed an arm around the Asian beauty. Mysti gave Hollister a searing look, then turned to me and wrinkled her nubbin of a nose. "What happened to you?"

Hollister chuckled. "Looks like little dude got on the wrong side of a fist."

"It was a serious question," Mysti sneered.

"Go-go boy misfire," I replied, hoping the intrigue of the statement would appeal to the couple.

"Whatever," Mysti huffed through her glossy pink lips.

"Let's hit it." Hollister clapped her hands and fired two finger pistols at the exit. She came across as a take-charge kind of gal with an attitude that said *What you see is what you got a problem?* I liked her immediately. I got along well with big personalities. We balanced each other out.

Mysti, on the other hand, was quietly hostile. I couldn't tell if she was pissed that I was cock-blocking her date with Hollister, pissed at Hollister for some other reason, or just generally pissed. What the two women saw in each other was a mystery. They went together like a tiara and sweatpants.

I followed the women out of Hunters and into the parking lot. Hollister drove a newer-model two-seater Porsche.

Knowing nothing about sports cars yet appreciating this one's undeniable sex appeal, I provided my review: "Snazzy."

Hollister gave the roof of the car a little thump. "Hayden, meet Mo. My other girlfriend."

Mysti rolled her eyes. "Still not funny."

"Let me guess," I said. "Short for momentum?"

"Toni Morrison. Bold, Black, beautiful."

"Oh, the author."

Hollister seemed impressed. "You know her?"

"Just the name, I'm afraid. Never read her."

Hollister gave a quick nod that seemed to say *Thought so.* She slipped behind the wheel while Mysti and I stood next to the open passenger-side door and considered the one available seat. Hollister leaned toward us. "You two getting in or what?"

Mysti answered with an irritated growl, took the seat, and crossed her arms. She stared straight ahead with an angry pout.

I shuffled my feet. "Um, so—"

"Get in, little dude," Hollister said.

I bent down so I could make eye contact with her. "I can see you're tight on space, so maybe if you just give me Burley's address, I can meet you there."

"Sit on Mysti's lap."

This broke Mysti's silence. She gave me a look that nearly blew my hair back. "Don't even think about it."

"Then share," Hollister said merrily. "You can both fit."

Mysti growled again but scooted toward the gearshift. I squeezed onto the sliver of seat she'd made available. I could close the door only by resting half my butt on the armrest built into the door. The driver's side of the car was equally crammed; the seat was pushed back all the way, and the top inch of Hollister's mohawk brushed against the moonroof.

Hollister said, "Don't get too comfy. It's not far to Burley's place." She launched out of the parking lot with a force that threw my head back against the headrest. Shifting gears, she floored the accelerator. The car flew down the street with the speed of a Michael Bay film.

Fifteen minutes into the trip, Hollister hadn't let up on the gas pedal. Her approach to driving—twice the speed limit with no time for stop signs or red lights—didn't discriminate between a lifesaving race to the emergency room and getting to a birthday party.

My susceptibility to motion sickness had me inhaling and exhaling deeply as I tried to keep my eyes directed on the road ahead. It wasn't easy. One second I was leaning against the door, the next I was pressed against Mysti, who would squirm and shove me away. During a short stretch of straight road, I allowed my focus to stray and noticed Mysti's reflection in the windshield. Her eyes were fixed on me; she was giving me a death stare.

Hollister turned on the sound system, and out spilled a male country voice singing *The hardest thing for me is not falling hard for you.*

"Oh, nice," I said. "Stanley Kellogg. I like this song."

This got a head turn from Mysti. "Really? You don't seem remotely country."

"Neither are you, babe," Hollister said. "But you came around."

"Whatever," Mysti huffed, and flipped down the visor, revealing a small mirror. She pulled a lipstick from her clutch and, despite the jerky ride and cramped quarters, went about applying a thick glossy coat of pink L'Oréal with the steady hand of a surgeon.

"One minute to Sodom, kids," Hollister announced. "Hope you're down to party, little dude. Burley's events are epic."

Party? Getting drunk was the last thing on my mind. I was on a mission to find out what Burley might know about Camilo, and I needed her to take the dog off my hands.

"We've arrived at our destination." Hollister steered Mo hard to the curb, hit the brakes. She leaned forward to see me on the other side of Mysti. "Better watch yourself in there, little dude. You're so pretty some lady might mistake you for a young butch and drag you off in her camper van."

Chapter Eight

Gentle Giant

There were so many pickups and SUVs and Subarus lining the street that Hollister had to park a block away. Even at that distance, the unmistakable four-on-the-floor beat of house music reached our ears. The volume steadily increased with every step we took toward the thumping, ranch-style house that had seen better days. The lawn would have needed mowing were it ever watered. The street numbers affixed to the house were crooked and craved paint—as did the house itself. The screen door had a large rip in it. There was no point in knocking; the front door was propped open by a case of empty whiskey bottles.

Once inside, Mysti dropped me fast, like I was her little brother at the mall. Hollister, on the other hand, squeezed my shoulder and said, "Okay, little dude, let's see if we can find Burley somewhere in this hothouse of sin."

Hollister kept calling me "little dude," which I'd yet to decide whether I found offensive or endearing. Most guys who were into me described me as cute, which I tolerated, or adorable, which, while admittedly flattering, I detested. Gurgling babies were adorable. Frolicking puppies were adorable. A grown man, regardless of his size, was not adorable. How I longed to overhear a guy say, "Damn, Hayden is hot," or "You know Hayden? Total stud!" The topic—one I'd put considerable thought into—had been the subject of one of my first blog posts, "Too Cute to Be Hot?" I'd struck a nerve with my readers; the post earned a record number of likes (fourteen) and comments (six). The online debate had been intense. So much so that I'd taken the unprecedented step of authoring a follow-up post, "Too Cute to Be Top?" In that second installment, I asked why the bigger guy usually assumed he'd be taking the top bunk. In my case, pretty much all guys were heavier and taller, yet not necessarily bigger in all respects.

I followed Hollister as she bobbed and weaved from room to room, frequently stopping to exchange hugs, kisses, high fives, and even one chest bump with the houseful of women. I understood it was a party and that Hollister had come to have fun, but I was anxious and impatient. I had come to talk to Burley, and the constant social interruptions were killing me.

The crowd was a mix of types, some similar to Hollister, giving off a masculine vibe, while others were more like Mysti, decidedly femme, dressed in curve-hugging dresses with meticulous attention to hair and makeup. And then there were those ladies who lacked any distinctive style, who looked to be dressed for a weekend pilgrimage to Costco.

One trait, however, was shared by all the women: these ladies knew how to party. I didn't see a single person without a drink. Everyone was dancing or engrossed in loud, animated conversations or part of the four-person game of drunken Twister taking place on the dining room floor. How the rail-thin woman in a short cocktail dress managed a left-hand-red without spilling a drop of her rosé was no less mind-boggling than anything staged by Cirque du Soleil.

Somewhere during our home tour, Hollister had acquired a bottle of Gentleman Jack, and she was now busily guzzling it down like Gatorade.

"So . . . you think we can keep looking for Burley?" I tried.

"Relax, little dude." She offered me the bottle. "We'll find her soon enough."

Relax? I didn't have all night. Still, Hollister was cool enough to have given me a lift, and I didn't want to offend her by turning her down. Besides, what was one little sip? *Ah, screw it.* Considering the weekend I'd had, I deserved some fun.

I took the bottle, put it to my lips, and tipped it back.

Ay caramba! The back of my throat burned like a blowtorch. I should have known better. My occasional hard cider or pale ale had left me ill prepared for eighty-proof alcohol. That said, once the flames died down, the whiskey did hit the spot. So much so that I surprised both Hollister and myself by taking a second, long pull.

"Easy there, little dude. I offered you a swig, not the whole freakin' bottle."

"Oh, sorry." I wiped my lips with the back of my hand.

It was curious to hear Hollister say "freakin'" instead of dropping an eff bomb, which was inarguably more satisfying. Maybe she was just warming up her cussing? Or perhaps it was verbal variety? Or maybe, and I hoped this wasn't the case, she thought I might take offense? But Hollister wasn't the type of person to edit her vocabulary—or much else—for anyone.

She laughed. "Ah, I'm just effing with you, Hayden."

And there it was: for a woman who seemed unafraid to go anywhere, the eff word was one step too far. I made a mental note of this curiosity. In the unlikely event we spent more time together, I'd like to know why.

She gave my back a hard slap, sending me stumbling forward a few steps.

"Drink up. I know where Burley keeps her stash; plenty more where this came from. Now. Where is our mostest hostess?"

Relieved that the search was back on, I followed Hollister as she plowed through the living room full of dancing, drinking women. The most generous way to describe Burley's design sense was eclectic-vintage. A Georgia O'Keeffe print of a lurid lavender iris set in a seventies-era frame of small mirrored tiles hung above the fireplace. On the mantel stood a lava lamp, a basketball trophy, two pewter candlesticks (with no candles), and a tall beer stein overflowing with coins. I gave the tableau a critical eye. "Lived-in" seemed to sum it up nicely.

Hollister and I navigated our way to the outdoor deck, which stood about five feet above the backyard. Like a ship's captain on the lookout for land, Hollister surveyed the sea of women below. "There she blows," she said, using a finger pistol to single out a woman standing next to the fire pit. "She's hard to miss, am I right?"

Her target in sight, Hollister hustled down the steps and marched across the expanse of uneven brown lawn at double her usual brisk pace. I jogged to keep up, needing two strides to match one of hers, as we closed in on Burley, a six-and-a-half-foot-tall, three-hundred-pound giant of a woman. Burley leaned down while Hollister stood on her tiptoes to accommodate an exchange of cheek kisses befitting a meeting at a Parisian café. That a woman was named Burley was unexpected, and yet I was one thousand percent certain I'd never met anyone with a name that suited them better.

"Burley, meet Hayden. Hayden, this here is Burley, queen of the ball."

Burley was so imposing that even someone the size of Hollister looked puny standing beside her. Burley had a second notable characteristic: a pair of waist-length gray pigtails.

"Yowza, what happened to your eye, fella?" Burley said, "You look like a raccoon with an eye patch."

I raised a finger, ready to explain why the double reference was unnecessary, but I thought better of it. Instead, I decided to employ Camilo's name immediately and set the conversation in the right direction. "Your friend, Camilo, kicked me in the face."

Burley pondered my explanation, then slowly nodded her watermelon-sized cranium.

"Sounds about right. Big shoes. Red. No laces."

Hollister rolled her eyes as if she'd heard this commentary before. "Listen up, Burley. Hayden here is looking for Camilo. He's not here, is he? You know where he might be?"

Burley craned her arms skyward. "Depends on the stars." It was now obvious—Burley was totally baked. I'd smelled pot throughout the house, so I shouldn't have been surprised. And the Willie Nelson braids should have tipped me off.

I didn't expect Hollister to do my talking for me, so I said, "I was with Camilo last night. This morning, Camilo left at some point for some reason. The cops found his truck in an empty parking lot. The door was open and the engine was running."

Burley's head rocked on her shoulders as she pursed her thin lips. "Running? I don't think so. I got bad feet."

Oh boy.

Sidestepping the confusing topic, I tried for simplicity. "Where is Camilo?"

Burley nodded. "Camilo is . . . " We waited for her to continue, but she appeared to have departed to another psychic plane. I looked to Hollister for help. She raised her hand as if to say, *I got this.*

"Yo, Burley!" Hollister shouted. "Where is Camilo? Do. You know. Where. Camilo is?"

"Is there any cake left?"

"Burley, focus." Hollister let out a long sigh, indicating she'd been to this rodeo before. She got in Burley's face and shouted, "Burley, pay attention, will you? Answer the question. Do you know where Camilo is?"

I didn't imagine many people—men or women—who would be comfortable hollering into the face of someone as big as Burley. But Hollister didn't hesitate. She was like the giant-whisperer, except for the yelling part.

Burley reached deep into the pocket of her jean shorts, retrieved her phone, and after several long seconds said, "Yo, Milo-man, there's a guy here. Here with Hollister. They're looking for you. You should see this guy. Red hair . . . freckles . . . adorable. He's like one of those tiny Snickers bars you buy at Halloween . . . fun-sized." Burley laughed, coughed, then continued laughing.

Hollister yanked the phone away from her, ended the call. "Freakin' ridiculous."

Burley wasn't listening. She was looking skyward, seemingly captivated by the Little Dipper.

Hollister shouted up to her, "So you have no idea where Camilo might be?"

Burley surprised us both by answering, "Roy's."

The look on Hollister's face was anything but reassuring.

"Who's Roy?" I asked, directing my question to both women but knowing Hollister was the better bet for a coherent answer.

Again, Burley surprised me. "My brother," she said.

Hollister dropped her head, muttered under her breath. She looked at me, shook her head, then looked up to Burley. "What did Camilo want with Roy?"

"Roy?" Burley said. "That boy got no sense."

Hollister said, "Not asking *about* Roy. Asked what Camilo wanted *with* Roy."

"A gun. What else?"

Hollister turned to me. "Out front. Now!"

I said a quick good-bye to Burley and turned back to Hollister, but she was already halfway across the backyard. I caught up with her in the middle of the front lawn.

"You've got yourself a problem, little dude. Roy Driggs is a world-class asshole. I can't believe Camilo would've been stupid enough to go near him. But you heard Burley. She may be a little stoned, but if she said Camilo went to Roy's for a gun, then that's where he went."

The description of Roy should have worried me, but my mind was stuck on Hollister's assessment of Burley as being only a little stoned.

"So you can just forget any idea you might have of going to see Roy by yourself."

Hollister was right, of course. I had no business poking around in Camilo's disappearance or investigating a home break-in that now included a gun. As worried as I was about Camilo, I had to be sensible. This was a job for the police. I was out. My only remaining concern was to find a temporary home for Commander. And I was pretty sure it wasn't with Burley.

Hollister offered me the Jack. "Here, take a good last swig before we hit the road."

My hand stopped midway between us, frozen as I stared at her, wondering if I had heard her correctly.

Seeming to read my mind, she said, "Hey, we got ourselves a bona fide mystery here. A good guy has disappeared. If we don't find out what happened to him, who will? Seriously, Camilo's life could be at stake. Time to get in the game. Let's get it on, little dude."

Despite the cool night air, beads of sweat formed at my brow. "You mean now?"

"Party is lame. I know all those ladies. If you know what I mean."

"What about Mysti?"

"*Pfft.*" She waved a hand dismissively in the direction of the house. "That girl won't even know I've left. We'll be back in less than an hour. She'll still be nursing the same half glass of Chardonnay."

I didn't want to offend her, but I couldn't avoid the next question: "You sure you're all right to drive?" My eyes bounced from her to the bottle of Jack she held loosely against her thigh.

She dropped her chin against her chest, looked at me as if peering over eyeglasses. "Responsible. I like that." She dug in the pocket of her tight-fitting black jeans, pulled out her car keys, and tossed them in a slow arc in my direction. "You drive."

Would I regret following Hollister back to the car? After crunching the numbers, I determined it was an 85 percent lousy idea. What accounted for the other 15 percent? Three things: I was enjoying this flirtation with a bolder, more outgoing version of myself; I liked this Hollister, and for some inexplicable reason, I'd decided it was important that she like me back; and in all likelihood, Camilo needed our help—perhaps desperately so.

After adjusting the seat and the mirrors, I started up Mo. Hollister said she knew the way to Roy Driggs's place. It was about a half-hour drive. I shifted into first and crept away from the curb. When I got the speedometer up to twenty, Hollister gave my knee a friendly squeeze. "You got this, little dude. Nothing to worry about."

I nodded but kept my eyes fixed ahead on the road, my hands firmly at two and ten.

"Except for the dogs," she said. "When we get to Roy's, we'll most definitely want to be on the lookout for the dogs."

Chapter Nine
Me and My Lady

Driving through a light-industrial neighborhood, we'd already passed a moving company, plumbing supplier, cemetery stonemason, auto-glass repair shop, and oddly, a Pentecostal church that had set up shop in a large warehouse. The house of worship had one of those road signs on wheels parked at the curb that said, *Your most powerful position is on your knees*. I logged the phrase as a possible headline for a future blog post.

Hollister's directions had been spot-on, and we arrived at Roy Driggs's thirty minutes later. The street was eerily quiet, the purr of the Porsche's engine and the crunch of tires on gravel the only sounds. Occasionally I glimpsed headlights or taillights a few streets ahead or behind, but they veered off in other directions before getting any closer.

The sign on the chain-link fence read *Driggs' Dolls*. Judging by the look of the enclosed, dark, heavily wooded, and wildly overgrown property, Dolls had to be a brand of ammo or some sort of specialty hunting equipment—or perhaps a code word known only to a tight-knit group of armed-to-the-teeth survivalists. On the other side of the entrance gate, a cracked cement sidewalk disappeared from view behind a wall of bushes twenty feet ahead, where the pathway curved off to the left. There wasn't a single vehicle parked anywhere within a block. If there were cars, trucks, Harleys, or repurposed military vehicles on the property, they had crept their way deep within the compound through a large gate off to the right.

Like the sidewalk, the road went a short distance before becoming lost in a tight thicket of trees and brush. As I peered into the darkness, the tiny blond hairs on my forearms stood and shivered. I looked at Hollister.

"Told you," she said. "Roy ain't to be messed with."

My ability to swallow had disappeared somewhere between Burley's house and Roy's compound. I croaked, "Perhaps we should come back in the morning. You know, when it's light out. More people around."

"Nah, we've come all this way. Sunshine won't make Roy any sweeter. Besides, I thought you wanted to find Camilo. I sure as hell do. So you going to open that gate or what?"

Hollister was right. I had come for answers. Camilo's life might be at stake. Our visit could not be put off until morning.

My fingers trembled as I raised the latch on the rusted metal gate. My feet were leaden. Still, I was going in. Hollister eased the gate shut behind her. Though we weren't trying to sneak in, something about the scene's dark creepiness cautioned me against making any unnecessary noise.

However, I wondered if staying quiet might not be the best idea. Surprising Roy—a gun dealer—at home after dark couldn't be wise. Maybe we should make our presence known?

A menacing growl came from somewhere off to my right.

"That's not good," whispered Hollister.

I snapped my head back in her direction. "What the—"

"Told you, the dogs."

We could try to make a run for the house or whatever shelter lay ahead, but if the distance was too great, the animal would chase one of us down before we reached safety. But if we turned and ran the short way back to the front gate, we might have a chance.

As I turned slowly, a second, louder growl came from behind me. *Stupid, Hayden, stupid.* Hollister had warned me about the dogs—plural. Why hadn't I followed up on that crucial piece of information? And why in the hell hadn't she taken the threat more seriously?

"If you knew the dogs were dangerous, why did you have us creep inside the property?" I snapped.

Hollister looked slighted. "How was I to know he'd have them out roaming about? When I was here before, they were barking up a storm and throwing themselves at the fence, trying to get at me and Burley. With it being so quiet, I assumed they were inside."

"Bad assumption!" I said, louder than intended.

I sensed the dogs inching closer. We had unwittingly presented them with the exact situation they'd been trained for: unfamiliar intruders sneaking onto their property. Though my legs were locked in terror, my voice dealt with the fear in its own way. "Help! Roy Driggs! Call off your dogs! Roy!"

Hollister reached out, grabbed my arm roughly. "What the hell? Shut up. You trying to get us killed?"

I yanked my arm free of her grip. "No, I'm trying to save our skins." I paused, hoping to hear a reply, but heard only the dogs' low, guttural snarls. I screamed, "Roy! Help us! Roy!"

An intense flood of light flashed on from high up in the trees, blinding us. "Who in Hades is out there?" boomed a man's voice.

"Roy Driggs!" I shouted back, my right hand shielding my eyes. "Your sister Burley sent us. My name is Hayden. I'm here with my friend Hollister. We came to talk to you about Camilo Rodriguez." A new wave of fear washed over me. What if Roy had something to do with Camilo's disappearance?

"Bullet! Winchester! Down!" Roy commanded. The growling stopped. The blinding spotlights were doused, replaced by several low-to-the-ground outdoor lights that illuminated the path ahead.

"I suggest you get yer asses over here," Roy shouted.

Hollister and I hurried up the sidewalk and rounded a bend. About fifty feet ahead of us sat a trailer. Standing on its small porch was what looked like a refrigerator with a beard—the whole Driggs clan ran extra-extra-large. Roy must have been six foot eight inches tall and 350 pounds. He was cradling some sort of long gun.

Every cell in my body was screaming *Run!* But that had ceased being an option the moment we'd closed the gate behind us. All Hollister and I could do now was play out the situation and hope it wasn't as dreadful as it appeared.

When we got to within twenty feet of the porch, Roy raised his weapon and removed the toothpick from his teeth. "That's far enough, you two."

He wagged his head, causing a ripple effect down his foot-long gray beard. " 'Bout now I'm thinkin' to myself, what kind of moron comes creepin' onto another man's property in the dark o' night? I mean, that type of idiot's just itching to get his head blown off."

I cut a glance at Hollister, whispered, "See? What'd I tell you?"

She cocked her head. "Really? You might want to be more solution oriented about now."

"Shut up!" Roy hollered. "I got better things to do than listen to you two lovebirds squabble in my yard."

Hollister and I shared a look, telegraphing the same thought: could this bozo think there was even the slightest possibility that we were together?

I couldn't control the wavering in my voice. "We're sorry to disturb you, sir, and we apologize for coming at this hour. Burley, your sister—"

"I don't need you to tell me who my sister is."

Thankfully, Hollister decided to join the conversation. "You probably don't remember me, Roy, but we met once before. I came here with Burley. Anyway, Burley said Camilo might have come to see you. We're looking for him and thought you might be able to point us in the right direction."

"Who are you? FBI? ATF?"

Seriously? "Um . . . no sir, we're not law enforcement—"

Hollister elbowed me, hard.

"Ah hell, son, you think for one goddamn second I'd think you was the feds?" Roy's sinister laugh reached down my throat and squeezed my stomach. He eyed me intently, said, "Looks like you were in a scrap recently." He pointed his bearded chin toward Hollister. "The missus do that to you?"

It took me a moment to realize Roy was referring to my black eye. I decided to skip his ridiculous assumption that Hollister and I were a couple. "No, sir. Camilo kicked me."

This news seemed to please Roy. A crooked grin lifted the edges of his scraggly mustache. "Now I reckon Camilo had reach on his side, along with a good fifty-pound advantage. So if that's the worst of yer lickin', I'd say you got off easy. What do you think, son? You get off easy?"

I looked up at Roy. "Yeah, I guess so." With him standing on the elevated porch, it was like gazing up at a redwood—a malcontented, armed redwood.

"Best come on in, bring your lady." Roy returned the toothpick to his mouth.

"Thank you, sir." But I wasn't thankful, and I was pretty sure Hollister wasn't either. Though whether she was more put off by Roy's general horribleness or the fact that he'd subjugated her to being "my lady" wasn't yet clear. What I did know was that I absolutely, positively did not want to go inside that trailer.

Still, I managed a step forward.

"Little, ain't ya? I didn't know better, I'd think you'd come trick-or-treating." Roy stepped into the long, skinny house on wheels, apparently expecting us to follow. I pictured him thirty years ago—overweight and big for his age—bullying some small, terrified kid who had tape on his eyeglasses in the middle school bathroom. He'd graduated from stealing lunch money and giving wedgies to selling guns and verbally abusing strangers. He'd been playing his twisted game his entire life. We were just the latest target.

"Well?" I whispered to Hollister.

"We either go inside or make a run for it. Neither one of us is outrunning those dogs. If it were just one dog, I'd say run for it. My legs are longer than yours. But with two dogs . . ." She shook her head at the situation, started up the steps.

My knees shook so badly I worried they'd buckle as I followed close behind her. That I allowed her to go first wasn't lost on me. But Hollister would have been furious had I attempted an act of chivalry by strong-arming her and taking the lead. However, that wasn't why I held back. The regular Hayden had returned, and he was terrified.

Inside Roy's trailer, I was hit by a one-two punch to my senses. The first was the overwhelming odor of Mentholatum. It smelled as if Roy and the entire room had been sprayed with Vicks VapoRub. The second was without question the most bizarre thing I had ever seen in my twenty-five years of living. Hundreds of sets of tiny eyes stared at me from every direction.

Roy gestured broadly. "This here's the wife's nonsense. Though you'd be goddamn amazed how much some of these plastic munchkins are worth. See that one there?" Roy pointed to a doll that occupied a miniature rocking chair next to the electric fireplace. The doll had freaky oversized round eyes the size of quarters and brown wavy hair in the style worn by movie stars of the 1940s. "What you got there is a fifteen-inch German googly. She's worth seven thousand, if the wife's estimate's correct—which it usually is."

There must have been over a thousand children's dolls lining the walls of Roy's trailer. They sat on floor-to-ceiling shelving and, aside from a series of foot-wide trails snaking across the carpet, occupied every inch of flat surface in the small living room.

Roy pointed his toothpick at me. "You realize you're damn lucky *my* missus ain't here at present. Had she heard someone making a ruckus in her yard after sundown, she'd have skipped the pleasantries and blown yer heads off. Me, I'm more neighborly. I like to say howdy-do before I neutralize a threat. That what you are, son? You and your lady a threat?"

I wished Roy would stop addressing only me while disregarding Hollister. So far she'd let it slide, but I had a feeling that, even being on the wrong side of a gun, she had her limits. Her twitchy fingers and clenched jaw suggested that Roy was fast approaching it.

"No, sir. As I said, we just wanted to ask if you knew where we might find Camilo."

Roy squinted his bloodshot eyes, considering this. "It's a free country. A customer stops by, whatever business he may want with me is private. So even if I did, and I'm not saying that I do, but even I did know something, I'm not about to betray client con-fee-dent-she-ality."

"Here's the deal, Roy." Hollister's voice startled me. "We're friends of Burley. So unless you want word to get back to her that you were a total dick to us, you'll stop screwing around and tell us what you know about what's going on with Camilo."

As Hollister spoke, my eyes grew wider. I was in awe of her bravery. Or recklessness. Either way, she was my hero. Roy held the gun, but Hollister was the badass.

Roy sat back in his large recliner, its arms covered by two doilies, and made an exaggerated show of checking his grenade-size wristwatch. "Getting late, so I'll tell you what you want to know. Have I seen Camilo lately? Okay, sure. He came here a few nights ago—Wednesday, to be exact. I sold him a gun. What kind is between him and me. He didn't say what he wanted it for, and I didn't ask. Now I'd like the two of you to get the hell out of my house and off my property."

Hollister nodded and started to leave. I held her arm, which earned me a withering look. "One last thing, Roy," I said. "How did Camilo seem to you?"

"Seem to me?" Roy snarled. "Are you seriously still questioning me?"

Hollister stood, tugged on my arm. "Time to go, Hayden."

I stayed put—we'd come this far. "Did he seem angry? Scared? Worried?"

Slowly, a lopsided grin, rivaling that of a jack-o'-lantern's, spread across Roy's face. "I'll tell you what he seemed. That boy was scared out of his mind."

That Camilo had been frightened seemed to amuse Roy.

"Mexican boy got all them muscles but afraid to use them. Pathetic, if you ask me."

"He's Venezuelan," Hollister said.

"Say what?"

"Ven-e-zue-lan." Hollister emphasized each syllable as if she were slapping Roy's face.

Roy shrugged. "Whatever."

Again, Hollister tugged at my arm, and again I held my ground. "You can read people pretty well, can't you, Roy? You'd have been able to tell whether Camilo had wanted a gun for protection or if he had been aiming to, you know, be the one to start something?"

My question appeared to intrigue Roy. He sucked on his toothpick, scratched the squirrel nest on his chin. "Tell you this, that boy was in an agitated state." He shook his head knowingly. "Too scared to be the aggressor—them's the over-confident ones, all puffed up, talking a big game. Camilo was meek as a mouse. All 'Yes, sir,' 'No, sir,' 'How much, sir.' When I handed him the gun, he turned white as a sheet. Not easy to do when you look like him." The smile returned to Roy's cracked lips. "That boy wasn't looking to cause trouble. That boy was afraid trouble was looking for him, and he was shaking in his boots."

Chapter Ten
Mates on Dates, Post No. 21

The encounter with Roy Driggs had been rewarding in two respects. First, Hollister and I had learned important information: Camilo had indeed gone to visit Roy and bought a gun, and he had been frightened—of what we were determined to discover. The second positive outcome was that I had a good topic for a blog post.

MATES ON DATES: Boo Is for Bully

I owe you all an explanation. You are probably wondering why I am taking on the topic of bullying in a dating blog. I promise to make it relevant, but you have to stick with me through the first half ☺. Recently I had an unpleasant encounter with a person who was a bully. Trust me on this. One thousand percent. When I think back on his behavior, I realize what he got out of being nasty was the power of being a jerk—there was nothing I could do about it.

This notion of "nothing I could do about it" stuck with me. When all is said and done, what makes a bully a bully is using one's power over someone else and getting off on getting away with it.

About a year ago, I was dating a guy named Tony (some of you may know Tony). We'd been hanging out for almost two months when he started showing up late, seeming disinterested, and on a few occasions canceling on me at the last minute. I soon learned that he had started dating someone else: Ashton. (Now to the second half of this post, where bullying meets dating.) Guess how I found out?

One day I was standing next to Ashton in the showers at the gym. As Ashton was lathering his sculpted body from perfect head to perfect toes with Hermes body wash, he told me that he and Tony had been seeing each other for weeks. Imagine the sting of humiliation. Ashton had made a classic bully move—just in a dating context. It didn't help when I found out that everyone but me had known about Tony and Ashton.

Minutes later, when I confronted Tony in the locker room, standing before him in only a towel, Ashton walked up. By way of explanation, Tony said only this: "Why? You want to know why, Hayden? Look in the mirror, then look at Ashton."

Tony, too, as it turned out, was an emotional bully. There were a million ways to tell me that he wasn't feeling it between us and that he was interested in someone else. But choosing cruelty wasn't cool.

And so, fellas, to my point in all this. Bullying comes in more forms than the clichéd playground menace stealing lunch money from littler kids. Boo to bullies in all their forms. C'mon, guys, there's already too many haters out there. We don't need to add to their number. When treading the dating waters, we owe it to one another to do so with care and compassion for the other person. Be honest but appreciate a person's feelings; acknowledge that they have their vulnerabilities—even the hot guys do (or so I'm told).

In conclusion, be good to each other. The more good you put out, the more good you'll get. What could be a better way to date!

Till next time, I'm Hayden.

And remember, if you can't be good, be safe!

Chapter Eleven
Duty Calls

Had it not been for Commander, I would have slept even later than two in the afternoon. The lack of sleep on Friday night—coupled with last night's late adventure with Hollister—had left me exhausted. The past forty hours of sensory overload had been the opposite of the chill last few weeks I had planned before the new school year began and I'd have to memorize the names of 150 new students. And hallelujah for that. So far I had spent my time off in relaxation mode: reading, movies, the club, running in the park, dinners at my aunt's, repeat. I was in dire need of a good shaking up. I just hadn't realized it. That said, half the weekend's excitement would have sufficiently checked the box. Already I had been given a story I would be retelling for the rest of my days. And yet "The End" seemed far from being written. Camilo was still missing.

During the drive from Roy's compound back to Hunters, Hollister had railed against social injustice and lectured on the impossibility of us "sitting this one out" while "a brown brother was deep in it." I'd conceded that Camilo was in some sort of trouble but argued that it was the police's job to get to the bottom of his disappearance. That comment had triggered a long rant on institutional racism. "The police don't care about a gay guy who dances at a bar for a living," she'd insisted. "But this Black girl sure as hell does."

We would have gone back and forth the entire trip had it not been for what she said as I cautiously eased Mo into a parking spot at Hunters. "Back there at Roy's"—she slapped the dashboard—"you have to admit that was really something. The way we marched in there, stood our ground, and demanded that dumbass answer our questions. We went in there determined to get information valuable to our case, and damn it all if we didn't get it."

Correcting her embellished account of events was what the old Hayden would have done, but doing so would have caused me to miss her point: *Hollister considered us a team.* Any doubt I might have had about my read of the situation was erased when she punched me in the arm and said, "You and I are one hell of a team. Hollister and Hayden, like Batwoman and Robin!"

I winced at my downgrade to sidekick, though I appreciated the spirit of her comment. "More like Spiderman and Batwoman," I suggested. "Equal billing, while acknowledging we bring our unique talents to the partnership."

She responded with a hoot, and we sealed our pact with a fist bump. As she left me standing in the Hunters parking lot, she fired her finger pistols at me and shouted, "Tomorrow, partner! Tomorrow we ride!"

Was tomorrow today or tomorrow? We'd left many of the details of our newly formed crime-fighting duo up in the air. Both nervous and excited, I was ambivalent about going through with whatever it was Hollister and I had agreed to. Who was she, anyway? Larger than most in life, without question. But it seemed that with Hollister there wasn't much space between bravery and recklessness. Envious of the first, I feared the second. Hayden the Disney character versus Hayden the Marvel hero. The opportunity to rewrite the script of one's life didn't come around very often. Yet my brain slid back to its default setting, chipping away with a pointed argument as to why I should pull the covers back over my head and refuse to leave the apartment. Meanwhile, a sweet but incessantly bossy bull terrier lay on the floor, chewing the heels of my new sports socks.

Buzz-buzz-buzz-buzz-buzz. My phone on silent skittered across the nightstand. The number, bearing a 760 area code, was not in my contacts, yet it felt vaguely familiar. The police would have a local number, as, I assumed, would Camilo or Hollister. Though it was possible either one of them could be borrowing a phone.

"Hello?" I answered with a rush of nervous excitement.

"Hi, hon."

"Oh. Hi, Aunt Sally." I hoped my groan wasn't audible. My aunt was good to me, but I paid for it in patience and a very open mind.

"You sound surprised it's me."

"You're not calling from your phone."

"How'd you know?" She seemed genuinely baffled yet delighted, as if I'd guessed the name of her favorite gospel singer.

"The number you're calling from isn't in my contacts."

"That's clever of you. No, you're right, it's your grandfather's phone. His ancient flip phone finally went kaput."

"Why didn't he keep the same number?"

"Oh, you know him. He said the NSA was probably tracking it. Better to start fresh. Anyway, sorry to bother you on your day off—"

"I'm a teacher. They're all days off till school starts," I reminded her.

"Well, I hope you're getting some quality R and R. You work so hard. So thin. I was telling your grandparents that you look too thin. I heard something on the news that said being too thin is not healthy. Middle-aged men need a bit of tummy fat to stave off . . . now what was it? . . . oh, I don't recall at the moment, but still, a little flab around the midsection wouldn't hurt you."

"I'm not middle-aged. I'm twenty-five."

"Of course you are, hon. I'm just saying you could use to put on a few pounds is all. Your grandparents agree with me, I might add."

"They're both skinnier than I am."

"Yes, dear, but they're both in their eighties, now, aren't they?"

Had it been anyone else on the other end of the line, I'd have lost my temper. But no one in my life deserved a longer fuse than Aunt Sally. She'd been there for me during my senior year of high school when I'd lost my mom. Naturally an introvert, I had turned further inward with Mom's passing. If I relied on only myself, my logic had been, others couldn't let me down, or disappoint me, or die on me.

The following year had been the hardest of my life. Aunt Sally, Mom's only sibling, took me in and smothered me in support. The transition from aunt to surrogate mother had been—and continued to be—a tricky one. But to her credit, Aunt Sally respected boundaries, knowing she would never replace my mom. And yet she so relished having someone besides a long series of cats to care for that she occasionally overstepped. She couldn't help herself. For my part, I struggled to achieve a fair balance between accepting her love and help and not resenting her for being alive and able to give it.

Then there was Aunt Sally's faith. She was evangelical. I was agnostic at best—and gay, there was always that, which heavily influenced my perspective on religion. And so we compartmentalized our relationship, avoiding two aspects of our lives that largely shaped us.

"Listen, hon, I hate to ask, but I need you to do me a favor."

"I will if I can," I replied, allowing myself some wiggle room.

"Jerry is out of toilet paper, so well, you know, it's the kind of thing that can't wait till I'm back in town."

Jerry was in his nineties and lived next door to my aunt. She'd been doing his grocery shopping, wheeling his trash bins to the curb, and running him to doctor appointments ever since his second stroke three years ago. He was a sweet old widower whom I'd gotten to know a bit when I'd filled in for my aunt on a handful of occasions.

"Sure, no problem," I said.

"Today? Again, I hate to ask, but you know, can't-wait sort of thing."

"Yeah, yeah. I got it. I'll head out shortly."

Minutes later, as I wrestled with Commander for control of my shoelaces, I shook my head at this comedic turn—anticipating a call from a missing dancer, the police, or an intimidating lesbian, only to receive an urgent request for a TP run.

For a moment I considered taking Commander along (he did so love to ride in the car), but I was reluctant to complicate the errand and prolong the visit with Jerry. Then again, I could do with some good karma points, and Jerry might get a kick out of Commander. I reached for the leash.

Chapter Twelve
TP Run

After a quick stop at the store, I arrived at my aunt's town-home in the Phinney Ridge neighborhood. The three-level, beige-colored home was attached to Jerry's identical-twin unit. He'd no doubt heard me opening the garage door to my aunt's place, as I could see his tall and slightly bent frame in the rearview mirror. He was standing in the driveway and staring into the dark garage with a look of concern.

"Hello, Jerry," I called out in my friendliest voice, adding a cheerful wave for good measure. "It's Hayden, Sally's nephew. I brought you toilet paper."

He nodded. "Hello, young man. Sally isn't due back for another few weeks, so when I heard the door—" He leaned over to see past me. "Is that a dog you got in the car?"

My guess that Jerry might like Commander had been slightly off: Jerry *loved* Commander. And though Commander seemed to like everyone, he seemed to take to Jerry with more excitement than to anyone other than Camilo. I shouldn't have been bothered by this, but after I had taken Commander in, fed and walked him, even let him hijack the lower half of my bed, I did feel a tad bit slighted.

Commander found a stick in Jerry's small, fenced-in courtyard, and the two of them played fetch. I watched from a metal lawn chair that had once been teal. Most of the paint had flaked off, laying bare a rusting frame that seemed to suit the surroundings: overgrown lawn, fence missing a few slats, and a once-ornate birdbath now stained and filled with brackish water. I shuddered to think about the condition of the inside of Jerry's house.

It turned out I had nothing to worry about; his home was spick-and-span. His clothes, however, were a wreck. I convinced him to let me do a few loads of laundry. As the washing machine chugged away, I kept a close eye on my phone. Jerry watched a *Wheel of Fortune* marathon, and Commander took a nap, his head on Jerry's lap.

With the last of the laundry folded, I said good-bye to Jerry with a promise to return soon with his new BFF. Jerry was sad to see Commander go, and for a fleeting moment I considered leaving the dog with him, as that would solve my problem of finding the dog a temporary home. But supervised visits were one thing; leaving the muscular, strong-headed dog with frail, elderly Jerry could be asking for a broken hip.

After promising Jerry another playdate on Tuesday, Commander and I set off for home.

Halfway across the bridge, my phone vibrated in my pocket. It wasn't until I hit the first stoplight that I was able to check the voice mail.

"Hey, little dude. It's Batwoman. I'll pick you up. Call me."

The moment had arrived. Was I in? Or was I out? Once I returned Hollister's call, there'd be no going back. Until now,

I had allowed myself to flirt with the notion that I would join forces with this unpredictable and somewhat frightening woman. But apprehension slithered into my thoughts. I granted myself the time remaining in the drive to Orca Arms to make a final decision as to whether I was going to suit up for the game or leave my cape hanging in the closet. One minute I was cheerfully folding an old man's skivvies, the next, consumed by an existential crisis.

Could I give up on Camilo? I was beside myself with worry about him, and Hollister's arguments had left me with zero doubt that we were his best chance of being found.

And what about Hollister? Was I prepared to disappoint her? Or would I take a risk and do what felt dangerous and entirely outside my comfort zone?

Who would win out? Regular Hayden? Or the new adventurous Hayden that both thrilled and scared the crap out of me?

Turning into the apartment complex, I had made my decision. It was me I was dealing with, after all. Maybe someday I could be that guy—that aspirational Hayden—but not today. I wasn't ready.

Arriving at my assigned space in the carport, I blinked and rubbed my eyes. A smile sprang loose on my face. I felt lighter. I was suddenly—and this is the only word to describe the feeling—*giddy*. I parked the car into the space next to mine, a rule violation that drew a twenty-dollar fine, which would be nothing compared to the hellfire Sarah Lee would reign down upon me if she caught my car in her space. But I didn't care. *Bring it on, Sarah Lee.* Besides, what choice did I have? My own space was occupied by a black Porsche.

Chapter Thirteen
Happy Hour

Hollister and I agreed that our investigation should begin at Hunters. We would see what we could find out about Camilo from a not-sky-high Burley. According to Hollister, Burley was a fixture on Sunday evenings. I hoped we would catch her before she had one too many.

I'd never been to Hunters on a Sunday night, too anxious as I was about prepping for class and getting a good night's sleep. My "school night" observance had become so ingrained that even during the summer months or on Sundays before Monday holidays, I'd stay in with *Sixty Minutes*, followed by *Masterpiece* on PBS.

Nothing drew a crowd to a bar like a good happy hour, which there was: two-for-one microbrews and two-dollar well drinks. Yet that wasn't the main reason the parking lot was full. Sundays were karaoke night at Hunters, and Burley Driggs was both MC and a featured performer.

We are all guilty of stereotyping. I would have bet my meager 401(k) that Burley's go-to would be a Stanley Kellogg cover or some Texas Roadhouse standard. Correct answer:

heartland rock. Specifically, Bruce Springsteen. Standing on the makeshift plywood-on-pool-table stage towered giant Burley Driggs. If she had changed her clothes since I had last seen her holding court in her backyard, I couldn't tell the difference: cowboy boots, jean cutoffs, and a fringed buckskin vest over a flannel shirt. There was one noticeable modification: Burley had rolled her long braids into two Princess Leia pinwheels that hugged her large head like earmuffs. She was midstream of belting out "Born to Run," and she was killing it.

Hollister picked up on my astonishment, nudged my ribs. "Burl isn't half-bad, is she?"

My mouth gaped like a fish. No words did justice to what I was witnessing. Burley could sing. Oh, how she could sing. Her performance brought to mind one of those popular television shows where everyday people amble onto the stage, step up to the microphone, and either wow the judges or elicit hand-covered titters and cringes from the panelists and crowd. In one famous episode, a frumpy middle-aged British woman had strutted onto the stage in sensible shoes and dress. What came next, a knock-your-socks-off rendition of an iconic *Les Misérables* aria, had shocked the audience. Burley's boot-stomping, sky-punching, throat-popping performance was every bit as impressive. The Hunters crowd whooped and clapped as she mocked a curtsy.

"Standing O," Hollister shouted into my ear. "Every time. Standing O."

Technically we were all already standing. Still, I had no doubt that every last trans, girl, boy, butch, femme, boi, bear, otter, twink, twunk, jock, daddy, and label-defying, tribe-blurring person in attendance would have sprung from his, her, or their seat in appreciation.

Burley invited the next performer, a tall and elegant pretty boy, onto the stage. Awkwardly rocking his hips, he launched into an energetic—if not particularly on-pitch—send-up of Madonna's "Like a Prayer." We caught up with Burley at the bar; Hank pushed a tumbler of clear liquid on ice in her direction.

"The race is on," I whispered to Hollister.

She scrunched her face in confusion before understanding that I was referring to the drink sitting in front of Burley. "That's seltzer water. Burley doesn't drink alcohol."

"But last night . . ."

"Weed, yes. Booze, no." She pointed her chin toward Burley. "Ask her yourself."

Hearing Hollister's voice, Burley turned, raised her glass. "Cheers, and ask me what?"

"Hey, Burl," Hollister said. "Little dude wants to know why you smoke pot but don't drink."

"I, uh—"

"You look familiar," Burley said, examining my face for a hint of recognition.

"I was at your party last night. I'm Hayden."

Burley nodded, took a long drink of water. "Yeah, I remember. Who could forget that shiner?"

Odd as it was, I didn't mind having a notable characteristic that was something other than my hair, my freckles, or my size. "That's me," I said rather proudly.

"My tum." Burley patted her ample belly.

When I realized that would be the extent of her comment, I looked to Hollister for interpretative help; she just shrugged.

"Liquor doesn't agree with me," Burley explained. "Wreaks havoc on my GI."

The boy on stage had reached round two of the chorus, and I realized we'd be losing Burley to her master-of-ceremonies duties every few minutes for the entire night. A direct line of inquiry was in order. "I don't suppose you've heard from Camilo?" I asked.

"Not a peep," she replied. "Not like him, either. Not like him at all. I don't think there's been a day in the five years I've known that boy that passed without a text or a call. Hank told me about what happened, how they found his truck in some parking lot, no sign of him, his place torn up. Sounds bad to me. Real bad."

Applause from the crowd.

"Be back in a jiff." Burley bounded for the stage.

Hank joined the conversation from behind the bar. "Don't know if this is important, but about six months back, Camilo asked to drop Saturdays from his schedule. I thought he was crazy. Biggest night, hands down. And I don't need to tell you how popular he is." He winked at me as if we shared a tantalizing secret.

"Didn't make any sense to me," Hank continued. "Every guy would kill for a spot in the Saturday night lineup."

"He say why?" I asked.

"That's the weirdest part," Hank said, wiping down the bar. "When I asked, he just laughed and said, 'The animals need me, bro.' "

"What the hell did that mean?" Hollister said.

"Didn't know then, don't know now. Camilo, always the jokester. He just left it at that."

"And he never worked another Saturday night?" I asked.

Hank shook his head. "Not a one. A few weeks later, he dropped Wednesdays too. But I'd almost expected that. Wednesdays are pretty slow. Guys don't make much money. Only the newbies get excited about midweek gigs. A good test for the fresh meat."

I wondered if Hank would last a full day at any job with a competent HR department. As it was, the dancers at Hunters would have to grin and bear it, which hopefully wouldn't require any one-on-one time with Hank.

On the stage, Burley coaxed a bashful woman with long bangs hiding her eyes to the mic. A minute later, she returned to the bar. "What's with these women and Alanis Morissette? One second a chick is too scared to get up there, the next she's screeching 'You Oughta Know' at the top of her lungs." Burley reached for her tumbler.

"You're Camilo's best friend," Hollister said. "The police track you down yet?"

"Police?" Burley took a long, slow drink of water. "What the police want with me?"

"It's been nearly two days since Camilo disappeared. You'd think they'd want to talk to you, talk to somebody." Hollister's tone said her words shouldn't need explaining. She turned to me, narrowed her eyes. "But only if the cops care about finding him."

The start-stop conversation with Burley lasted through another five numbers, reflecting the crowd's diversity: pop, ballad, rock, show tune, and folk. Burley announced the night's winner—I'd not realized a competitive element was at play—and the meek woman with long bangs reluctantly crept onto the stage to collect her punch card for ten free drinks.

Hollister and I retreated to a quiet corner of the club where the pinball machines stood blinking but silent. We recounted what we had just learned from Burley: Camilo was in his final year studying computer science at a local community college; the only family she'd ever recalled Camilo mentioning was a sister, Daniela, whom no one had ever met; he'd never had a boyfriend who had lasted longer than a few months—the last was some guy named Riley or Rory, whom Burley had immediately detested (too much beauty, attitude, and cologne, in that order); and "Commander could take a dump in Camilo's shoes and still get a treat" (a piece of information I could loosely corroborate).

"And let's not forget Camilo giving up his Saturdays," I said. "There could be something to that."

Hollister sat back on her barstool. "I have to disagree with you there, little dude. Remember what Hank said about Camilo saying something about 'the animal needs me'? Camilo was talking about Commander. What else could he have meant?" She scanned the room, appearing to search for someone, then noticed I had gone quiet. "What? That look on your face. Out with it. Say what's on your mind."

"Animals, not animal."

"Come again?"

"Camilo said, 'The animals need me.' If he'd been referring to his dog, wouldn't he have said 'animal'?"

"Maybe, maybe not. Hank could have heard him wrong, too."

"But even that wouldn't make sense. Why would Camilo trade his week's biggest paycheck to sit at home with his dog?

Besides, he kept Friday nights. Why not give up Fridays and keep Saturdays? No, something's not right about it, Hollister. Whatever Camilo meant when he said, 'The animals need me,' had nothing to do with Commander."

Hollister raised her hands in surrender. "Okay, okay. Point to Hayden."

Another silence settled between us. Again her focus shifted to the crowd. She slowly moved her head from right to left.

"You looking for someone?"

Keeping her eyes on the room, she said, "Mysti. That girl is making a mess of me. I can't live with her"—she cut me a glance—"can't live without her. Said she'd be here, but I don't see her. Typical."

"Maybe she got held up, just running late."

"Could be." Hollister let go a long, overdone sigh. "With Mysti, it could be a million things. Her hair. Her parents. Her job. Her car. Her clothes. Her apartment. Her parents—did I already say her parents?"

"Yes," I said cautiously.

"Asian. South Korean, but otherwise very WASP-y. Big into the yacht-club scene. Some dudes collect cars; Mysti's father collects sailboats. Ever heard of such a thing? I went with her once to their uptight club. Only once. We had shrimp cocktails and Chardonnay while wearing all white. First and last time this girl will ever wear all white. Things we do for love, am I right? At least we weren't trapped on a catamaran with her family. Her parents gave her a speedboat for her eighteenth birthday. She has never completely forgiven me for topping out the speedometer as we jetted across the sound—not that she was scared, just that her hair got messed up. Anyway, about her family, Mysti won't come out to them. She goes on and on about the shame it would cause her parents. Just imagine how much fun it is to visit them at their Magnolia mansion and be introduced as 'Mysti's good friend.' Ironically, they think I'm good for her. They think of me as a coconspirator. Every time we visit her parents, her mother pulls me aside to enlist my help in getting Mysti to accept one of the dates the parents have arranged for her."

"Sounds awkward."

"It's effed up is what it is. And then there's Cynthia. Always there's Cynthia."

"Should I ask?"

Hollister just shook her head, whispered something I couldn't make out.

"So . . . tomorrow's a new day." I tried for an upbeat vibe. "How about we try to find the sister or the most recent ex? Or we could visit Camilo's school. Maybe a professor or classmate might know something."

"Yeah, sounds good."

Her heart wasn't in it, at least not at that moment. It appeared lipstick Mysti was Hollister's kryptonite. That someone so seemingly self-involved and aloof as Mysti could so completely deflate someone with the vitality of Hollister was a testament to the power of love. Or tortured love. Or torturing oneself in pursuit of love at all cost. I wondered whether Mysti was truly special to Hollister or if she merely occupied a space Hollister longed to fill.

I'd been there. I'd suffered two months of snarky, belittling comments from Tony because while we were together I wasn't alone. Shortly after we first met, I'd thought Tony was *the guy*. When we started dating, I'd thought he felt the same way. The honeymoon phase of a relationship is supposed to last only so long, but I'd never lost that thrill with Tony. Over the weeks we were dating, it became apparent that he could take or leave me. In the end, he chose the latter.

But not before he'd started going out with Ashton.

One night Tony and I were out dancing. Afterward, Tony complained that Ashton was "too perfect," going so far as to inventory each of Ashton's bothersome blemish-free attributes: teeth, hair, nose, body, clothes, job, laugh. The whole package.

Upon reflection, this should have rung alarm bells. Learning the truth had been the emotional equivalent of wading into a pool of piranhas I'd mistaken for a koi pond. And so whatever it was that Hollister felt for Mysti, I wasn't one to judge. At least not yet. Not until I knew her better.

My suggestion to call a rideshare was rebuffed; Hollister insisted on driving me home. Before I climbed out of the car, we agreed to meet for coffee the next morning at a place I'd never been to but had always wanted to try: Slice, the popular cake and pastry shop. According to Hollister, it also poured Seattle's finest espresso. From there, we would decide our next move.

I hoped that after having a good night's sleep, Hollister would rebound and regain her enthusiasm for our investigation. Then again, if she didn't, a small part of me would be relieved. Outwardly I had embraced our adventure, but I'd never shaken my reservations. My naturally cautious inner Hayden had yet to catch up with the bolder version of myself I was putting out there.

When Mo's taillights disappeared around the corner, I turned toward the stairs and noticed a white piece of paper pinned beneath one of the Prius's windshield wipers. As I'd reparked the car in my assigned spot before leaving with Hollister, it wouldn't be a scathing note left by Sarah Lee—at least not about parking in her space.

I pried back the wiper, expecting some notification about recycling bins or a change to the lawn-sprinkling schedule. But the note wasn't from Orca Arms, whose bulletins were typed and printed on aqua-blue letterhead. This message was conveyed in a hurried scrawl of red ink: *Whoever you are, back off.*

My head snapped right, then left, and back again. Could the person who'd left this still be lurking somewhere nearby, ready to attack? I hurried up the stairs, nearly tripping over my own feet. I bolted the door before peering out the blinds, looking for some sign of movement in the overlapping shadows. I saw only stillness.

The feeling of safety was short-lived, however. Commander needed to go out before I could turn in for the night.

After digging in the toolbox I kept stored at the back of my closet, I retrieved the hammer I had only ever used to hang a few pictures. With the comforting weight of the weapon in one hand and a leash in the other, I descended the staircase.

Commander sniffed around the lawn, exercising prolonged choosiness in locating just the right spot to relieve himself. Enough time passed that I started to relax—if someone had been out there hiding in the shadows, they would have acted by now.

Suddenly, a flash lit up the yard. I jumped, spun around, startling Commander. *Yap!*

"Caught in the act," Sarah Lee declared from the balcony. With a sneer, she waved her phone in the air. "Wait till Mrs. Weiser sees this. Even if you're rid of that mongrel before she's back, here's proof you violated your lease. My cousin Meg is looking for a place, and guess what? Yours is perfect. So you might as well start packing now, you freaky little munchkin."

Sarah Lee slammed the door to her unit before I'd switched emotions from panic to anger. As an avalanche of expletives filled my brain, I realized her quick retreat was for the best. Hurling insults in her direction would only further escalate neighbor hostilities. Still, I couldn't allow Sarah Lee a complete shutout victory. Since only Commander would hear me, I shouted up toward her door, "*Little* and *munchkin* are redundant, Sarah Lee!"

Chapter Fourteen
And So It Begins

What had happened to summer?

Seattle had happened to summer.

I shook my small, pale fist at the heavens. Today's overcast sky and drizzle were an unforgivable violation of the pact we Seattleites had with the weather gods. In return for enduring a relentless string of gray and sloppy days throughout the other ten months of the year, we expected—no, more like desperately needed—summer to be sunny and warm. Today was July 21.

Inside the front door, I sat on my knees and dried three of Commander's paws with an old Star Wars bath towel from my childhood. His fourth paw, the back left, he declared off-limits. Giving up on a job that was only 75 percent complete would have, under most other circumstances, been a non-starter, but Commander's flare-up of crankiness startled me. Could that paw be sensitive for some reason? He didn't favor it when running or walking, so I'd never thought it might be hurt. I concluded that it was more likely that the dog had a three-paw time limit and had become impatient with my fussing. I disentangled him from the towel and watched him trot toward the kitchen, leaving a curious trail of a single wet paw print across the linoleum.

The distance to Slice, the bakery where I was to meet Hollister, was no more than three miles away, but I hadn't accounted for rush-hour traffic. I'd be late. I drummed the steering wheel with anxious energy. I hated to be late. I prided myself on arriving to work early to ensure that my class started at the morning bell. I showed up at airports two hours before the flight time. Whenever meeting someone for a date, there'd I'd be, sitting in a booth, reviewing the menu and checking my riotous red hair in the reflection of the window, a minimum of ten minutes before the time we'd agreed to meet.

When I was growing up, my mom had kidded me about my zeal for punctuality. "Slow down, Hayden," she'd say with that lovely smile of hers—the memory of which never failed to make me teary eyed—"the world will wait."

I switched on the radio and caught the tail end of the news about a missing man. His red pickup truck had been abandoned in a parking lot early Saturday morning. The announcer asked that anyone with any information about Camilo Rodriguez contact local police immediately.

Over forty-eight hours had passed since I'd awoken alone in the dancer's bed. Whatever had compelled Camilo to sneak out of the house in the dead of night must have been either preplanned or something he had been called to do at the last minute.

But if his early-morning mission had been orchestrated ahead of time, he wouldn't have invited me over. I could easily have caught him slipping out. Why put himself in a position to have to explain anything? And why risk leaving me alone in his house? Not knowing each other went both ways. Of course, I'd never steal from him or mistreat his dog or burn his house down, but he couldn't have known that.

The only explanation was that someone had called Camilo—no, I would have heard the phone ringing. Someone had *texted* Camilo, and the message had been so urgent that he'd driven to meet someone in that parking lot.

Which parking lot? The police hadn't shared that bit of information.

But then I'd not informed them that Camilo had recently bought a gun. Should I? Wouldn't they just tell me that buying a gun wasn't a crime? Worse yet, they would ask how I knew about his buying a gun when I had claimed I didn't know anything about him.

My biggest fear, the one neither Hollister nor I had said out loud, was that Camilo was dead. If he was alive, he was hiding or someone was holding him against his will. In either case, why leave the pickup behind with its engine running and the door open?

Only one thing made sense. He'd been kidnapped.

My head simmered with thoughts to share with Hollister. More than anything, I wanted to tell her about the creepy note left on my aunt's car.

I clomped up the creaky, warped stairs to the entrance of Slice. Each step of the old wooden house was bookended by pots of enormous red and pink geraniums. Someone had hand-painted each pot with a sign of the zodiac. I spotted mine, Cancer, on the second step. The crab's garish pincers outsized its plump, red-orange body. What sign had Camilo said he was? Taurus? It must be that one there, a pair of horns attached to a brown blob with hooves.

The aroma of fresh coffee welcomed me as I stepped inside the bungalow-turned-bakery. I took in a deep and satisfying breath before walking over to where Hollister had claimed a spot at a corner table near the window. She glanced up from her coffee mug, wisps of steam wafting up toward her mohawk. "You're late."

"Sorry. Traffic." I peeled off my rain jacket, took the seat across from her. "I don't ever come this way at this hour."

"Excuses only satisfy those who make them." She cracked a smile. "My flute teacher used to say that every Thursday afternoon when she'd caught on that I hadn't practiced."

"You play—"

"Ah, ah, ah." She raised a finger, gave a slow wag. "We don't ever talk about the flute."

I proceeded to tell Hollister about the news report on the radio and that the cops must be taking Camilo's disappearance seriously. She sipped and listened silently. When I finished, she gave her mug a little shake. "I need a refill. Can I get you something?"

"Actually, I haven't eaten a bite."

"Well then . . ." Hollister was on her feet and halfway to the counter before I realized I was supposed to follow her. I perused the selection of croissants and strudel, scones and turnovers, each perfectly browned or sugared or precisely topped by a dollop of chunky fruit filling.

A voice boomed from above me. "I'll be a monkey's uncle; it's the fun-sized sleuth!"

I recognized the voice instantly. My head followed my smile up, up, up to where Burley stood on the other side of the counter, swaddled in a white apron seemingly the size of a bedsheet. Her long hair was braided into a single ponytail wrapped around her head like a coil of rope—held in place by two long chopsticks.

"How about a blueberry muffin? Just pulled them out of the oven."

I raised my eyebrows, turned to Hollister. "You weren't going to tell me?"

"Why spoil the surprise?"

Never had I wondered about Burley's day job. Still, I'd not have been surprised to find her reconstructing a diesel engine, operating a backhoe, or welding together two I beams (though I doubted that welding masks came large enough to fit her head). Oil and grease, yes; powdered sugar and frosting, no.

"Burley owns the place," Hollister said, "Family business. She took it over from her father about ten years ago. Was either her or her brother. You've met Roy, so I needn't explain. Burley was reluctant at first, but after a while she got used to it, then good at it. Then really good at it."

Burley returned with a muffin the size of a cantaloupe. As she pushed the white plate across the countertop, she noticed the look on my face. "Have you seen these hands? They don't do dainty."

My eyes bugged. "I'll need Hollister to help if I'm to have any chance." I reached for my wallet. Burley waved me off.

"On the house. I appreciate you and Hollister trying to find our boy Camilo. I know what people think. Latino, gay, suspicious circumstances, must be mixed up in some bad business, so something bad happened to him. That's the easy read. That's the story that lets us off the hook of caring and getting our butts in gear to find that boy. The truth is, Camilo is a good person. Works hard. Studies hard. And is committed to building a good life for himself. He isn't a criminal. He doesn't go near drugs. He doesn't trick. Bottom line, he doesn't deserve whatever has happened to him. Now, I'm not a defender of our girls and boys in blue, but I don't distrust them as completely as Hollister here. But make no mistake, there isn't anybody out there looking for him that truly cares about finding him."

"Except for us," Hollister said.

"Except for you." Burley nodded. Her gaze suddenly shifted to my hair; she squinted and tilted her head slightly as if examining a strange insect that had landed on my head. "Little-known fact," she said. "Ginger is good for dogs with heart problems."

I stared up at her, wondering what the hell she was talking about.

"When I was little, we had a Chihuahua with a murmur."

Most people would have asked a follow-up question, her non sequitur as impossible to ignore as a furious itch. I had no such trouble; my only thought was to wonder how little a *little* Burley could be. Hollister, on the other hand, took the bait.

"So . . . what happened?" she asked. "Heart failure?"

"Snatched by a falcon." Burley shook her head slowly, followed by a moment of reverential silence. "To this day, I can't look at a bird without reaching for my slingshot."

"Did you ever get another dog?" I managed to ask.

"Funny how things turn out," Burley said. "Yes, but in a roundabout way. I got Roy an adorable set of brother-and-sister pups as a birthday present many years later. I thought they might soften him a bit—you know, give him something to nurture and care for, like my experience with our little Cucaracha. But those dogs of Roy's"—she shivered, her mountainous shoulders shaking like a tremor—"they turned out just like him. Big and mean."

"Word," Hollister said.

Wanting to flex my firsthand knowledge of Roy's dogs, I added, "The only thing capable of flying away with those dogs is a Nazgûl on a Fellbeast."

Now the dumbfounded looks landed on me. I'd overestimated the number of *Lord of the Rings* fans in attendance by two.

Hollister seemed ready for a subject change. "So, Burley, we should let you get back to your oven. Little dude and I need to plan our day."

Before we began the debate about which avenue of investigation to pursue, I told Hollister about the note—*Whoever you are, back off*—that someone had left on the car.

"So they know who you are," she said, tapping a long purple-painted nail on her ceramic mug. "They must be watching Camilo's house. They saw you there. How else could they know about you?"

I covered my muffin-filled mouth. "When did they become *they*?"

"Just a matter of speaking is all. Why? That bother you?"

After pausing to swallow, I replied, "Sounds like we're outnumbered."

"Odds are as good that we're dealing with more than one person as we are a single individual. Either way, we need to be careful. They know who you are."

Wiping crumbs from my chin, I said, "Well, not technically. Otherwise they'd not have addressed the note to 'whoever you are.' But I get your point. They could pick me out of a crowd."

Hollister held up a hand. "That's too soft a softball to swing at."

"And they know where I live."

"Technically, they know where you park."

"Touché, madam."

It took as much time—twenty-five minutes—for me to consume a huge muffin as it did for us to agree that our next move would be a visit to Camilo's college. We bused our table, said our good-byes to Burley, and climbed into Mo.

Chapter Fifteen
Caught in the Act

Hollister declined my offer to drive us, which was fine by me. I attributed her refusal to ride in my aunt's car to the whacky religious stickers on the back windshield and bumper. I also expected she wasn't comfortable anywhere other than behind the wheel. The only reason she'd let me drive us to Roy's had been her drinking at Burley's party. While Hollister's driving style never failed to do the impossible in turning my knuckles an even lighter shade of white, I knew my cautious approach to the road—sticking to the speed limit, obeying stop signs, and not needing to treat a light turned green as the equivalent of a starting gun—would make her crazy.

Hollister pointed the car toward Capitol Hill.

"You have a boyfriend?" Hollister asked.

"Negative."

"And why's that?"

"Got dumped."

Her eyebrows shot up. "His name?"

"Tony."

"Well, Tony's an idiot."

"Ha, on that we agree."

Hollister turned serious. "Mysti, on the other hand . . . she's got a big heart. Just gets in her way."

I shifted in my bucket seat. As much as I wanted to know more about Hollister and be supportive, I was wary of asking the wrong question and inadvertently facilitating the conversation's swerve off course and into a dark alley. I'd seen how the topic of Mysti could send Hollister into a tailspin. I didn't want to see her getting down or distracted from our mission. Still, I had to say something.

"Well, I don't know about Mysti, but you seem like a good egg."

She sputtered a laugh. "That so?"

Shrugging, I said, "Yeah. But I'm probably wrong. You're probably a horrible person, pretending to be all Batwoman-good when you're all Alice-evil."

After I explained Alice's comic book role as Batwoman's archnemesis, Hollister said, "I just try to do my best, little dude. That's all I can do."

"Imagine a world if everyone did that."

"Dream on, brother."

The next few miles sped by in comfortable silence. I had successfully redirected the conversation away from the valley of Mysti and up to a higher plane, where it now rested, waiting for a second wind. The swish, swish of the wipers kept time with the hum of the defroster, pushing a gentle breeze against the windshield. I relaxed, letting my head fall back against the headrest, and took in the passing view of Capitol Hill, a dense urban neighborhood situated just east of downtown and between the hospitals of First Hill on the south and Lake Union to the north. Capitol Hill had evolved from a cluster of lovely old brick buildings to mixed-use complexes offering city dwellers gourmet doughnuts and high-concept fusion cuisine on the ground floor and tiny-roomed apartments stacked above.

"You grow up around here?" I asked.

"Chicago. All my family is still there."

"Brothers? Sisters?"

"Three brothers, two sisters. All Baptists, except for my brother Daryl. He's in the Army, stationed in Germany."

"What brought you out here?"

"Work."

I realized I had no idea what Hollister did for a living. She dressed well; her clothes seemed high quality, made from only leather or denim or cotton. Boots, no jewelry. She drove a newer-model sports car and apparently didn't work weekends or Mondays. These observations did little to narrow the universe of job candidates beyond a typical nine-to-five gig. However, her hair provided a directional clue: the mohawk was by any measure a bold statement that would stick out in any work environment other than, say, the music industry or a tattoo studio. With hints of crimson among the black, the hedge-like strip of hair was precisely trimmed at about six inches tall, three inches wide, with the sides of her head clipper-cut to nearly scalp level.

Learning that Burley was an award-winning baker had set a high bar in the improbable-jobs guessing game. I eagerly awaited Hollister's answer to my next question: "So what is it you do?"

"Artisan."

"Artisan," I repeated. "As in making things with your hands?"

"Precisely."

This answer delighted me immeasurably. "And what do your hands make?"

"Furniture."

It took some pressing to learn more, as Hollister wasn't forthcoming with information about her craft. At first, I thought she was being tediously private, and then I worried she might be embarrassed. The truth was she was exercising modesty, because to talk about her work would be to reveal she was something of a rock star in her industry. Her line of furniture, Holl&Wood, had been featured in numerous magazines, including *Architectural Digest*, *Elle Decor*, and *Dwell*. Her clientele included your run-of-the-mill billionaires and several Grammy and Oscar winners. She'd moved to Seattle to join a small, selective guild of craftswomen and be nearer the forests and the natural resources required for her trade.

Rather than enjoying the opportunity to talk about her success, Hollister seemed restless or bored and answered my questions without embellishment. Learning what I did about her business was due only to my persistence. It was when she said, "And that's enough about that," that I got the message that a topic change was in order.

"Do you get back to Illinois to visit your family often?"

Hollister downshifted; the campus was nearby, and the search for a parking spot was on. "Not much to get back for, unless you count arguing as a reason. If you hadn't noticed, I like girls, and in my family, that's unacceptable because it's unacceptable to God." She rolled her eyes. "Whatever."

"Is that why you don't swear? Because you were brought up in a religious household?"

She chuckled. "Uh-huh. You ever hear of parents threatening to wash their kids' mouths out with soap if they cuss? In my house it was more than just talk. Me and my siblings even gave it a name: Dove tongue."

I loved Hollister's laugh—big and joyful and genuine. I couldn't help but laugh whenever I heard it, and it made me happy to think I'd played a role in bringing on the moment.

"Are you close with any of your siblings?"

"Daryl is the one person who doesn't care about me liking girls. He's not gay himself, just doesn't look at it as a big deal. Maybe it's his being in the military."

"How do you mean?

"I don't know," she chuckled. "Maybe shooting at people and getting shot at yourself puts things in perspective. Who a person wants to have sex with shouldn't much matter in a world that is always experiencing some war or atrocity. I mean, if my dad wants to devote a sermon to the societal perils of an LGBTQ agenda, it's his right. But honestly, what a waste of time. I'm not a problem. To him and the way he sees the world, I am a disappointment. That's his problem, not mine. It took me years to realize that, by the way. Daryl helped a lot. But if religious folks want to do something godly, why not focus on helping people rather than demonizing them? Look around. Enough men are doing the devil's work right here on earth. How about we humans put a little more focus on them?" She turned her head, partially to address me but also to see over her shoulder as she backed the car into an open space. "What about you? Family?"

"My mom passed away from breast cancer when I was in high school. My dad was never really in the picture. No brothers, no sisters. I had a sister. She was older by five years but died shortly after she was born. My closest family are my grandparents. They live in Palm Springs. And there's my mom's sister, Aunt Sally, who lives here in Seattle."

"The Prius," Hollister said.

"The Prius," I confirmed. "My mom wasn't religious. She taught biology. Not that that explains it entirely, but I do think her study of science played a big part in shaping her beliefs."

Hollister put the car in park, shut off the engine. "She ever knew you were into guys?"

I nodded. "I came out to her my freshman year. I wasn't proud. I wasn't brave. I hated the way I felt. I thought it was so unfair; why me? Why do I have to be the statistic, the one in ten to like boys? I was fifteen and already convinced my life would be miserable."

"Was she cool with you liking guys?"

"She gave me a speech. It was long, but I'll never forget how it ended. She said, 'Listen, son, you want to get through this and become a reasonably happy person, you don't need to love the idea of being gay, but you do need to appreciate that being gay is just another thing about you that makes you lovable.'"

Hollister reached over the stick shift and hugged me, the left side of my face pressed into the smooth leather of her jacket. "Your mom sounds like a very cool lady."

"Yeah, you two would have liked each other."

"She'd be proud of you, Hayden. You're a good man."

Man. Had anyone ever before referred to me as "a man," good or otherwise? That I had become a grown man struck me as a minor revelation. The transition from boy to man hadn't occurred with the flip of a switch; it had been a long and steady creep, marking its progress in a series of tests, each imparting the lesson that the world didn't solely revolve around me. Hollister had summed up a personal ethos as compelling as any I'd ever heard: "I just try to do my best." I could get behind that. As a man, I'd try to do the same.

I joined her on the sidewalk, and we headed down Broadway toward campus. The clouds broke, allowing a shaft of sunlight to shimmer in the puddles and warm our cheeks. Turning the final corner to the main entrance, we nearly bumped into a trio of students; they pushed and shoved each other in jest, like puppies wrestling on a lawn. The cutest among the group, a boy who looked to be about twenty, thin with a bit of blond scruff on his chin, gave me a look. *That* look. Slyly, while opening the door to the building, I looked back at him as they zigzagged away. The boy wore his jeans well, like only a lean body could. I held my gaze an extra few seconds in the hope he'd turn back and confirm the connection.

"That's not obvious," Hollister said.

Spinning around, I tried for a look of confusion. "Sorry?"

"Don't even," she said. She held up two fingers to her eyes. "I'm not blind."

"Oh, I . . ." Why did I feel like I'd just been caught skimming cash from the register? Hardly was a quick flirtatious glance something to feel guilty about. I was single, after all.

"Relax, I'm just teasing. He was cute—young, but cute."

"Yeah," I said, happy to let it drop. I followed Hollister inside.

She stopped, suddenly serious. "So, with that young boy, I guess you'd be the daddy?"

"Not funny."

Hollister threw her head back, laughed. "Maybe that'll be your new nickname: Little Daddy."

I groaned, shook my head. "Let me know when you're finished."

"Okay, okay. I'll stop. We got work to do. What's the plan, anyway? Hang out by the computer lab and classrooms, then what? Ask around? Why should anyone talk to us? Who do we say we are? What's our business in looking for Camilo?"

My only issue with Hollister's questions was that she'd not posed them earlier. Though what really rankled was that I hadn't thought of them myself. During the car ride over, I'd allowed us to lose focus and talk about ourselves when we should have been tightening up a plan. Maybe that was why I felt slightly guilty about staring at that boy: my concentration should have been on our mission to find Camilo.

The fourth student we asked knew the computer science department's location within the building's five floors and a maze of hallways. As luck would have it, she was on her way there. Although she knew who Camilo was, they "ran in different circles," as she put it. She did, however, know who Camilo did hang out with: Tanner and Paul.

Chapter Sixteen
Total Waste

Geeks. There was a time when being a geek placed you at the bottom of the K–12 social ladder: at the lunch table sitting across from the nerds. Truth be told, if there was a difference between the two tribes, I couldn't tell you what it was. Since my days of having lunch in public school cafeterias, several popular television shows had featured awkward brainiac protagonists as oddly charming, earning them a newfound degree of cool. As I considered myself half nerd, half pocket-gay jock—a term that combines my decent tennis game with the somewhat familiar term *pocket-gay*, as in, "Why, he's so little, I could put him in my pocket"—I was gratified by this turning of the tables.

Such thoughts sprang to mind because Hollister and I had just met Camilo's closest college friends, Tanner and Paul. Geeks. One thousand percent geeks.

Knowing what I knew of Camilo, I couldn't picture him hanging out with these two. Whereas Camilo was full of life, gregarious and jolly—and gay—these guys were hard to read, awkward, straight, and displayed no interest in physique or appearance. They did both have one distinctive feature: Tanner sported short, blue-dyed hair; Paul had dreadlocks. They also shared an unexpected and impossible-to-ignore use of the sort of body spray favored by teenage boys, the kind with names like Rebellion and Turbo. What bound them to Camilo was a senior project they wouldn't discuss.

After shrugging away most of our questions about Camilo, Tanner and Paul did spill that Camilo had become increasingly flaky over the past few months, canceling meetings at the last minute, arriving late, leaving early, and generally not pulling his weight. On this topic, Tanner and Paul were effusive. So much so that Hollister and I had to wait until their rant subsided before I was able to interject the obvious question: "Why? What caused the change in Camilo's behavior?"

"That stupid new job of his," Tanner scoffed.

"Stupid is right," Paul agreed.

"Total waste of a brain."

"Waste of gray matter. Even stopped hanging out with us at Festers."

Tanner answered our baffled looks. "Video games, pinball, that sort of thing. Open late. We go most nights."

Desperate to stop them from getting distracted by tales of Festers, I held up my hands, hoping the crossing-guard signal would be respected. "Back to Camilo's job, what job was that?"

"At that stupid pet store," Tanner said.

"A pet store." Paul rolled his eyes, which from behind his improbably thick glasses gave the effect of the room tilting.

"What pet store?" I asked, the urgency in my voice matching Hollister's posture. She looked like she was about to reach across the table and throttle them.

"Farkingham Phallus," Tanner said.

"Sorry, Fark—"

"Stupid-ass name," Paul said. "We call it Farkingham Phallus. It's really Barkingham Palace."

"Barkingham Palace?" I looked to them for confirmation. They shrugged.

"Told you it was stupid," Tanner said.

Chapter Seventeen
In the Blink of an Eye

Mo's navigation system pointed us westward. With Hollister behind the wheel, we made it across town in less than half an hour. I'd never heard of a pet store named Barkingham Palace, but then I didn't own a pet and seldom traveled to the northwest part of the city. It seemed to me there were two types of pet stores: big-box chain and local mom-and-pop. Within those categories, they were all pretty much the same, I thought.

How wrong I was. Barkingham Palace was a single-story cinder-block building painted a glossy periwinkle blue with a facade that had been artfully painted in a trompe-l'oeil to look as if it were supported by golden columns. Someone had added crenellations to the roof line to give the appearance of a castle parapet. The store's sign, which stretched above the front window and entrance, was formed from individual letters fabricated to look like they were cast from solid gold.

The main window display—modeled at roughly 10 percent scale—rivaled that of the New York Macy's during the Christmas season. Carrying the title *Alice in the Palace*, the case's decoration included three exquisite chandeliers hanging over a palace hall surrounded by little gilt mirrors. A doll-size table, set with an appropriately scaled tea service, was covered end to end with plastic replicas of cakes and cookies. Assembled around the table sat the six main characters of *Alice in Wonderland*, all of them represented by stuffed toy animals. The role of Alice was depicted by a Yorkshire terrier wearing a light-blue dress with a white apron front. A placard next to her informed customers that Alice's outfit was *Available in most sizes.* The Mad Hatter was portrayed by a French bulldog promoting a burgundy leather collar with black stitching: *Handmade right here in Washington!* The White Rabbit was played not by a white rabbit but by a white poodle sporting a red cape, and the Cheshire Cat was represented by—what else?—a chubby cat wearing a purple-striped sweater. Rounding out the party was the Queen of Hearts miscast by a slim boxer with a tiny silver tiara awkwardly strapped to its head. *All items by special order.* If the mind-bending exhibit was any reflection of the owner's personality, I was both curious and concerned. As creative and well executed as the display was, the overall effect suggested an imagination slightly unhinged.

On the drive over from the college, Hollister and I had agreed that we'd split up once inside the store, pretending to be single shoppers to double our odds of learning something valuable. She would peruse the dog aisle, and I'd take cats. I'd argued that my recent experience with Commander made me more suited for canines, but Hollister had refused to trade, her argument being, "I'm a dog person. I'm going to the dog section. End of negotiation."

Entering through the store's front door triggered a chorus of trumpets to herald our arrival. The horns faded out, leaving a cheerful orchestral arrangement of "We're Off to See the Wizard" floating through the aisles.

The inside of the store was like being dropped into a gum ball machine. There was up-close color everywhere I turned. The aisles fanned out at various odd angles. There was a long service counter at the back of the store, split into two sections, each marked by a large overhead sign. One read *Pet Check-In*, which I assumed was for grooming and boarding services, and the other *People Check-Out*, for store purchases.

The store's two other customers appeared to be dog owners—both were perusing the *Woof* section. Hollister soon joined them. I headed to the *Meow* aisles. There were birds on sticks, mice with bells, ribbed rubber balls, and dozens of other human creations sure to bewilder, if not entertain, man's second-best friend. I was admiring the astonishing assortment of cat toys when an overwhelming waft of gardenia filled my nose.

"Looks like some lucky pussy is in for a special surprise."

I spun around and was face-to-face with a middle-aged woman who brought to mind a word I didn't think I'd ever used before: buxom. The lenses in her gold-framed eyeglasses were the size of drink coasters, and her gray eyes were enormous and unblinking. While well put together, her clothes were in a style popular with the female characters of 1980s television dramas—silk blouses, long jackets with shoulder pads, and big hair. This woman had dyed-blond curls piled atop her head like rickety scaffolding. She was midfifties, heavyset, and appeared to apply her makeup with a trowel.

"Allow me to introduce myself. My name is Della Rupert, proprietress of Barkingham Palace. I sincerely thank you for coming in today. So, love bug, you finding everything you're looking for?"

"Um . . . yes, thanks. Just looking."

"You know that is just the best thing, really it is. Just looking allows one to stay open to the possibilities. It's such a rarity these days. I have oodles of customers who just dart in and out, quick as you please, like they're in a race for their lives. Mind you, I am delighted they can find what they're looking for, but I can't help but think they're missing out. Just look around you. We just have so much to offer. So much to see. So much you would never discover unless you are just looking."

"Yes, I see that."

Della's still-unblinking eyes, magnified by her quarter-inch-thick glasses, had me transfixed.

"Your first time?" she asked.

"My first time?"

"Visiting us here at Barkingham Palace?"

"Oh, yes. I just moved to town." Why I said this, I didn't know.

"Oh really," she said, drawing out the words.

I sensed Della's interest in me had just shifted into a higher gear. "A newbie to our wonderful city. Isn't that just lovely?"

"Seattle is very nice. I like it a lot." This was true.

"You know, love bug, you are just the most adorable thing. Those eyes of yours are quite something. Now, what color is that exactly?"

"Hazel."

"My, my, hazel eyes and red hair. Why I never. And those freckles. I imagine the girls pester you somethin' awful."

Adding to Della's list of oddities was that she spoke in a singsongy way, yet her face appeared to be set in wax. I wished Hollister were here to witness the conversation—I'd never capture its weirdness in my retelling. Though bizarre as it was, I sensed that Della was flirting. I doubted she would be as interested in talking to me were Hollister present.

"Oh, but just listen to me, will you? You'd think I'd forgotten what year we're living in. I'm sure it's not just the girls who are beating down your door. Am I right?"

"That's . . . um . . . nice of you to say."

"Pishposh. I'm just saying what my own two eyes can see. So did you and your pussy move here for work?"

Della's use of the word *pussy* was weirding me out. "Yes, for work," I replied. "Leonard, my *cat*, seems to like it too." Another lie, but this one seemed to be necessary.

"Oh, how lovely. What line of work, if you don't mind me asking?"

"Web designer." Yet another lie, but at this point . . .

"You don't say? What a marvelous vocation. With everything going online these days, I'm sure there is no end to your opportunities. The whole world all in a digital dither. Why next thing I know, I'll wake up, find out I've been replaced by a robot or an algorithm or some such. All the more reason to maintain the irreplaceable virtues of a high-touch, personalized customer service experience as long as possible."

"I'm sure you're right. Listen, I was wondering if a friend of mine was working today?"

"Oh." Her magnified eyeballs telegraphed surprise. "A friend, you say? Now who might that be?"

"His name is Camilo."

"Camilo?" she repeated, and blinked for the first time. "Camilo, did you say?"

"Yes, that's right."

"No, no Camilo under my employ."

"You're sure? I swear he said he worked here."

A long pause followed. Della pressed an index finger to her lips, displaying a nail painted the same light-blue shade as the building's exterior. "You know, sweet pea, I'm afraid you must have the wrong store. Perhaps this friend of yours intended to apply? Wouldn't that just be a hoot? If your friend gave you the wrong information? Now, where have I misplaced my manners? I introduced myself but never got your name."

"Blaze." I had no idea where this came from. I just opened my mouth and out it spilled.

"Blaze?" she repeated. "Well, lovely to meet you, Blaze . . ."

"Thurston." Suddenly I recalled the name's origin.

"Blaze Thurston," she repeated slowly, as if to commit to memory my nom de guerre (thanks again to Mrs. Gasquet). "Well, Blaze, you really must forgive me, but I have other customers to attend to. I do hope you enjoy your visit to Barkingham Palace. If I can be of any further assistance, don't you hesitate to give Della a shout." She turned and shuffled off down the aisle, aiming for a woman rummaging through a shelf filled with rawhide bones.

I headed toward the exit, my pace reflecting my need for fresh air. I'd been inside the store for only a short while, but Della's suffocating presence had made the encounter feel like it lasted an hour. From the corner of my eye, I could see that Hollister was surprised to see me leave so soon. She followed me outside, slid into the driver's seat. "Well?"

"I met the owner. Her name is Della Rupert. That lady is one creepy chick."

"Oh my God, you reek of her perfume." Hollister waved a hand in front of her nose.

"Tell me about it. She must bathe in the stuff."

"So what did you find out?"

"Get this: she says she doesn't have anyone named Camilo working for her."

"But Tanner and Paul said—"

"She's lying. I know it. One thousand percent lying."

"How can you be so sure?"

"She blinked."

"Say again?"

"She blinked. The only time she blinked during our entire conversation was when I said the name Camilo."

"Damn, damn, damn. Anything else?"

"She is worried. She made a point of getting my name."

Hollister punched me in the arm. "Why in the hell would you give her your name? We already have to deal with whoever left that threatening note on your car."

I produced my coyest smile.

"What?"

"Meet Blaze Thurston."

"You can't be serious."

"I was caught up in the moment. I felt like a spy. A spy needs a cover."

"You've been watching too much Netflix."

"Ha! You said you were like Batwoman."

"To you, but not to strangers. And Blaze Thurston? How'd you come up with that?"

"Porn star."

She shook her head, but I could detect the crack of a smile. In true Bond fashion, I raised a single eyebrow. "That's not all I discovered. Take a look at the cars in the parking lot."

Hollister scanned the area. "I see them . . . and?"

"Which one of them belongs to the owner, Della Rupert?"

There were five cars in the lot, including Hollister's Porsche. She immediately ruled out the massive four-wheel-drive as being much "too dude." Next, she eliminated the tiny compact, as she'd seen Della from across the store and doubted the woman could squeeze herself behind its wheel. Two cars remained. One was a modest midsize import, and the other was big and luxury and American.

"Got it," she said. "The new silver Cadillac sedan."

The personalized plates were the clincher. They read FURBALL.

"Now what?" she said.

I checked the clock on the dash. "We come back at five, when the store closes, and follow her."

"And in the meantime, I say we find the sister, Daniela."

Daniela Rodriguez. Common first name, extremely common last name. Where to start? We didn't know if Daniela lived in the area—or the country, for that matter. A quick search on social media resulted in twenty-two possibilities within the state alone, half of them offering nothing beyond a last name and first initial. Camilo's phone would no doubt have her contact information, but he'd taken it with him—and even if he hadn't, it was probably password protected. Same for Camilo's computer, but someone had stolen it when they'd ransacked his house. The police must have ways to find Camilo's sister, should they decide to use them. Hollister and I had only our wits and determination.

Hollister slapped the steering wheel. "His house! If we can get inside Camilo's house, do a thorough search, we will find something. And maybe not just related to the sister, either. We might find the smoking gun."

"I hope not!"

"I meant figuratively."

"Oh," I said, relieved. "But wait." My worry rushed back. "We can't break into Camilo's already-broken-into house. If the police catch us, they'll think we're part of this whole mess."

"We are part of this whole mess, little dude."

"Yes, but not in a criminal way. We're just trying to do the right thing. Find a good guy that something bad has happened to. Neither of us has said it, at least not out loud, but we're trying to save Camilo. If we can find him in time, we just may save his life."

"Exactly. So given what's at stake, don't you think it's worth taking the risk? We need to search his house."

I bunched my lips and blew out a long breath. I didn't like where this was headed. What Hollister proposed was reckless, teetering on dangerous. My focus was on the probability of us getting caught and arrested. Hollister read my apprehension.

"How about this?" she said. "We wait until dark, go in the back. The place is empty, right? We use flashlights. We wear gloves. We stay for one hour. Just one hour. We find whatever we can find and we're out. No one will ever know."

This I couldn't do. No matter how much Hollister tried to reassure me that nothing would go wrong, the possibility of being handcuffed and thrown in jail shredded my insides. I'd heard about prison. *Look at me!* I'd be a sheep thrown to the lions. No way.

"Let me think about it," I said.

Hollister started up Mo. I could see she was frustrated. "Fine. I'll take you back to your car."

"Unless . . ."

"What?" she said, her voice reflecting her disappointment. She kept her eyes set on the road ahead.

"Remember at karaoke? Burley had mentioned Camilo's ex-boyfriend, a Ryan or Rory or something like that. She couldn't remember exactly."

"Yeah, I remember." She looked at me from the corner of her eye. "So?"

"We have the entire afternoon. Let's find him."

Chapter Eighteen
Down a Dancer

Back to where it all began: Hunters. As it was just past noon on a Monday, the front lot was empty. However, behind the building, a tan Chevy was parked by the back door, propped open. The place was dark and smelled of stale beer and popcorn. A digital jukebox illuminated a corner of the bar. A now-familiar song spilled from the speakers: *And still the easiest thing I've done is falling hard for you.*

Hollister and I found Hank, the club manager, busying himself with some paperwork at the bar. He must have heard us come in the back. He looked up, seemingly not at all surprised to see us standing there.

"Hey, Hollister, what's shakin'?" he said, before adding, "Hey, Hayward."

We returned Hank's hellos.

"Cops were just here," he said. "You just missed them."

My stomach dropped. I looked at Hollister. If she shared my alarm, she didn't show it. She pulled out the stool next to Hank.

"Good," Hollister said. "It's about time the police took this situation seriously."

Too worked up to sit, I steadied myself by planting a hand on the bar next to Hank. "What did they want?" I asked, afraid to hear the answer.

"What do you think?" Hank said. "Questions about Camilo . . ." He shifted his focus from his papers to me. "And you." The dread must have been apparent on my face. "Don't worry about it, man. I told them what happened that night, how you got that shiner. They were, you know, just checking out your story. As you'd expect, they had lots of questions about Camilo: how long he worked here, what he was like, friends, family, if he'd changed somehow recently, started hanging out with new people. That sort of thing. I told them what I could, and they left."

"Did they seem satisfied?" I asked.

"Guess so," Hank said. "When it comes to Camilo, I only know what happens here. That's all I could tell them."

Hollister scooted her stool closer to the bar. "Listen, Hank, the other night Burley said something about Camilo having a boyfriend—"

"Ex-boyfriend," I said.

"Ex-boyfriend," Hollister repeated. "Burley wasn't sure about the name, though. A Riley or R-something. We were—"

"Ryan," Hank said. "You don't know Ryan?"

Hollister arched her brows. "Should I?"

I shook my head, though he'd asked Hollister.

Hank punched some numbers into a calculator. "No reason, you liking women and all. But if guys were your thing, you would very much like to know Ryan."

"And why's that?" she asked.

"On a ten-point scale, Ryan is an eleven." Hank beamed as if he deserved some credit for the guy's attractiveness. "Hottest dude that's ever worked here. Dancer. For a while, anyway. It was good for business. It was bad for business."

"How do you mean?" I asked.

"Great for Ryan," Hank explained. "He made more money in one night than most guys do in a month. But he took the lion's share of the tips. The other guys complained. They didn't make enough to make it worth their while. So one by one, they refused to dance on the same nights as him. It's no good having a solo show. No matter how smokin' hot the guy is, the crowd likes a variety of eye candy."

"Sounds past tense," I said. "I take it Ryan doesn't dance here any longer?" Hank didn't need to answer the question. I came to Hunters often enough that I would have noticed an eleven on a ten-point scale. Given the club's current lineup, Camilo was the hottest dancer by at least two full points.

Hank shuffled some papers. "Quit."

"He give a reason?" Hollister asked. The song on the juke-box ended, and an eerie quiet took over the dark space.

"Something about a better gig. Better hours. Ten times the pay. I remember that part distinctly." Hank opened a thick black binder, started to make entries on a ledger page. "Granted, I don't pay much per hour. Tips are where the boys make their money. But still, Ryan must have been raking in a thousand a night. So when he claimed he was going to be making ten times that, I just laughed, wished him well."

"This is where he met Camilo, though, right?" I said. "They dated?"

"Yeah, could be. Camilo was here throughout the months Ryan was around. Camilo was the only guy who could hold his own in tips when dancing the same night as Ryan. I saw them leave together on a few occasions. But you know, these young guys. Is it for one night? Two? The hotter they are, the shorter the romance. Always someone new. Trust me on that. I've been working this bar for nearly twenty years. There is always someone new. Hey, if I looked the way they do, why not? Why not get it while you can?"

Hank appeared to be lost in wistful thought, his fingertips frozen on the spreadsheet before him.

"So back to Ryan," Hollister said.

"Yeah, what about him?" Hank said, snapping back to attention. "Why the interest in him, anyway? You think he might know something about Camilo's disappearance?"

Hollister tapped her nose. "Know where we can find him?"

Hank flipped to the tab at the back of the binder. "His address should be in here. I needed it for payroll, W-2s, et cetera. I can't promise it's current, but here it is. Ryan Waddell. Seventy-eight ninety-eight Cornelia Court. Here in Seattle. Somewhere out by the locks, I think."

Reaching for a paper coaster on the bar, I asked to borrow a pen and wrote down Ryan's full name and address. On our way out, Hank shouted, "You find Ryan, tell him to give me a call. I'm short a dancer."

Chapter Nineteen
Eleven on a Ten-Point Scale

Was I eager to meet Ryan Waddell and hear what he could tell us about Camilo? Without question. Was that why I found myself—inconceivably—wishing Hollister would drive even faster? I wish I were a better person and could truthfully answer yes. Fact is, I wanted to see with my own eyes what this eleven looked like. Images of cover models raced to mind, along with a few celebrities and the one-in-a-thousand guy I'd randomly pass on the streets or, if fortunate, catch changing in the locker room that made me think, *Lucky jerk, you hit the genetics jackpot!*

"You ever been with an eleven?" Hollister asked, an eyebrow raised. Once again, she'd caught me off guard while also being freakishly in tune with where my mind was at the moment.

"Camilo came closest. A nine-point-two. However, the system is highly subjective. How about you?"

Her look of discomfort told me she hadn't expected the question turned back to her.

"You've seen Mysti. What would you say she is?"

Uh-oh. I must be careful here. My without-thinking-it-through reply was a seven. I was downgrading heavily (two full points) for her bad attitude. That's if I was honest. But honesty isn't always the best policy. Sometimes what a friend needs most is someone to shut up and listen to her—even if what she is saying is overblown, even when she knows it herself.

"What's your answer?" I tried.

"Twelve," she said, not missing a beat.

Oh boy. To think how deeply I had almost stepped in it. But come on, a twelve? Even recognizing that this game of slapping a number on a person by looks alone was a bit (a lot?) degrading, Mysti was no twelve. Hollister had gifted Mysti at least five bonus points. And for what? Infatuation? Amazing sex? Love? Whatever the reason, I didn't see it. Before, I'd managed to dodge the topic of Hollister's relationship with the Asian femme fatale, but now I sensed there was something Hollister needed to unload. As a friend, I needed to invite the opening of the floodgates.

"What's with you two?" I ventured, striving for a broad opening that would allow her to take the conversation in the direction of her choosing.

"Goddamn girl makes my heart bleed."

Waiting for more, I sat silently. As seconds became minutes, I realized the subject of Hollister's romance with Mysti had met with a slamming of the brakes. Had that been all Hollister wanted to share? Or had her admission of pain forced a retreat back into silence? Having only my gut to rely on, I decided not to push it. I'd shown I was open to listening. The ball was in her court.

Sleek and modern described the homes on Cornelia Court. The two-story white box with the large black numbers *7898* next to a five-foot-wide glass front door was no exception. Parked in the middle of a two-car driveway was a sleek mat-gray motorcycle. Hollister parked Mo in front of the house.

"You sure you wrote down the right address?" she said.

I nodded. "When Ryan told Hank he'd found a job making ten times the money, he wasn't kidding."

"Could be his parents' place."

"Maybe, but I don't see any parent riding that," I said, pointing to the motorcycle with *Ninja* painted across the gas tank.

"Damn," she said. "A Kawasaki H2R. That's like a fifty-thousand-dollar bike."

"You know motorcycles?"

"Past girlfriend was way into it. You know, during the gay pride parade, the ladies on motorcycles that kick things off."

"Dykes on Bikes," I said, pleased I knew what she was talking about. Hollister and I had little in common, so I relished any overlap in life experience.

"That's right." She nodded and chuckled. "Cynthia was head of the pack. She's a tiny thing, too, never looked right straddling that much horsepower."

I had a joke on the tip of my tongue but decided I didn't know Hollister well enough to risk it.

"What about you?" she said. "You ride?"

"Just the other day, as it happens."

This intrigued Hollister. "Let me guess. Honda?"

"Schwinn."

"Hilarious."

"I'm serious." I explained my recent ride on the borrowed girl's bicycle. The image gave Hollister a good laugh.

"Ready to do this?" She drew two finger pistols, aimed them at the house. I sensed Hollister shared my eagerness to speak with Camilo's most recent ex-boyfriend. Days were slipping by with no sign of Camilo, and we were desperate to learn something that would progress our investigation.

The sidewalk leading to the front door was a series of large, disconnected cement slabs, interspersed by lawn, perfectly cut, lush, and the only green on the property. Stepping up onto the platform before the door, Hollister and I exchanged bewildered looks.

"Do we knock on the glass?" With my hand as a visor, I peered into the room beyond.

"Beats the hell out of me. You'd think a house this fancy, they'd have sprung for a doorbell."

"Can I help you?"

I jumped at the unexpected sound.

We both looked up and at either side of the doorway. We couldn't discern the direction from which the voice had come.

"Hello?" The voice again, more insistent. "Can I help you?"

Hollister gave me a shrug.

"Hello," I shouted. "We're here to see Ryan."

"You don't need to yell. I can hear you just fine. Who are you?"

"My name is Hayden McCall."

"My name is Hollister."

"We're friends of Camilo Rodriguez," I added.

Silence.

"Hello?" I shouted.

"Seriously, you don't need to yell," the voice said. "Come in. I'll be right down."

With a soft click, the door swung open.

Had I ever wondered what living in a modern museum would feel like, I'd just stepped into the answer. White on white on white. Angles, angles, angles. High ceiling. A massive black-and-white photograph of a black rhino took up an entire wall.

"Should we take off our shoes?" I whispered to Hollister.

"No, but thanks for asking." The voice again, now from a specific direction. Someone was descending the open steel staircase. The bare feet were attached to long, toned legs, followed by a thin waist, broad chest, broader shoulders, and then . . .

I heard Hollister catch her breath.

Ryan Waddell. Jet-black hair, longish and falling across emerald-green eyes. Full red lips. Like his surroundings, his face was a composition of ideal proportions at perfect angles. He wore drawstring linen shorts the color of a dove and a torso-hugging, sun-bleached yellow tank top emblazoned with the name of some gym in Barcelona. Not muscly, but muscled. His olive skin had a smoothness that invited one's touch. I wanted to touch it very badly.

"I'm Ryan," he said, his baritone warm and soothing, like a generous splash of Baileys on a chilly night. "You say you're friends of Camilo's?" He extended a hand. A gold Rolex watch and a burgundy leather bracelet with thick black stitching hung loosely around his wrist. "Hell of a thing, Camilo disappearing like that. I still can't believe it."

Ryan ushered us into the main living area, where we lowered ourselves onto a semicircular light-gray leather sofa, the thin cushions surprisingly comfortable. Like a concerned therapist, he sat on the edge of the furniture, elbows on knees, hands clasped beneath his square jaw. "Now," he said, "is there something I can do for you? Do you know anything about Camilo? Tell me how I can help."

Hollister took the lead, explaining that we were talking with anyone who might help us locate Camilo. As she spoke, her voice started to rise, conveying her frustration over not making more progress in finding him. I felt her, but my churning stomach was how I expressed my angst. If Camilo was alive, there was no guarantee he still would be an hour from now. The situation's urgency increased by the minute.

Ryan listened intently, appearing both sincerely worried and intensely curious about what we'd found out so far.

I should have been focused on the conversation, but my mind wandered off to picturing Ryan and Camilo together. No one would question the two of them sharing a fitting room at James Perse, or splitting entrées at a candlelit table, or doing each other's backs with sunscreen on a Malibu beach. That Hollister and I were trying to find Camilo was unquestionably the right thing to do, but somewhere along the way, I had developed a secondary motivation: a relationship with Camilo. Although it was a naïve fantasy, I'd wondered if perhaps our one night together could lead to a legit date—*and from there, who knows?* But now, staring across the glass coffee table at Ryan Waddell, I realized how foolish I'd been.

Hollister continued piloting the conversation. Ryan confirmed that he and Camilo had gotten together on a few occasions after work and gone out on a few dates but said they had never been serious and that the casual relationship had not lasted long.

Otherwise, Ryan couldn't add anything to what we already knew. Hollister and I knew more about Camilo than Ryan did. First off, Ryan said he didn't know Camilo had a sister.

Really? I didn't question him on that, but I found it hard to believe. In my blog, *Mates on Dates*, I'd recently devoted a post to topics of conversation for a first date. The post had received the most comments to date, with most guys agreeing that asking a date about his family was a terrific way of showing interest and gaining critical insights about him.

Another thing Ryan claimed to know nothing about was Camilo's computer science studies at the community college. Good lord, what had those two ever talked about? Or had conversation not been central to how they spent their time together? According to Ryan, after a few weeks of seeing each other, neither of them was "feeling it." There had been no hard feelings either way, and they'd parted as friends. Since then, Ryan hadn't seen Camilo for several weeks. They'd last run into each other at a concert, said their hellos, and that was that.

Hollister then took the conversation in a different direction. "So why'd you leave your gig dancing at Hunters? With your looks, you must have made a killing."

Inside I winced. Too personal. Why ask a question that had nothing to do with Camilo? Hollister had seemed impressed with the house, but how Ryan made his money was none of our business. And why bring up his good looks?

People must tell him all the time how attractive he was—either that or they just stared too long for him not to notice their admiration.

To my relief, Ryan seemed to take the question in stride; he smiled, said, "Something better came along."

"Oh yeah? What's that?" Hollister said.

My hand reached out to Hollister's arm before I considered how she might react. "I'm sure Ryan would rather not talk about work."

Hollister batted away my hand and gave me a look as if I'd just farted loudly. Again to my relief, Ryan seemed unfazed. "Corporate work. Terribly boring, but speaking of which . . ." He shifted his weight, glanced upstairs.

Sensing the conversation was coming to an end, I made my contribution to the interview: "By any chance, have the police come by to speak with you? You know, to ask you about Camilo?"

Ryan sat back against the sofa. The question seemed to knock him off-balance. "Gosh. I never considered that. But you're right. It's probably just a matter of time. I mean, if Camilo remains missing, they'll have to talk with everyone who knew him. Like you two are doing now. It seems you're one step ahead of the police."

It could be nothing, but his use of the past tense was disturbing.

"You'd like to think the police would be ten steps ahead of us," Hollister said, anger simmering in her voice.

I was no mind reader, and yet I imagined Hollister thinking that had Camilo looked anything like Ryan—meaning, white—the police would have already found him.

Ryan escorted us to the door. He placed a hand lightly on each of our backs as we crossed the shiny marble floor. The gesture suggested he knew how to handle people. Outside on the landing, Hollister and I exchanged promises with Ryan to call the other party as soon as one of us learned anything worth sharing. As we'd gotten Ryan's telephone number from Hank, we told Ryan we'd text him our contact information. Ryan thanked us for looking for his friend, and as the door closed on his magazine-cover face, his eyes threatened tears. "Whether it's you or the cops, I just hope someone finds our boy."

Back in the car, Hollister noted the one undeniable conclusion from our meeting. "That is one good-looking man."

"Coming from a lesbian, that's saying something."

She frowned. "I may not want to sleep with a dude, but I can appreciate beauty when it's sitting across from me. He your type?"

"Are you kidding? Ryan's anyone's type."

"Surprising how little he knew about Camilo."

"He did seem genuinely worried, though." Another topic for my blog sprang to mind. I filed it under *amicable breakups*.

Hollister started the engine. "You ever see one of those telenovelas on Univision?"

"Once or twice, not all the way through. Too much drama."

"Yeah, well"—she shifted into first gear—"if there is one thing you can count on, it's the pretty boys that are always up to no good."

Chapter Twenty

Mates on Dates, Post No. 22

My blog was due for a new post. Fortunately, a topic had been on my mind. It had started with Camilo (surprise, surprise), evolved when I'd met Mysti, and then solidified into a concept after a half hour spent with Ryan Waddell.

MATES ON DATES: Two Points for Being Nice
We're all guilty (shouldn't we all feel a bit guilty?) of judging a person's attractiveness on a 10-point scale. You know, "He's a 9," "She's a 10," that sort of thing. While the measure is subjective, it's also reasonably accurate within a range. For example, if a number of people say a person is an 8 or 9, few others are likely to say that the same person is below a 6. More or less, we all apply the same general standards for what we find attractive—look no further than magazine covers, movie stars, models, etc.

What I'm proposing is a more comprehensive measure on a *12*-point scale. This new system allows added points for being nice and deducts points for being a jerk, jackass, or scoundrel.

I recently met a guy I would safely say is a 9 (trust me, boys). After spending some time with him, I realized that he was genuinely nice! This finding added to the attraction I felt for him. Shouldn't that be worth something? Surely being kind accounts for as much as beautiful eyes? Or a nice chest? Using my new 12-point scale, I awarded this guy 1.5 points for being nice (2 points, btw, I'm reserving for people who are both privately and professionally good, such as nurses, smoke jumpers, and kindergarten teachers).

Conversely, I recently met an attractive woman who was rude to me. Had my only way to judge her been by looks alone, I'd say she was a 9. But, again, applying my new and improved measurement system, I think she deserves to have 2 points deducted for being all-around unpleasant. You can do the math.

So, guys, I invite you to try out my new 12-point system. Next time you want to judge someone, look beyond the haircut, cheekbones, and toned bod. When you're swiping right or messaging someone, or you first see them waiting for you at the bar, hold your judgment. Give them a chance! There might be a couple of points there you can't see upon first glance.

Till next time, I'm Hayden.

And remember, if you can't be good, be safe!

I hit save and stored a duplicate copy in the cloud.

Chapter Twenty-One
Knock, Knock

Jerry's not answering his phone. Could you check on him?

I read the text from Aunt Sally en route back to Slice, where I had left the car. Hollister had some errands to run on her own, and so we had agreed to meet at my apartment at four thirty and then head back to Barkingham Palace before it closed for the night.

Although it would add an easy twenty minutes to the drive, I decided to swing by Orca Arms and pick up Commander. Jerry loved the mutt, and Commander had been cooped up for the entire morning and probably needed to go out.

The space in the carport next to mine was empty, signaling no Sarah Lee. For her to leave her apartment always and without exception entailed taking her orange Volkswagen Beetle, its corny dashboard vase never absent a daisy. I'd witnessed her on a delightfully sunny day drive to the other end of the complex—a distance no farther than two blocks—drop off a rent check at Ruthie Weiser's, turn around, and drive back.

Commander and I took what had become our usual stroll around the courtyard. Also as usual, he selected the spot where he would relieve himself with the care of a farm-to-table chef picking the day's produce. Back inside the apartment, I found the backgammon board—thinking Jerry might be interested in a game—and an old can of tennis balls for him to play fetch with Commander.

Suddenly the dog stood tall and growled, his ears swiveled toward the door.

Someone knocked on the door.

Had I known it was Sarah Lee, I might have pretended not to be at home, but surprise, there she stood, one fist on an ample hip, the other shaking a piece of paper in my face.

"One of your slutty boyfriends left this on my door by mistake."

The sheet of paper was folded in half, as had been the one left under the car's windshield wiper. Under the seething glare of my neighbor, I read it: *I told you to stay away. I won't ask again.*

"I didn't know you were so desperate that guys had to warn you off," Sarah Lee said. "So you know, I made a copy to show Mrs. Weiser. This, along with that"—she pointed a chubby finger down at Commander—"is sure to get your gay ass evicted."

After tucking the note in my pocket, I tried my utmost to look gleeful. "Well then, no need for me to worry about the orgy I'm hosting later. I thought it best to keep it to under twenty guys, but now"—I shrugged—"just be warned. If all the moaning and banging get too loud, you might want to step out for a few hours. I doubt earplugs will cut it."

Sarah Lee narrowed her eyes to mere slits. "You're disgusting."

The backgammon board under my arm and leash in hand, I pushed past her, locked the door behind me. "Ta-ta," I said over my shoulder.

On preceding occasions, meeting Sarah Lee's anger with my own hadn't proved successful. Would this new approach of outrageous deflection work? Descending the staircase to the carport, I wasn't sure, and yet I made it to the car without hearing anything shouted at me from above.

After getting Commander into the back seat, I was about to close the door when the unthinkable happened: still nothing.

Chapter Twenty-Two
The Secret of All Old Men

"You need to plug your phone in," I explained to Jerry. "It's not like the one with the cord on the wall. This one needs to charge its battery."

"I know, I know. I just forgot is all. I know how it works."

Did he? Jerry had no computer, no internet, and no idea what I had been talking about when I suggested that he stream the old western and World War II movies he liked so much. And yet he was sharp—and adamant about his knowledge—so who was I to doubt him?

The offer of a game of backgammon didn't delight Jerry half as much as the notion of playing fetch with Commander. Before I would let him go outside, I insisted he put on a sweater. The last thing I needed was for him to catch a cold on my watch.

Returning to the same chair in the small yard, I sat while Jerry tossed the ball for Commander. The simple and yet complete joy with which he watched the dog race around the yard was contagious—for the moment, I was content, unburdened by the weight of worry I'd been saddled with ever since the police first knocked on Camilo's door.

Jerry broke the spell when he asked me what I'd been up to since I'd last been by to see him.

I thought my world of liking guys and police visits was likely to confound someone of Jerry's generation, and yet I surprised myself by telling him all about the Camilo situation: how we'd met, the circumstances surrounding his disappearance, how I'd joined forces with Hollister and we were conducting our own extremely amateur investigation. Jerry listened with interest, consuming the minutest of details, as I knew he did with his collection of World Wars I and II nonfiction. When at last I'd finished, we were back inside, sitting at the Formica kitchen table, sipping tea, and setting up the board.

"Your eye looks a lot better," Jerry said. "Still a tad black-and-blue, though."

"Yeah," I said. "I notice fewer people staring."

"Ha. People do love to stare. Wait till you get to be my age; then it's constant. The looks don't bother me, though. It's the assumption that just because I'm old, my brain must have atrophied that sticks in my craw. The truth of the matter, Hayden, this old man is smarter than he's ever been." He tapped the side of his head. "There's over nine decades of learning and experiences in here. My only little history vault. Lived through idiot bosses, inept politicians, and mean relatives. But I've also been blessed to have had my share of marvelous friends and family."

"Were you ever married?"

"Ha! As if I could ever forget my wives. Been married twice. The first didn't take. Still, we were together for twelve years. It took her that long before she decided she just didn't like me that much. My second wife, Sandra, we were married thirty-eight years. How old are you, Hayden?"

"Twenty-five."

Jerry nodded as if he already knew this. "I was married to Sandra thirteen years longer than you've even been alive. Boggles the mind."

"Any children?" I'd always been curious, as there were no framed pictures of children—or, more expected, grandchildren—to be seen anywhere in Jerry's home.

"Lillian, my first wife, and I tried. Sandra wasn't interested, which at that point in my life, since I was then in my early forties, was a relief." He chuckled. "Listen to me, running my mouth. The curse of living alone. I get an audience and there's no stopping me."

"I asked you. You're not boring me, if that's your worry. I like chatting with you."

And I meant it. I spent so much time in my head, it was a relief to get a glimpse into someone else's. And listening to Jerry was night and day from talking to guys my age. Their issues were my issues, and while there was comfort in commiseration, it could also become mind-numbing. Jerry offered a been-there-done-that perspective. He was reasonable. He was wise. I decided I liked him very much.

"So what do you think happened to this Camilo fellow?" Jerry stirred his English Breakfast tea with a small silver spoon.

"That's just it. I have no idea."

"That's not true." Jerry lifted the cup to his lips with two hands, one to steady the other.

I flashed a look of consternation that was my go-to whenever one of my students was misbehaving. "What do you mean that's not true? Yes it is."

"No, sir, I don't think so." He took a careful sip. "Having an idea and knowing for certain are not the same thing. You have an idea. So what is it? Do you think this Camilo fellow faked the whole thing? Ran away?"

I shook my head. "No, not for a second."

"Well, there you go! You don't know, and yet you do have ideas. You think Camilo went with someone willingly?"

Again I shook my head. "No. Someone forced him."

"Now we're getting somewhere." He pointed a bent finger at my cup. "Your tea is going to get cold if you just let it sit there."

I took a sip, swallowed fast. It was too hot. "How do you drink this?" I waved a hand in front of my mouth. "I just scalded the bejesus out of my mouth."

"I'm old."

"I'm not sure that explains it."

"You'd be amazed at how comprehensively that does explain things." After another sip, he continued, "So who took him?"

"I don't know."

"Don't backtrack. Did Camilo know whoever it was that took him?"

"Yes."

"Why do you say that?"

"He hadn't planned on leaving that night. Otherwise he'd never have invited me to his place. He certainly wouldn't have had me spend the night. Someone had contacted him, likely by text, to meet him. Given that it happened in the middle of the night, whatever caused him to leave would have been something urgent. He must have known the person who sent the text. Nothing else makes sense."

"I agree," Jerry said. "How about a biscuit? Tea is always better with a biscuit."

"Okay, sure."

"They're above the toaster." He flicked a finger toward the ancient avocado-colored appliance. "Bring the box."

Stepping over the slumbering Commander at my feet, I went to the cupboard. The door opened to an astonishing number of pill bottles. So this was what getting old was like. I turned back to Jerry. "How many of these are prescription?"

"Aside from the fish oil, all of them."

"Wow."

He laughed. "More like holy crap! At least that's what I yell each month when the bills start pouring in."

I set the box of biscuits on the table. "How are you feeling these days?"

"Old! That's how I'm feeling. Old, old, old, and it sucks, sucks, sucks. So how about we do not talk about the most uninteresting thing imaginable and we do talk about something that is pretty damn fascinating."

"Back to the Camilo saga?"

"Yes, please." He fussed to open the box of biscuits. "Damn packaging. Hand me the scissors, will you? The top drawer next to the toaster."

Until this afternoon, the closest I'd heard Jerry come to swearing was a random "heck" or an occasional "darn." I was unsettled by his casual use of a legitimate swear word, and I was too curious not to say something. "Um, so why all the cussing?"

"Because your aunt's not around, that's why. Now let's get back to business. So we think whoever lured Camilo to that parking lot must have known him."

"Yes," I agreed. "And when Camilo got there, something happened, something so unexpected and so fast that he didn't have a chance to shut off the truck's engine or to close the door to the cab."

"Good. And . . . ?" Jerry cut the cellophane from a fresh tray of biscuits.

"And?" I shrugged. "I don't follow."

"Whoever had been waiting for him in that parking lot, were they in a hurry?"

"Yes, of course. Otherwise, they would have shut off the engine and closed the door to the truck. But they didn't, which was a mistake. Someone noticed and called the cops."

Jerry crunched a biscuit and swept crumbs from his lap to the floor. Commander, sensing food, sat up. "Whoever was in that parking lot waiting for Camilo wasn't just rushed; they panicked. That tells you something about them, now, doesn't it?"

"They weren't prepared . . . or they hadn't thought it through . . . or Camilo didn't react as they'd expected. Or maybe someone was approaching, and they wanted to leave before being seen?"

"Excellent. All reasonable possibilities." Jerry tossed a biscuit to Commander.

I wished he wouldn't. He was teaching the dog a bad habit, and I'd be the one to have to deal with his begging.

"How many, do you think?" he said.

"To be honest, zero. I'd rather you didn't feed him from the table."

Jerry batted away the comment. "Not biscuits, assailants. How many persons were waiting at the parking lot for Camilo? One? Two? More?"

"I don't know." Seeing his scowl, I said, "Okay, okay. Two."

"Interesting. Why two?"

"Camilo is young, fit, strong. Assuming even that the other person could match him, it would have been a fight. And that would not fit with the assumption that the encounter happened fast."

"Ah"—Jerry waved a biscuit in the air—"but what if that one person had a gun? They could be as small as you and still be quite convincing."

I realized I'd forgotten to tell Jerry about the gun Camilo had bought from Roy Driggs. Once I'd corrected that omission, Jerry said, "And what do you make of that?"

"Two guns? There would have been a shootout. Noise, chaos, sirens. Total mayhem. So yeah, I'm sticking with two persons against one."

"And why not three? Why not more?"

"Unnecessary. Perhaps another person was waiting in the other car, but only two people needed to be involved in Camilo's abduction."

"Ah, the car." Jerry lifted his cup, realized it was empty. "More tea?"

"If you like."

"Mind putting the kettle back on?"

Standing at the stove, I turned my back to him while fiddling with the knobs, figuring out which one went with which burner. "Larger rather than smaller," I said.

"What?" he said. "I don't follow."

"The car. It would have been larger. Nothing like a compact. Nothing like my car. Camilo is a bigger guy. I don't see anyone easily or quickly stuffing Camilo into a hatchback. More likely the other car was roomy. Then again, it could have been a truck or a van. Vans are used a lot in movies for abductions. Roll open the doors, throw the victim inside, easy peasy."

"It could be just as you describe."

"You think so?" The back left burner started to glow red.

"Beats the hell out of me."

"What! Then why—"

"Because you need to give voice to your thoughts, Hayden. Think it all out loud, poke and prod the various possible scenarios. That's how you form hypotheses. Without them, no matter how iffy, you're flying blind. Keep in mind what's most probable, and then start ruling things out when contrary evidence presents itself. That is how you solve a mystery. Slow. Steady. Relentless thinking."

He was right, of course. The answer to Camilo's disappearance was not going to fall from the sky. It would take time. It would take work. And sound thinking. Hardly was I brilliant, but I had a good brain. And together with Hollister—and Jerry's ninety-plus years of accumulated wisdom—I might solve our mystery and find Camilo before it was too late.

Throughout our investigation, my mood had bounced between high and low, confidence and doubt. On more than one occasion, I had decided to chuck it all. But now, at this moment, I felt optimistic. As Jerry had just said, we just had to move smartly and methodically.

"How did you get to be so wise, old man?" I raised a brow, grinned.

Over the whistle of the kettle, he said, "The secret of all old men"—he tossed a biscuit to Commander—"I managed to live a long damn time."

Chapter Twenty-Three
Caught on Camera

The snarled traffic between Jerry's townhome and Orca Arms had gnawed my patience to a thread. The time was already ten minutes past four. Barkingham Palace closed at five. After I coaxed Commander out from the car's back seat, we raced up the stairs to the apartment. As I unhooked his leash, my phone buzzed, alerting me to a text. Hollister's message was unexpected, so much so that I read it twice to make sure I'd gotten it right: *Something came up. Busy rest of day. I'll call tomorrow.*

Huh?

Once the surprise wore off, I was both disappointed and relieved. The mix of emotions were the same ones I'd felt when I learned I hadn't gotten the assistant principal job I'd recently applied for. It had been a long shot and I'd worried about the pressure and the long hours, but no one likes rejection. In the present case, I was grateful to avoid an argument with Hollister about her crazy idea to break into Camilo's house. Still, I was bummed that we wouldn't be following

Della Rupert. There was still time to get to Barkingham Palace before it closed for the night. Traffic on the bridge had been light traveling the other direction. If I left now . . .

Yes! Why not? I was capable of following a car on my own. Besides, the Prius was far less conspicuous than a Porsche, and I was the more cautious driver—less likely to attract Della's attention. I gave Commander a pat on the head and grabbed my keys.

*   *   *

Five o'clock. The silver Cadillac with FURBALL plates hadn't moved. I parked across from the store and retrieved a ball cap from the pocket in the door. Della didn't know this car, but if I got too close while trailing her, she might catch a glimpse of my hair in the rearview mirror—and to see my hair was to recognize my hair. For good measure, I slipped on a pair of my aunt's oversized sunglasses kept in a sleeve on the underside of the sun visor.

I should have figured closing up shop would take a while. Ten minutes passed before the store lights went out, and another ten minutes ticked by before Della Rupert emerged from the store's side door and bustled toward her car.

Immediately things got off to a rough start. Rather than turning left out of the lot, as I'd expected, Della turned right, forcing me to pull a U-turn in traffic. At the first intersection, she accelerated through a yellow light. I had to run a red light not to lose her. She then engaged in a series of bobs and weaves, changing lanes when even the slimmest opportunity presented itself. Figured. Just when the job called for Hollister behind the wheel of Mo, it was me instead in my aunt's gutless compact.

The nerve-racking chase kept up for miles until a temporarily closed lane suddenly forced me left. I ended up at a red light right next to the Cadillac. Others might have slipped lower in their seat, but as that wasn't an issue with me, I just kept my eyes focused on the road ahead. This strategy, however, didn't last long. The Donna Summer pumping loudly from the sedan was too much. I had to look over. Della wasn't just singing along; she was belting it out, shimmying her padded shoulders and drumming the steering wheel to the beat. I wasn't concerned about her seeing me; she was absorbed in her own disco world. The spell was broken only by the changing of the light. Della floored it. And we were off.

My batting average in guessing what would happen next had, since the night I'd met Camilo, been abysmal, so watching Della pull the Cadillac into the waiting line for the Bainbridge Island Ferry shouldn't have surprised me. But still, the ferry?

I managed to get two cars between us before joining the lane for loading. It turned out the speedy journey through the city hadn't been for nothing—no sooner had I put the car in park than I needed to shift into drive. We were boarding. Minding the attendant's instruction, I steered to the port side of the ferry, where I crept up close to the next car's bumper and shut off the engine. Della was already out of her car and heading toward the staircase leading to the upper decks.

Stay put or follow? Risk being spotted or possibly miss seeing something important? I checked myself in the mirror, shoved unruly clumps of red hair under my cap, pushed the large sunglasses up the bridge of my nose, and reached for the door handle.

For a bigger woman, Della moved briskly. By the time I reached the staircase, she had already disappeared onto the second or third level. Odds were on the second—as it was half the distance—but lately the odds hadn't been my friend, so I continued climbing the stairs to the topmost deck. After a circumnavigation of the outdoor perimeter and a careful scan of the indoor seating areas, it was clear I had overshot: she was on level two after all.

Under the best of conditions, a hot dog wouldn't appeal to me. This was a disinclination not shared by Della. She was pumping ketchup into a tiny paper cup when I found her in the cafeteria, her brown plastic tray laden with three hot dogs and cola in a giant cup. Pretending to peruse the sticky laminated menu, I watched her from the corner of my eye. She set up shop at a nearby table, its legs bolted to the floor. Her head bounced to an invisible beat as she squeezed mustard from a packet.

After buying a bag of chips, I found a booth next to a window with a direct line of sight to the proprietress of Barkingham Palace. Oddball? By anyone's measure. Had Della lied about knowing Camilo? If Tanner and Paul were to be believed, yes. But none of that made her complicit in Camilo's abduction. Looking across the galley at her, I realized I wasn't surveilling a criminal mastermind. I was witnessing a middle-aged woman engaged in her own little hot-dog-eating contest. Hardly was this revelation worth the nearly forty bucks for the round-trip fare. Should I continue the adventure and follow Della to wherever she lived on the island? It would be several hours before I made my way back to the city. Hollister was fortunate to have had something come up that prevented her from coming along on this fruitless escapade.

Twenty minutes later, Della was still driving. Following her had become easier with fewer vehicles on the road so far out into the sticks. As each mile clicked by on the odometer, I was sure we must be nearing the end of the island. Coming around a bend in the road, I caught sight of taillights pulling off the road into a driveway up ahead. I hit the brakes and steered the car over to the shoulder. A moment later, the Cadillac moved forward and disappeared from view. Not sure what I'd find, I drove slowly up to the driveway. It led to a tall, black iron gate. Like a coat of arms, a large golden emblem adorned its center and featured the letters *D* and *R* in a looping script font. Beyond the gate, an asphalt drive curved off to the left and disappeared beyond a twenty-foot-high hedge. Whatever lay at the end of the drive promised to be a grand estate. And if I could trust my bearings, it was a grand *waterfront* estate.

I felt light-headed, tightened my grip on the steering wheel. I wished Hollister were here. She had to see this to believe it. A discreet mailbox had been designed into a stack-stone pillar that also housed an intercom and a sophisticated-looking computer screen. I jotted down the address: 6969 Bounder Road.

My attention was distracted by a slight motion somewhere up and to my right. I leaned forward over the dashboard to see better. Someone had affixed a camera to the top of the fence, and its wide lens pointed down at the car. Suddenly a crackle sounded from the speaker in the intercom. Before the person on the other end had a chance to say anything, I slammed the car into reverse and sped back down Bounder Road, toward the ferry terminal and home.

Chapter Twenty-Four
Guilty as Charged

Climbing the stairs to my apartment, I heard voices. As I neared the top of the landing, the backs of two men came into view. They were standing in front of Sarah Lee's open door. One of the men looked great from behind. Though he was trim, he had a fantastic butt, hugged by navy trousers.

The men must have heard me jangling the keys to my door; they both turned.

"Speak of the devil," Detective Zane said, spreading wide the arms of his black bomber jacket. "You're just the man we want to talk to."

From inside her apartment, Sarah Lee poked her head out into view, glared. "I hope you lock him up and throw away the key."

Detective Yamaguchi looked taken aback. "That's not the way it works, miss."

"Whatever," she huffed before closing her door.

I invited the police officers inside. Detective Zane was delighted to see Commander. The dog rolled onto his back and eagerly accepted a profuse belly scratching from the handsome cop.

The brief pleasantries dispensed with, Detective Yamaguchi said they needed to check on a few things. The tone in the room turned serious.

"May we?" he said, gesturing toward the small two-seater sofa, the only furniture other than my bed that could accommodate more than one person.

"Be my guest," I said, lowering myself onto the only chair I owned: a secondhand office chair, its black mesh efficiency at odds in a room dominated by a mattress and tennis posters.

"Seems you've been busy," Detective Yamaguchi said.

Had this to do with following Della? Had she seen me after all? Could she have written down my license plate? No, that couldn't be—it was my aunt's car. So what did he mean by that?

Detective Yamaguchi continued, "We came by earlier. You were out. You didn't answer our calls."

I yanked my phone from my pocket. *Damn it.* Now and again, I forgot to take the ringer off silent. There they were: two calls from the same local number that had come in over the past two and a half hours. While I had been crisscrossing Elliott Bay, the police had been looking for me.

"You were the last person to see Camilo," Detective Yamaguchi said, "so it's likely you have information that would be helpful to our efforts to find him. I know we already spoke with you, but we may have missed something. We'd like to go over a few details with you again. Is that all right with you?"

"Yes, of course. Anything to help." My mind raced. There was what I knew when I'd last talked with the detectives, which was very little. And then there was what Hollister and I had learned since then, which was a lot. To reveal any of my newfound knowledge would demand I explain how it had been acquired. I didn't imagine the police would be too pleased to hear that Hollister and I had been conducting our own investigation.

"Camilo has a sister, named Daniela," Detective Yamaguchi said. "Do you know her? Do you know how we might get in touch with her?"

I answered truthfully, "No. I have no idea."

"Do you know anyone who might know how to get in contact with Daniela?" he asked.

"I don't. I'm sorry."

The ease with which the detectives moved past the topic suggested they had expected my reply.

Detective Yamaguchi continued, "Earlier, you said that you assumed Camilo must have taken his phone with him the morning he left and that you didn't know his phone number. Is that correct?"

"Yes," I said.

"And he never called you? Not a single time? Maybe you want to check your phone to make sure?"

I shook my head. "Camilo never called me. He couldn't. He doesn't have my number, just like I never got his."

Again, neither of them seemed surprised at hearing this.

"Now Camilo's computer," Detective Zane said, "you're sure it was on the kitchen table when you first left Camilo's home that morning, after the initial police visit?"

"Yes."

"And then when you returned later that afternoon, when you found his home had been broken into, you noticed the computer was missing. Do we have that right?"

"Yes."

"Did you touch the computer?"

"No."

"Was there anything on the screen?"

"It was a laptop. It was closed. So no."

"Can you describe it for us again?"

My hands helped provide the dimensions. "About so big . . . maybe twelve by fourteen inches. Black. I didn't catch the brand. It wasn't as thin and sleek as some. Decal from his college. Looked heavy."

"No papers lying nearby? Documents, flash drives?"

"No, I don't think so. But honestly, I had never set foot in Camilo's house before that night. I was in the living room for only a few minutes before we went into the bedroom, so it wasn't like I was familiar with the place. But I can tell you that Camilo was extremely tidy. Might even say a neat freak. So while I'm not one hundred percent certain about, say, a flash drive or some other small thing lying around, there weren't any papers or stuff like that. Later, when I went back, the place was a total mess. Had something been missing, it would have been hard to tell."

"And yet you spotted the missing laptop. Why is that?"

"The laptop was obvious. It had been right there on the kitchen table. Later, only the mouse pad and charger were there."

"Do you have Camilo's email address?"

"No."

My initial panic had subsided. The police had come seeking answers to particular questions, all of which I assumed were textbook: find and interview the family, track his phone, read his emails, find something incriminating on his computer. I knew nothing about any of it. Apparently the detectives hadn't made any progress along those lines either.

So what *did* they know? The police had possession of Camilo's truck and complete access to his house; they could search and fingerprint the bejesus out of both of them. They could track his phone, but if it wasn't on, that was a no-go. Hank had said they'd gone to Hunters and confirmed my story of getting kicked in the face, but he hadn't said whether he'd given them Burley's name. Burley had told us about the gun, Camilo's ex-boyfriend, Ryan, and Camilo's computer science studies, which had led us to Tanner and Paul and the revelation of Camilo's second job, which had led to Della Rupert. If the detectives knew any of that, they weren't saying. And if they didn't know any of that, what did that say? Was it possible that Hollister and I were making more progress than the authorities? From what I could gather from the detectives' questions, the answer was yes. Still, they seemed to be actively investigating—despite Hollister's belief that the police weren't doing everything they could to find Camilo.

"One more thing, Mr. McCall," Detective Yamaguchi said. "In your earlier statement, you described Camilo as being 'upbeat.' What did you mean by that?"

This question seemed odd. "Um. Just, you know, in a good mood. Happy."

It was a muted reaction, just a twitch of the mouth, but I sensed Detective Yamaguchi was for once pleased with my answer. Perhaps they needed to rule out that he was depressed and hadn't run away. Or worse.

"Did you see Camilo use any drugs when you were with him?"

"None."

"Did his behavior seem at all unusual?"

"He wasn't high," I said, letting my annoyance show. It was wrong to assume that just because he was young and danced at a bar, he must be a drug user.

The detective held up his hands in defense. "You understand we just need to get an accurate picture of the situation. The more we know about him, the better our chances of finding him."

"Well, again, he wasn't high. Just happy. He didn't seem like a user. Had I thought for a second that he might be, I wouldn't have gone back to his place with him."

The detectives shared a nod—a signal, it seemed, that they'd gotten what they'd come for.

"Oh," said Detective Yamaguchi, "just one last thing. Did you know Camilo was here in the country under DACA protection?"

"Sorry?" My look of shock must have provided an adequate answer.

Detective Zane added, "His DACA renewal deadline is coming up. Just thought you might want to know." He concluded the visit by giving Commander a second round of belly scratching, which gave me a final moment to decide whether to tell them everything I knew. As Detective Yamaguchi opened the door to leave, I reminded myself that I had never lied to the police. Detective Zane followed his partner onto the landing.

All I had done was ask around, as any friend would do, as anyone who cared about another human being *should* do—as the police should be doing a lot more of.

I closed the door.

Had I convinced myself not to tell them about the gun and Della Rupert so Hollister and I could continue what we started?

Guilty as charged.

Chapter Twenty-Five

Mates on Dates, Post No. 23

My recent encounter with the clean-cut, devilishly handsome Detective Zane had inspired a *Mates on Dates* post. I placed my fingertips on the keyboard and waited for inspiration to strike with an appropriate title.

MATES ON DATES: Look, but Don't Touch!
Right out of the gate, I'm offering a confession: recently I found myself lusting after a guy who I thought might have fascist leanings of the German World War II variety. I know, I know, inappropriate, to put it mildly. For argument's sake, let's say I had been right in my character assessment and that the guy (I'll call him "Mr. Z") was indeed twenty shades of despicable. However rotten Mr. Z's insides, they hadn't spoiled my appreciation of his chiseled features and the way his tall, toned frame filled out his blue uniform (that's all the hint you get ☺).

My observation that a good-looking creep is still good-looking is hardly a revelation. But is there anything to the notion that a characteristic that should make a person verboten (to continue my Germanic theme) can produce a perverse attraction all its own? We all know the signals: the sexy sneer, the freaky skull tattoo, a barely legal cousin tanning in a Speedo in the backyard. What is it about the edgy, the naughty, and the taboo that sets our pulses raising?

The best I can come up with is that we seek a thrill we don't get from "the guy next door." We're aroused by a dude our better judgment says we absolutely, positively should have nothing to do with. But here is the caution! While looking, even flirting, may be harmless, touching can kill—*if not mortally, then emotionally.*

So what's all this got to do with dating? Dating is trial and error. You may have a winner on Tuesday, a total dud on Thursday. You may want a second date with Sylvester, the third romp with Gilles, or memory loss and hand sanitizer after Chad. But the goal for most of us trying to stay afloat in these dating waters is to find a keeper. And a keeper is the guy with whom you are simpatico, maybe not in all things (how boring would that be?) but with enough overlapping interests that you can join together in pursuit of them. Your partner in the game of life should inspire and motivate you to be your better self—and don't forget it's your job to do the same for him. So the next time you ask someone out or you are on the fence about whether to accept an invitation for a date, ask yourself: does he seem like a bad boy or good guy? If he is a member of the first camp, feel free to look, ogle, flirt, stare, and fantasize, but DO NOT TOUCH! We're looking for a spark, not a third-degree burn. Be good to yourself by holding out for the guy who promises to be right for you.

Oh, and as for Mr. Z? Good news! My suspicions about him were wrong. I found him online. He's half Jewish!

Till next time, I'm Hayden.

And remember, if you can't be good, be safe!

I ran spell check and printed out a copy of the post to review later. I was eager to crawl into bed with Agatha Christie. I was deep into her book *And Then There Were None*. There were five down, five to go, and I was excited to see who would be next—and by what grisly means they'd meet their end.

Commander hopped up onto the bed. I parted my legs, making him a little nest between my knees. After turning three complete circles, he plopped down onto the blanket as I reached for the book.

Chapter Twenty-Six
Help Wanted

Hollister called. She apologized for bagging out on me the night before. Her excuse: Mysti had felt neglected, and so for the sake of their relationship, Hollister had needed to hang out with her. I said I understood (I didn't). I was eager to fill her in on my discovery of 6969 Bounder Road, the second threatening note, and the detectives' visit—along with the bombshell that Camilo was in the country because of his DACA status. For all that, I decided it was better to talk in person. We agreed to meet at Slice in an hour.

When I arrived, Hollister was already at the same table by the window. "Top of the morning, Batwoman."

She tipped her mug. "Robin."

"No, no, no. We've been through this before. Spiderman, please."

"What, you don't want to wear a kick-ass cape and sexy tights? Fine by me. Wouldn't be my choice."

"Have you seen Spiderman? Sexy bodysuit. Even covers the entire head"—I pointed to my hair—"like a space-age hairnet. What could be better?"

"A cape."

"Nah, I'd just trip over it, get it caught in doors. A regular nuisance."

Hollister changed the mood by launching into a tirade on the topic of Mysti. *Ugh.* I was excited to share the news of recent events, and Hollister wanted to talk about the drama swirling around her girlfriend, whom she described as "super demanding." As Hollister told the story, she had explained to Mysti that she'd been hanging out with me to search for Camilo, but Mysti was convinced Hollister had been getting together with her former girlfriend, Cynthia.

"A million!" Hollister said. "That's how many times I've told that girl nothing is going on between Cynthia and me."

As Hollister recounted her history with Cynthia, I found myself—unexpectedly—seeing Mysti's side of things. If I had kept an accurate count, Hollister and Cynthia were on their fourth breakup, which could only mean they had gotten back together on three previous occasions. Mysti was understandably fearful that the cycle would complete itself yet again. There was more. As messy as the situation was with Mysti, Cynthia had vowed to not give up without a fight.

"I told Mysti—again—that it was over between me and Cynthia. For real. But Mysti refuses to believe me. One minute it's crazy sex; the next, she's throwing a skillet at my head. That kind of drama will kill a person."

"Literally."

"So anyway, little dude, I needed to take a short time-out from our mission, tend to my girl."

I said it was cool (but it wasn't). Camilo was missing. Hollister's love triangle was starting to get in the way. I knew I should say something. Instead, I told myself it probably wouldn't happen again. Hollister was, after all, fully committed to finding Camilo. And yet I couldn't shake the feeling that her girlfriend issues were becoming a recurring theme.

"So, your turn," she said. "Tell me about your night."

"In a minute. First, I need a coffee and something to eat."

"Espresso, please. And thank you." She gave me an air smooch. "Burley knows how I like it."

Burley had filled the pastry case with a fresh assortment of baked goods, each one more tantalizing than the last.

"No two ways about it," Burley said. "Peach scone. Let me heat it up for you."

For today's hairstyle, Burley had wound a single long braid into a pretzel-like formation that perched on top of her head, its height threatening a collision with the whipping blades of the ceiling fan.

I reached for my wallet. Again she waved me off. "As long as you keep up the hunt for our boy, it's on the house."

"No, really, I insist."

Burley looked amused. "Do I look like the kind of gal you want to insist to?"

I sputtered a nervous chuckle. "No, ma'am. Can I get a cappuccino too, please?"

"One shot or two?" She turned her attention to the espresso machine.

"One. Listen, Burley, the police came by my place last night. Same questions about Camilo. Did he take his phone? What about his computer? Where's his sister? They seem to be taking his disappearance seriously."

She sniffed dismissively above the hissing steam.

"Have they talked to you?" I asked.

Burley looked down, eyes showing concern. "Talk to me? Why would they want to do that?"

"You're his best friend. Any progress that Hollister and I have made is only because you pointed us in the right direction."

Slowly she poured milk into a cup. "I don't talk to the police."

"Yeah, I know it can be intense, but—"

"I don't talk to the police." She pushed my cappuccino across the counter. "Did Hollister want a single or double?"

"She said you'd know."

Burley rolled her eyes. "I should make it a decaf, but then you might not live to see the afternoon."

"So Hank didn't tell the police about you? That you're Camilo's best friend?"

Burley pressed grounds into a portafilter. "Hank values his ability to walk, so that would be a no."

The next question would be a hard one, but I had to ask it anyway. "You, of all people, must have known that Camilo was a Dreamer. Why didn't you tell us?"

Burley grabbed an oven mitt, retrieved my scone, slid it onto a plate, and finished with Hollister's espresso. Only then did she turn back to me. "Camilo has DACA status. You know what that means?"

"Deferred Action for Child Arrivals. It's a policy that allows some young people to stay in the country if they came to the U.S. as children."

"I know what DACA is, Hayden. I was asking if you understood what it means to Camilo. His status gives him the legal right to be here. He may not have been born here, but he's as American as anyone else. And one hell of a lot better than most. Still, the police aren't going to go to the mat for him, now, are they? As for me not telling you, I didn't because it's not my private information to share. I suspect that's why Hollister chose not to tell you either."

"Wait. Hollister knows that Camilo is illegal?"

"You need to stop saying that, Hayden. It makes Camilo sound like a criminal. The boy couldn't help it that his parents weren't citizens."

"Where are his parents?"

"Government sent them back to Venezuela several years back."

"Oh God. And Camilo's sister?"

Burley tossed the oven mitt onto the counter. "No idea. She might have gone back with the parents. That'd be my guess. But Camilo made it clear the topic of Daniela, along with the rest of his family, was off-limits." Burley pointed her chin over my shoulder toward Hollister. "I suggest you get this coffee to Queen B over there while you still can."

"So I know for the next round, a single or a double shot?"

"A double"—she winked—"but I always make her a triple."

Balancing a saucer and two cups, I returned to the table. "All this time, you knew Camilo wasn't a citizen. Why didn't you tell me?"

"Burley tell you?" She looked incredulous.

"No, the cops did. And now I find out both you and Burley already knew."

Hollister dropped her chin, her thin eyebrows arched. "Now don't you give me that look. All puppy-dog eyes. How long have you known Camilo?" She stared, awaiting my reply. "What's that? A few hours? And Burley and I have known him for how long? Years?"

"Okay, okay. I get it. The news from the cops blindsided me is all."

"See why I don't trust the cops to do everything they can to find him?" She counted on her fingers. "Latino. Gay. Dancer. Dreamer."

"Speaking of the cops . . ." I told Hollister all that had happened the previous night. We sipped our coffees and shared the scone.

"What's that woman doing living in a waterfront estate?" she said. "You don't make that kind of money running a pet store. That place must be worth . . . I don't know how much, but a lot."

I reached for my phone. "I'm curious. Let's find out." After opening the browser, I punched in the address—6969 Bounder Road. Several old listings for the property appeared in the search results. "Here it is"—I whistled—"last sold two years ago for three-point five million." I scrolled through the listing pictures. "Holy Shakira, get a load of this place." I scooted my chair over to Hollister, shared my small screen. "There's forty-five hundred square feet of marble everywhere. High-end European appliances. Floor-to-ceiling windows with views of the city. Oh my God, is that a movie theater?"

"A lot of house for just one person," Hollister said.

"I wonder, does she live there alone?" As the next photo slid into view, I gasped. "A tennis court! A freaking tennis court on the waterfront."

"Rich people," Hollister scoffed. "Who the hell needs their own damn tennis court? The parks are full of them."

"Oh, no. No, no, no. Trust me, Hollister. You do need your own damn tennis court."

"If you say so. Seems indulgent to me. Though a wine cellar, now; I could get behind a wine cellar."

"Say no more!" I pointed to the next photo of a cedar-walled cave that looked to be nearly as big as my entire apartment. "You access it by elevator."

"Damn. Imagine the party Burley could throw in that place."

I bunched my lips, shook my head. "I don't see it. No room for the Twister mat."

"I meant the whole house, not just—" Seeing the smile on my face, she stopped. "Oh. Ha-ha, very funny."

"But seriously, folks, we can check the online property records; they're public." Four clicks later. "The property belongs to D.R. Enterprises. That's Della Rupert. It has to be."

Hollister checked the dates. "She bought the estate two years ago, meaning she recently came into money. A *lot* of money."

"Could be. Or for all we know, Della downsized."

"Either way, it doesn't add up. With all the money she must have, why bother with a pet store?"

I raised a finger, waiting to swallow. "Maybe the pet store does make that much money. Della does own the place, after all."

"Enough for a three-and-a-half-million-dollar estate? I don't think so. Not unless she's selling cocaine out of the back."

At her words, Hollister and I both froze, cups in midair. I watched as her brow furrowed, realizing mine had done the same.

"Might not be drugs," I said, "but there's something else going on at Barkingham Palace. Something that brings in a hell of a lot more money than kibble and catnip."

My next thought hit me with the force of a size-twelve high-top to the face. I gasped.

"What is it?" Hollister reached out, gripped my arm.

"Doesn't that remind you of anyone? New job. Gobs of money. Gobs of *inexplicable* money."

I watched as Hollister's eyes grew to cartoon proportions. "Oh my God," she muttered. "You think?"

I recalled what Jerry had said: *Think it out . . . prod the various possible scenarios . . . form hypotheses . . . then start ruling things out when the evidence presents itself. That is how a mystery is solved.*

"Follow me on this," I said. "Ryan was hanging out with Camilo. Ryan gets a new job that pays big. He gets Camilo in on the action. Camilo is now too busy, so he starts to drop the ball on his schoolwork with Tanner and Paul. All the guys know is that Camilo has got some new job at Barkingham Palace. Then suddenly"—I snap my fingers—"Camilo disappears."

"You two doing all right over there?" Burley called from behind the counter.

Hollister waved her over. "I want another set of ears on this."

Burley ambled over. I repeated the hypothesis I had just laid out for Hollister. "So we need to discover what's going on at Barkingham Palace," I summarized. "We find that out, we find Camilo."

The three of us exchanged looks, seeking comment or agreement.

"I don't see it," Burley said.

In an instant, my excitement deflated. Hollister seemed to share my letdown. She said, "Don't see what exactly?"

"Hey, friends"—Burley spread her arms wide as if inviting a bear hug—"guess what? I just won the super lotto. Mind if I cut you in on the jackpot?"

Hollister and I stared at her, utterly perplexed.

"Do I have to spell it out for you?" Burley said.

"Yes!" we said in unison.

"Why would Ryan share? He got himself a highly paid gig. Why let Camilo in on the action?"

"Ryan and Camilo dated," I said. "Ryan could have gotten Camilo the job while they were together. What other reason could there be?"

Hollister shrugged. "Needed another hand." She pointed toward a HELP WANTED sign taped to the bakery's front window. "Burley is looking for someone right now. Not so unusual."

"Yeah, but any job requires some set of skills. Burley needs someone with baking experience. So what did Camilo have to offer?"

"Good looks," Burley said.

"And?"

"The boy can dance," Hollister said.

"And?"

Burley crossed her arms, examined her gigantic orange Crocs as if someone had written the answer across her toes. Hollister bunched her lips in thought.

"And computer skills," I said in answer to my question.

Burley waved the tea towel she'd had draped over her shoulder. "Camilo is a whiz with computers. He got my whole system up and running in a single afternoon."

Hollister pointed a finger pistol at Burley. "Damn straight he does. He created a website for me in a day. It's the envy of everyone at the guild."

I sat back in the chair, my hands threaded behind my head. "And what's the one thing taken when Camilo's house was ransacked?"

"You may be onto something," Hollister said. "So what next?"

"I'll tell you what's next," Burley said. "You pay another visit to Ryan Waddell. If he won't fess up, you beat the crap out of him."

"Well, that's one approach," I said.

"Or you pay another visit to Della Rupert. If she won't fess up, you beat the crap out of her."

"Or before it comes to any of that"—I held up a hand to Burley—"we first make sure we're right about there being a connection between Ryan and Della. I say we follow Ryan, see where he leads us." I looked at Hollister; she drew another finger pistol, which I took as a yes. "So it's settled. You driving, or am I?"

Hollister stood up from the table, clapped me on the back. "You ever see Batwoman in the passenger seat?" Before I could answer, she finished her question: "I didn't think so."

Chapter Twenty-Seven
I Was Warned

There was no motorcycle in Ryan Waddell's driveway. Either he wasn't at home or his bike was in the garage. The only way to find out was to knock, but we wanted to follow him, not pay a social call. We'd have to stake out his place around the clock. As it was the middle of the morning, we agreed that Ryan was most likely already out and about. I imagined him doing bicep curls under a personal trainer's supervision or getting his bangs trimmed by a downtown stylist who went by only one name. Funny how I never imagined someone as good-looking as Ryan taking a number at the DMV. But for all I knew, he could be having his teeth cleaned at that very moment. Wherever he was, Hollister and I weren't waiting around. Besides, it made more sense for us to split up and use both cars.

After ten minutes of strategizing, we finalized our plan: one of us would come back later and begin surveillance, and we'd trade off every four hours. Whenever Ryan was on the move, whoever was on shift would trail him, alert the other by text, and continue with quarter-hour updates. Should anything major occur, we'd talk by phone.

After five games resulting in stalemates, my rock crushed Hollister's scissors. She was first up. We synchronized watches. She'd take me back to my car and would then return to Ryan's, starting watch at high noon. My shift would begin at four PM sharp.

The day was sunny and warm. How better to spend the afternoon than with Commander in Lincoln Park? It wasn't far from my apartment, so if I needed to dash somewhere to meet up with Hollister, it wouldn't add much to the travel time. Should things turn urgent, I would take Commander along.

As I pulled into the carport at Orca Arms, I caught sight of Sarah Lee and Ruthie Weiser advancing from across the courtyard. Sarah Lee marched ahead triumphantly; Ruthie, looking tired, followed a step behind. Although Ruthie hadn't been due back from Sedona for several days, there was no mistaking her. The owner-manager of Orca Arms had an older white woman's version of an Afro: ten inches of wiry gray hair sprang wildly from her head. She was midsixties, rail thin but farm strong. Not one for shooting the breeze, she engaged her tenants with the same efficiency she applied to watering the lawns and labeling recycling and compost bins.

As they approached, Sarah Lee flapped her arms, apparently to get my attention. Ruthie mustered an innocuous wave. I groaned. The doggy doo-doo was about to hit the fan.

Sarah Lee strode up, out of breath, cardio not a regular part of her routine. She planted her chunky ankle boots at shoulder width and folded her arms across her orange fleece vest, creating the image of an angry crossing guard. Ruthie stood behind her, appearing as though she'd just woken from a deep sleep.

"Hello, Hayden," Ruthie said. "Sarah Lee here has come forward with a complaint."

"He's got a dog in there!" She pointed up toward my unit, just in case there was any question among us as to where *there* might be. "Rules are no pets. Says so in the lease. He's violated your rules and should be evicted."

Choosing to ignore Sarah Lee, I smiled awkwardly at Ruthie. "It's only temporary. His owner's out of town. The poor dog had nowhere else to go. It was either take him in or turn him over to the pound. He is no trouble. Doesn't bark or bite. He's a model citizen."

Sarah Lee made an exasperated sound, like a muffled growl. "He's a dog. I reread the rules, Mrs. Weiser. It doesn't say anything about permanent or temporary. It says quite clearly in the plainest possible language, no pets. Hayden has a dog. He's broken the rules. And I'd like to know what you're going to do about it."

Ruthie furrowed her brow. It seemed Sarah Lee's last sentence hadn't struck the right tone.

"I'll ask you to calm down, please, Sarah Lee. I know what the rules say. I wrote them. But Hayden is a good resident and has always abided by the rules." Addressing me directly, she continued, "Now, Hayden, let's have your side of this story."

After an extremely abridged version of how I'd ended up with Commander—helping out a friend in need—Ruthie said she'd never met a bull terrier. I offered to introduce her to one that I hoped would charm her and soften her resolve to adhere to the letter of the law. Had a knife been handy, Sarah Lee would have plunged it into my chest.

The women followed me upstairs. I slipped my key into the lock. *That's odd.* The door was already unlocked. I swung it open, waited. Where was the *click, click, click* of toenails against the linoleum?

"Commander?"

Ruthie and Sarah Lee stood in the doorway and watched as I scurried around the unit's four hundred square feet. I poked my head into the bathroom and the closet. I dropped to my knees to check under the bed—no bull terrier.

"Very clever," Sarah Lee sneered. "But you can't hide him forever."

Still on all fours, I turned and looked up at her. "This isn't a game, Sarah Lee."

Ruthie looked utterly confused. "Do you or don't you have a dog?"

I scrambled to my feet. "Yes, but he's not here." Someone had taken Commander. The realization was a punch in the gut.

"Um, Hayden." Sarah Lee pointed to the refrigerator. Taped to the door was a white sheet of paper with a scribbled message in large red ink.

I warned you. Now see how it feels!

"What the—?" I muttered.

Sarah Lee and Ruthie had walked over to where I was standing; each of them read the message for herself.

Sarah Lee said, "That's just like the one that was left on my door by mistake."

"What the Sam Hill is going on around here?" Ruthie said. "Someone's been leaving threatening notes? And now they broke in here, stole this dog of yours? Did you call the police?"

As fair a question as this was, there was no way to respond to Ruthie's question without digging myself into a deep and very dark hole. As tenant and landlady, we got along well enough, but ours was not the type of relationship to withstand the full, truthful story. *You see, it all started with me getting kicked in the face by a go-go boy.* Ruthie would understandably conclude I was sketchy—probably on drugs—and ask me to move out.

"Vanilla," Sarah Lee said, sniffing the paper. "You smell that?"

Ruthie inhaled deeply through her nose. "Yes, I think you're right. Vanilla."

I sniffed. "I thought I caught a faint whiff of something unusual. You're sure it's vanilla?"

Sarah Lee scoffed. "Yes, Hayden, I'm sure. I'm a semiprofessional baker. So yes, I'm sure."

I had seen Sarah Lee delivering muffins and cakes and cookies to neighbors—*other* neighbors—and I'd overheard her television through the wall tuned to some baking contest filmed in the UK, so I didn't doubt her.

"Well," Ruthie said, turning the topic back to the string of written threats, "did you call the police or not?"

"I didn't, no," I admitted. "I just assumed the notes were, you know, a prank. What would the police have done, anyway? Leaving a note isn't a crime."

"Now one has been committed," Ruthie said, "and on my property. So if you don't call them, I will."

"Okay, okay." I raked a hand through my mop of hair in angst. "Yes, of course. I'll call them."

Ruthie pursed her thin lips, clearly going nowhere until she witnessed me making the call. Sarah Lee baffled me by looking more concerned than smug. My mind raced. If I called Detectives Yamaguchi and Zane, a proverbial dam would break, flooding my peaceful—save living next door to Sarah Lee—existence at Orca Arms while further implicating me in Camilo's disappearance. For a moment, I considered calling Officer Anand, but she'd just refer the matter to the detectives, resulting in the same outcome.

But what if . . .

There's a line in a movie (I can't remember the name of the film) when, in response to hearing the details of a harebrained scheme, a character says, "That's so crazy, it just might work!" With those words in mind, I looked at Sarah Lee, swallowed hard, and wiped an invisible tear from my eye. "Sarah Lee, would you . . . would you call the police for me? I don't think I can do it. Someone took Commander, and I . . ." I dropped my head into my hands and waited for her response. After too long a silence, I raised my head slightly and peeked through my fingertips. Sarah Lee stared at me, her nose wrinkled in disgust.

"Fine," she said with a drawn-out sigh. "But you owe me, Hayden. Like you don't already. My phone's in my apartment." She turned. Ruthie followed her out the door, apparently determined to see with her own eyes that the call was made, regardless of who made it.

Minutes later, they returned.

"They're sending someone," Sarah Lee announced.

How long would it take for the police to connect the dots? Sarah Lee would be on record as the caller, but surely she'd given them my name and address. There was nothing to do but wait.

Ruthie and Sarah Lee each took a seat on the small sofa, signaling their intention to stay put until the police arrived. While they looked on in silence, I searched for anything missing or any other sign of the intruder. I had left open the two windows at the back of my apartment—one in the bedroom, one in the bathroom—but gaining access to either window would have required that someone drag a ladder around the building to overcome twenty feet of flat cinder-block wall. Whoever did this must have picked the lock to my front door—still a ballsy move.

The police arrived much quicker than expected, and that both officers were women was also a surprise. They stepped inside just as my phone vibrated in my pocket. I gave the screen a glance as Ruthie and Sarah Lee introduced themselves. The text was from Hollister: *On the move with pretty boy.* I dropped the phone back into my pocket.

The cops wanted my version of events; I told them only about the three scribbled messages and the dog snatching. After examining the notes, the cops asked if they could borrow them. I handed them over. They took a look at the windows and door, agreeing that someone hadn't forced their way in—they'd gained entry with either a key or by picking the lock. All the while, the cops asked questions about unusual activities or strangers in the area. One question I couldn't answer was whether Commander had an ID chip. I explained that I was only watching the dog while his owner was away. That I wasn't the owner was a fact I couldn't avoid—Ruthie was sitting there, and my only chance of not being evicted was to stick to my story of helping out a friend by taking care of *his* dog.

Finally, I was asked the question I had known was coming and dreaded: "Who is the dog's owner?"

Again my phone vibrated in my pocket. I checked the screen. Hollister: *Pretty boy rides like a bat from hell. Out near airport.*

"You mind, sir?"

"Sorry," I said, setting down the phone.

"The dog's owner?" one of the cops repeated.

"Oh, right. Commander belongs to . . . Jerry, Jerry Millstein. He's an elderly friend of my aunt's."

The cops took this answer in stride but instructed me to get in contact with Mr. Millstein and find out if his dog had a trackable identification chip. They made the excellent point that just because someone stole a pet didn't necessarily mean they always kept it. I should notify the local shelters.

What followed was five minutes of excruciating slowness as Sarah Lee lectured the officers about the increase in credit card fraud she had witnessed at the downtown hotel where she worked. After suggesting that she call the department's cybercrime hotline for the third time, the cops walked away while she was still flapping her gums.

Yet another long five minutes passed, during which I reassured Ruthie that I would stay vigilant and alert to any strangers, make doubly sure my windows and doors were locked, and keep her apprised of any developments. She would call a locksmith to change the locks on my door and add a dead bolt. As for Sarah Lee, I thanked her for her help and left it at that.

With the women finally gone, I snatched up my phone, dialed Hollister's number. Technically it was up to her to phone me when she assessed the situation as urgent, but since I'd not been able to reply to her previous texts, I wanted to explain why and also get an update on the situation.

Hollister's phone rang five times before going to voice mail: *Here I am, rock me like a hurricane. Beep.*

"Hey, Hollister, sorry I didn't text back. The police were here. Somebody broke into my apartment and took Commander. Call me. Okay. Talk to you soon. 'Bye."

I paced the apartment. Every molecule swirling in my 125-pound mass screamed *Find Commander!* But where would I even begin? Della Rupert? Seemed farfetched. She didn't even know my real name, and nothing about this seemed like her doing. Then I remembered the first note had been left before I met Della. So it couldn't be her. Ryan? I hadn't met him either until after the first note had been tucked beneath the car's windshield wiper. So who?

Ten minutes later, hearing the ring I'd been waiting for, I lunged for my phone. "Hollister!"

"Hayden?"

"Oh," I said, recognizing the voice. *Aunt Sally.*

"Sorry, were you expecting someone else?"

Yes! "No. Sorry about that. How are you?"

"Fine, fine. Your grandparents, however . . . those two are a different story. You know that thing your grandfather does when he . . ."

My mind drifted off. I knew the thing my grandfather did. And I knew the thing my grandmother did after my grandfather did his thing. And how all those things drove my aunt crazy. I'd heard this story before. I switched to speaker and set the phone on the desk. My eyes went to the clock on the DVR. Only minutes had passed since I'd left the voice mail for Hollister, and yet it felt like an eternity.

"Isn't that just the funniest thing ever? Hayden?"

"Um, oh, yes. Hilarious."

My aunt continued to burn through topics: the weather (too hot), politics (too depressing), the air-conditioning setting (too high), and the air surrounding my grandfather (too gassy). Although there had still been no call from Hollister, I was too antsy to even half listen to Aunt Sally any longer; I said I needed to get going.

"Okay, hon, I understand. Listen, though, would you be a sweetheart and check in on Jerry, please? He's not answering his phone again."

"Seriously? I told him that he needs to charge—"

"Oh, I know. I've been over that myself. It's old habits, you know."

"It's too old and no habit."

"Yes, well, I'll let you tell him that."

As my aunt finally signed off, another call came in—this one from Hollister.

"Where are you? Did you get my message?"

"Yeah, yeah, but keeping up with that boy takes concentration. He can split the lanes; not so easy in Mo."

I shivered, imagining a car chase out of a Mission: Impossible movie.

She continued, "I called as soon as I could. So what the hell? Someone broke into your place? Took Commander?"

I filled Hollister in, hitting the main points.

"Damn," she said. "Another break-in, another note. And you have no idea who did it or why."

"That pretty much sums things up on this end. Where are you? What's going on?"

"Ryan's in some warehouse out here by the airport. I couldn't follow him inside the property. There's an electronic security gate."

"What's the business? Is there a sign?"

"Not that I can see, just a nondescript industrial park. Lots of giant white buildings with big garage doors, no windows. Ryan rode onto the property and disappeared behind one of the warehouses."

"Okay. Can you at least get an address of where you are?"

"Um, yeah. There must be something on the gate. Oh, there it is. Write this down, will you? Forty-two—"

"Hang on, I need to grab a pen." I hurried to my desk. The canister of pens and pencils had been tipped over. Teeth marks riddled the pens, and only fragments remained of a new set of number-twos. I snatched a yellow Bic and said, "Okay, shoot."

"Forty-two Commercial Drive East. According to the property directory, there are five buildings on the property, A through E."

"Got it," I said. "And you're okay? Ryan didn't spot you?"

"Pretty sure, but I'm not one hundred percent certain."

"Okay, cool. Keep me posted. Meanwhile, I'll dig into the online property records. See if I can find an owner."

"Will do, partner."

"And Hollister, stay safe, will you?"

"Sure thing, little dude. It's always good to have a plan B."

Chapter Twenty-Eight
Stop Wallowing

Each of the buildings located at 42 Commercial Drive East belonged to a different owner—it figured that I would need to sift through all five reports. After A through D were a bust, I held my breath, hit *Search*. The results populated the screen. I scrolled lower on the page to find the owner's name: D.R. Enterprises. I fumbled for my phone.

"Yo."

"Hey, Hollister, get this, building E belongs to D.R. Enterprises, the same entity that owns Della Rupert's estate on Bainbridge Island."

"So there's our connection. What the hell? Are we good at this?"

I chuckled. "We don't suck."

"Whoa, whoa, whoa. Little dude, Ryan's leaving the property. He's waiting for the electronic gates to open."

"Okay, I'll let you go. I know he's hard to follow on the Ninja."

"He's not on the bike anymore. He's driving a large white truck. Not a semi or anything like that, but still, it's at least twenty feet long. There's no writing on the cab or the sides of the trailer. Anyway, got to go. I'll keep you posted. Hollister out."

A white truck? Not that I'd envisioned a Mad Max–like War Rig, but the plainness of the vehicle was disappointing. However, the truck's lack of any messaging to reveal its owner was intriguing. Hollister's inaugural shift tailing Ryan hadn't been boring. Our schedule had us trading off in two hours. Until then, I'd do what I could to find Commander. The cops could be right: whoever had taken him intended only the taking part, not necessarily the keeping. His collar—burgundy leather with a miniature faux barrel—was unusual and would help to identify him, chip or no chip.

After making calls to a half-dozen public and private shelters in the area, I double-checked that my phone was on "ring" and had the volume turned up. Assuming Hollister kept to our schedule, she would issue her next update in fifteen minutes.

On the way out the door, my eyes fell on Commander's leash hanging on a hook by the door. Had whoever snatched him brought a leash of their own? Or had they carried him off? Had they hurt him?

I had to do something, so I decided to drive around the neighborhood. As unlikely as it was that I would find him, it wasn't impossible that once the intruder had opened the door to the apartment, Commander had made a run for it.

During the hour-long drive, I methodically crept down each north-south block, then crisscrossed, traveling east-west streets until the navigation on my phone alerted me that I was a mile from Orca Arms. I pulled over and asked various joggers and walkers if they'd seen a dog matching Commander's description. Each person's concerned look and promise to "keep an eye out for him" coincided with one of several updates from Hollister, which came in at quarter-hour intervals. While asking two lady power walkers if they'd seen a bull terrier on the loose, I received Hollister's first update: *Driving south on I-5.* Her second—*Traffic at standstill, accident?*—arrived as I interrupted four shirtless teenage boys playing two-on-two basketball in a driveway. The third and last, *Headed for airport*, hit my phone as I shouted through the car window to a solitary old man playing cards on his porch. I thought of Jerry and decided to check in on him. I turned onto Fauntleroy and headed toward the West Seattle Bridge.

Jerry may have been in his nineties, but he had the ears of a spaniel. He heard the car pulling into the driveway. As I opened the car door, he was already halfway down the front stairs.

"Where's my friend?" he said, peering into the empty back seat.

Jerry was a big boy, but I was upset enough for both of us. I told him another neighbor had begged to take Commander to the dog park. The look of disappointment on the old fella's face choked me up. Avoiding his eyes, I mumbled something incomprehensible about Sarah Lee and Commander.

"Hayden, is everything all right?"

That was all it took.

I wouldn't say I'm a crier per se, but it happens. My mom had said I was sentimental. I was reliable for a good cry at the end of cheesy romantic movies, during big showstopping solos, and, in the present case, around a teary-eyed old man who shared my fondness for Commander. Blubbering, I fell against Jerry's chest. He patted me on the back as the first wave of pent-up stress and worry gushed out. After a minute, I settled down enough to croak, "I'm sorry, Jerry. I didn't mean to lose it like that."

"Nonsense. Let's get inside. You can put the kettle on and tell me what's got you so upset."

Once inside the kitchen, Jerry pushed aside a magnifying glass and a newspaper occupying most of the table. My phone buzzed with a text from Hollister: @ *Intl cargo. What the F?*

Jerry slowly lowered himself onto his usual chair, nearest the window. "Just guessing here, but something's happened to Commander. Am I right?"

I looked up, nearly dropped my phone in the sink. *How?*

"You didn't think I'd buy the neighbor-and-dog-park story, did you? You're too responsible to entrust another's man dog to someone else. And you're too kind to disappoint an old man who gets a kick out of the silly mutt."

I filled the kettle, relieved to have a task that let me avoid eye contact. I had lied to Jerry and was embarrassed. I'd done it to protect his feelings. It turned out I was the vulnerable one. Pulling two cups from the shelf, I came clean, or as my grandfather would say, I fessed up. "Sorry, Jerry. I should have told you the truth. I just didn't want to upset you."

Jerry scoffed, but not unkindly. "When you tell yourself you're lying to someone for their good, Hayden, you're only lying to yourself. It's for *your* own good."

My head bowed over the kettle, I nodded.

"Grab the biscuits, will you?" he said. "Tell me what's happened. Maybe we can make some sense of it."

When I'd finished catching Jerry up on recent events—the series of threats being the focus—he asked to see the actual notes. The police had borrowed them, but not before I had snapped photos. I enlarged the screen on my phone.

Jerry reached for his magnifying glass and read them aloud in the order they'd been left:

Whoever you are, back off.
I told you to stay away. I won't ask again.
I warned you. Now see how it feels!

He sat back in his chair, snapped off a chunk of biscuit between his large, perfect white teeth (dentures?). He chewed with intense concentration, as though powering the gears spinning in his mind. "Odd, don't you think?" he said finally.

"Yes, of course it's odd. It's disturbing. It's totally messed up."

"Not really my point. Take the first note—*whoever you are.* Whoever left the note knew your car but not your name. So they don't know you well at all. Are you supposed to know who they are?"

"They must." I tried a sip of tea. Still too hot. "Otherwise, the notes are meaningless."

"On that, we're agreed. We'll come back to that. For now, let's consider the warnings—*back off* and *stay away.* It seems you're up to something and this person doesn't like it. Again, they must think you will understand what they're referring to—or, as you say, the threats are meaningless."

"There's only one biscuit left."

"It's got your name on it." He pushed the plastic container toward me.

"Should we make a run to the store?"

"Wouldn't hurt." He waved a bent finger in the air, promising something important. "And finally, the third note, *see how it feels*. They took nothing of monetary value, am I right? Just Commander?"

Covering my mouth full of biscuit, I mumbled, "That's right."

"How easily they could have grabbed your stereo or something of value."

Although I had no stereo, just a Bluetooth speaker, I got his point. And it was a good one.

"All they took was a living, breathing creature. The intention was to hurt you right here"—Jerry tapped his heart, barely avoiding the smear of mucus I'd left on his shirt while crying on his shoulder. "This isn't about something you're involved in, Hayden. This is about *someone* you're involved with."

"Yes, of course, I've known that all along. It's about Camilo. As long as you count one night, or a few hours, as seeing someone, it's Camilo."

Jerry took a sip of tea. "I don't think this is about Camilo."

"Of course it is. This is one thousand percent about Camilo. Or am I missing something?"

"How close you are, Hayden. Think about what you just said." Jerry smiled coyly. "What's missing is Camilo."

"I know that, Jerry. Everyone knows Camilo is missing."

"And there you have it."

"Have what, Jerry? All I said was . . ."

I cursed under my breath.

Suddenly, I got it. The threatening notes weren't about Camilo. There was nothing to be gained by warning me off seeing someone I couldn't possibly see. I'd made an amateur's mistake. The line connecting the dots from Camilo's disappearance to Hollister's and my search for him to the threatening messages had seemed deceptively straight and solid. Yet when one paused and examined the notes for what they said, as Jerry had just done—as I should have done—the truth revealed itself: this was about jealousy.

"I've been so freakin' stupid," I muttered.

Jerry dismissed my self-flagellation with a flick of his wrist. "So, who are you involved with? Who did you start seeing around the time the first note was left?"

"Hollister." I closed my eyes. My head rocked back. *Stupid, stupid, stupid.*

"And who would be jealous of you spending time with Hollister?"

"Mysti."

"Girlfriend?"

"Yes."

"Do you know her?"

"Only met her once."

"And from what you do know about her, could she have done this?"

"I suppose so. Hollister said she's needy and demanding." I dropped my head onto the table with a groan.

"Has Hollister ever suspected it might be Mysti?"

"No. At least I don't think so." I sat up. "No, check that. Hollister would have said something. She made the same error I did, skimmed over the notes' contents, went for the easy read, made simple assumptions."

"Slow and careful thought isn't for everyone, Hayden. It's humankind's greatest flaw. It's one thing to have this big brain"—he tapped the side of his head—"it's another to operate it wisely."

"You're saying I'm an idiot."

"Stop wallowing. It doesn't suit you. What I'm saying is you read the situation as most people would have. But you're not most people. You should expect more from yourself. Why? Because you're capable of more than most. I, for one, believe in you."

Again, I choked up. How long had it been since someone had said such a thing to me? I knew the answer, of course: seven years, three months. I'd lost more than my mom when she died. I'd lost a good chunk of me too—including the self-belief that only a parent or someone taking that role can instill in a person.

I reached out, gently squeezed Jerry's hand, bruise-colored with age. "Thanks, man."

He placed his other hand on top of mine, smiled. "If you really want to thank me, you'll take me to the store. I'm out of milk. Coffee without milk in the morning is a sadder life than I can bear to live."

Laughing, I said, "You said the same thing about biscuits."

"And truer words were never spoken."

"Oh yeah, what about tea?"

"Add it to the list."

Chapter
Twenty-Nine
Work in Progress

As I gathered up Jerry's canvas bags for our run to the store, my phone buzzed with an incoming update from Batwoman: *Argh waiting at cargo.* This message repeated itself in one form or another every fifteen minutes for the next hour.

After returning to Jerry's, I put the groceries away and started a load of wash. I had less than thirty minutes until I was to meet Hollister, so I needed to hustle.

The transfer of surveillance duty started easily enough. I found Hollister right where she'd said she would be: a parking lot in front of SeaTac's air cargo facilities. I pulled into a nearby space. As I approached her car, she said through the opened window, "Where's my coffee?"

Slipping into the passenger seat, I replied, "It's at Slice. So nothing has happened since Ryan went in there?" I tilted my head in the direction of the entrance.

"Nada. The bad news is that this gig is unbelievably boring. The good news is that pretty boy can't stay in there forever. When he does finally come out, you shouldn't have much trouble tailing him. I wouldn't say the same if he were riding the motorcycle, but the truck is manageable. Even for you."

"Easy now."

"Batwoman gets cranky when her caffeine runs low."

"This is Seattle. I have high confidence you can find a coffee shop."

"Your concern is touching." She grinned and punched my shoulder. "You got it from here?"

"Roger that."

"Great. Because Mysti is on my case. I need to get over to her place ASAP. She's having one of her meltdowns."

"Yeah, about that . . ."

"Oh damn, little dude. I'm so sorry about Commander. I know he's grown on you. I'm sure he'll turn up. Whoever is behind this is trying to get you rattled is all."

"Again, about that, Hollister."

"But seriously. I got to go. We can talk later, okay?"

She reached for the ignition switch. I grabbed and held her hand.

Jerking free, she snapped, "What the hell?"

"Hollister, it's Mysti."

"Mysti? What's Mysti?"

"The notes. Taking Commander. It was Mysti."

Hollister looked like I'd just taken a dump on the hood of her car.

"Have you lost your mind? You think it was Mysti who left the notes? Mysti broke into your apartment and made off with the dog? Why would you think that?"

As I pulled up the pictures of the messages, I repeated what Jerry had said about them. "See," I said, handing my phone to Hollister.

She stared at the photos, scrolled down, then up, then down again, examining each one. She didn't say a word, handed my phone back to me.

"Well?" I said.

Hollister slammed her fist against the dashboard. I jumped.

"It's not Mysti," she said.

I waited. The look on her face was impossible to read. Had I been wrong? If so, what had I just done to our budding friendship?

"Hollister, listen, please don't think—"

She held up a hand. "It's okay, Hayden. I get why you thought it was Mysti. At this point, I wish you were right."

"I don't understand."

Hollister laughed an unsettling laugh that lasted too long. She was freaking me out. Suddenly she stopped, shook her head. "What is wrong with me? I mean, something must be wrong with me, right? Why else would I let myself get mixed up with all Cynthia's craziness?"

"Cynthia?" There was being late to the party, and then there was showing up when the place was empty and it was time to sweep up the aftermath. How could I have not seen it?

She turned to face me. "Mysti didn't take Commander, Hayden. It was Cynthia."

How was it that a person's love for another could turn into an obsession of such intensity that they'd do what Cynthia had done? The thought frightened me. I worried about Commander.

"Would Cynthia harm a dog?" I said.

"I don't think so, but then I couldn't have imagined her doing this either."

"We have to call the police. You realize that, don't you?"

Hollister buried her face in her hands, groaned.

"Cynthia broke into my apartment. She stole Commander. We have to call the police, tell them it was her. They have to go rescue Commander, bring him back safely."

"She was doing so well, at least there for a while. Cynthia is bipolar. When she stays on her meds, she's okay. But when she stops taking them, she wigs out. You told me about the notes, but I never imagined it could be her. I mean, you're a dude. She has no reason to be jealous."

"Yeah, about that . . ."

"No offense, Hayden, but you're small and . . . that's quite the head of hair you have. Cynthia was at Burley's party that night. I guess she saw you with me, but only from afar. She must have mistaken you for a woman."

"And you're one hundred percent sure it's her?"

Hollister nodded. "Oh yeah. The second I saw the photos of the notes on your phone, I recognized the writing. The large, loopy letters in red is Cynthia, all right."

"You know where she lives? You can give the police her address?"

"Please, Hayden, no."

"Okay, fine. I'll call them. But I need the address."

"No, I mean no police."

"You're killing me!" First Burley had said no cops, now Hollister. But it was my apartment that had gotten broken into. And it was my dog—well, sort of my dog—that had been taken. I tried to appreciate everyone's sensibilities, but a line had been crossed. Cynthia, whoever she was, bipolar or not, was a criminal. We were calling the police.

"I want Cynthia's address, Hollister."

"I can't."

"Fine." I gripped the door handle. "I'll tell the police what I know. But since I can't give them her address—or last name, for that matter—you can expect them to be following up with you."

"Please, Hayden. They'll take her away and put her someplace. Lock her up. She just needs her meds is all. Let me do it. I'll go. I'll get Commander back. I'll convince her to get back on her meds."

While Hollister had been talking, my hands had bunched into tight fists. I was shaking with anger. "Hollister, would you listen to yourself! One minute you're all woe-is-me for dating crazy women, the next, you're trying to save them from themselves. Cynthia broke into my apartment! Do you get that? She picked the lock on my front door. She went inside my home. She stole Commander. She's a criminal. Sorry, but I don't care she went off her meds. I want my dog back. And whether she is hospitalized or thrown in jail isn't my problem. Now. Are you going to give me her address or not?"

"I hear you, Hayden. It's your call."

"Good, because—"

"But hear me out." She reached for my arm. "Please, just hear me out. What if we *both* go to Cynthia's? I'll talk to her, tell her that she either goes with me to the police or I'll call them right then and there. Either way, you'll get Commander back. Trust me, Hayden, this is a better way. Please."

"What if she's violent? What if she refuses? What if it turns ugly? Then what?"

"It won't. She doesn't get like that."

My blood started to simmer again. "How can you say that? When I asked if she could hurt a dog, you said you didn't think she would but that you weren't sure. Now that you're trying to talk me into this, suddenly you are sure."

"I'm asking you, as a friend, to do this for me. Please."

"As a friend, you shouldn't be asking. You're putting me in an unfair position."

"Please."

"You need help."

Hollister recoiled in shock. I had blurted words out in anger, and they'd landed a punch that seemed to cripple her resolve. I didn't regret saying it. It was clear that Cynthia needed help, and if Mysti was anything like her, she needed help too. But so did Hollister. There was a term for people who felt a desperate compulsion to save other people, even if it meant sacrificing their own needs in the process. Hollister had a savior complex.

"You're right. I'm messed up." Hollister looked as sad as a person could.

"Listen, we all have our issues. You care, just too much. That doesn't make you messed up, just a work in progress. Aren't we all?"

Hollister didn't move, didn't speak.

"Okay. Here's my offer. First, let's not forget about why we're sitting in this parking lot. It's four fifteen now. At five fifteen, no matter where things stand with Ryan, wherever we are, we call it a day. Then we go get Commander. You do your thing with Cynthia, but we're agreed that in the end, the police will be involved."

"What about Mysti? We had plans." Hollister slowly shook her head, pinched the bridge of her nose. "I can't not show up. She'll be furious."

The look on my face answered her question.

"Okay, okay." She blew out a long sigh. "I'll call her. She won't like it, but I'll tell her I'll see her tomorrow." She expelled another long breath, seemed to relax. "Thank you, Hayden," she whispered.

"One more thing. I have one condition."

Her eyes darted in my direction.

"We take Burley with us."

Chapter Thirty
That's One Way to Do It

After following Ryan and the white truck to the complex of warehouses on Commercial Drive, Hollister and I drove to Slice. We traveled separately, as neither of us was keen on leaving a car out by the airport. We had given Burley a heads-up that we were on our way and needed her to accompany us on an errand. We hadn't told her, however, what the errand entailed. When we arrived and did tell her, all she said was, "As long as we dedicate our mission to the memory of Cucaracha, I'm down."

Out of practical necessity (the two-seater sports car being a nonstarter), the three of us rode in the Prius. I drove. After sliding the front passenger seat as far back as it would go, Burley crammed herself inside. Pulling the seat belt across her fringed vest, she said, "This is like stuffing twenty pounds of flour into a ten-pound bag." Fortunately for Hollister, there was sufficient legroom behind me in the back seat.

Music was requested to put us in a "positive headspace" (you can guess who made this suggestion). I flipped the dial from NPR to KIK 86.5 new country, and we traveled merrily along, singing a three-part harmony to Stanley Kellogg: *The easiest thing I've done is falling hard for you.*

Hollister provided directions to Cynthia's apartment in the University District. According to Hollister, Cynthia was enrolled in the master's program for theater arts. The irony of her ex-girlfriend being in the drama department wasn't lost on anyone.

I parked on the street, and my two passengers dislodged themselves in clown-car-like fashion from the Prius. Cynthia's apartment was on the fourth floor at the end of the hallway. The plan was for Burley and me to wait around the corner by the elevators. Hollister would go in alone, not agitate Cynthia any more than she already would have with her surprise knock on the door. Once inside the apartment, Hollister would send Commander down the hallway to us, and we'd take him to the car. Hollister would stay with Cynthia and try to convince her to go with her to the police; if she refused, Hollister would join us in my car, and we'd phone the cops from there. That was the plan.

Although Burley and I were down the hallway and around the corner, the distance was not so great that we couldn't hear Hollister's knock. After a few moments, she knocked again. We listened to the door open.

"Hello?" a woman said. Her voice conveyed curiosity, as opposed to the familiarity I would have expected.

I looked at Burley. She looked confused.

"Is Cynthia at home?" Hollister asked.

"No, sorry, she stepped out."

Again, I looked at Burley. She shrugged, shook her head.

Hollister asked, "Do you know when you expect her back?"

"Mind telling me who you are?" The woman's voice had turned edgy.

"My name is Burley. I'm a friend of hers."

Although I didn't know why Hollister had used Burley's name, it seemed smart of her to not use her own. When it got back to Cynthia that a Burley had come around, the name would be familiar but a step removed from Hollister. But any description of the visitor would foil the deception: while both women were larger than most, Hollister was Black with a signature mohawk. Burley would never be confused with anyone else.

"Oh, yes," the woman said, "I think I've heard Cyn mention you. She just popped out to take Ralphie for a spin around the block. She should be back any minute. You're welcome to come inside and wait."

Burley and I exchanged alarmed glances, then shifted our eyes to the elevator's display of floor numbers. It read 3.

"It's probably Cynthia," Burley whisper-shouted. "Hide!"

I turned and hurtled for the fire door leading to the staircase as Burley leapt toward the hallway. We collided. I fell back hard onto my butt.

The elevator doors opened.

Commander, seeing me at eye level, bolted forward, yanking the leash from Cynthia's grip. He jumped into my arms. Burley spun around to face Cynthia. Having no way around Burley and me, Cynthia stayed in the elevator and started frantically punching a button, presumably for any floor other than the one she was presently on.

Burley said, "You stay here with Commander," then rushed into the elevator with Cynthia just as the doors closed behind them.

Hearing the commotion, Hollister, followed by the other woman, came running down the hallway. I had just climbed to my feet when they wheeled around the corner.

Seeing only me standing there, Hollister said, "What happened? Where's Burley?"

"Who are you?" the woman said. "Why do you have Ralphie?"

Ignoring the woman, I said, "Cynthia showed up. Burley is in the elevator with her." I looked up at the display. The car had just passed the second floor on its way down.

"There are two Burleys? What's going on?" the woman bellowed, now bordering on hysterical. "What have you done with Cyn?"

"Stairs!" I shouted to Hollister.

I heaved open the door to the stairwell and started down, taking two steps at a time. Commander was another two steps ahead, pulling on the leash. It was all I could do to hold on to him and not break my neck. Hollister was right behind me, followed by the woman, whose stocking feet on the slick cement staircase slowed her descent considerably.

At the bottom of the stairs, I burst through the door to the first floor. Burley was holding a screaming Cynthia in a headlock. A moment later, Cynthia's screams were joined by those of the other woman, who'd just entered the lobby behind us. Hollister approached Cynthia, which unfortunately didn't calm the situation. Cynthia only screamed louder, which I wouldn't have thought possible. Burley appeared nonplussed by the whole thing. She held on to Cynthia like a worn-out mother resigned to letting her toddler's tantrum run itself out.

The woman grabbed Commander's leash and tried pulling it from my hand.

"Give me back Ralphie!" she yelled.

"Stop it." I yanked the leash from her hand.

"I'm calling the cops!" the woman shouted. With the speed of a gunslinger, she drew a phone from the back pocket of her jeans.

While Cynthia continued her screams, Burley, Hollister, Commander, and I watched as the woman punched *911* into her phone. "Hello, police . . ."

Turning to Hollister, I said, "Well, that's one way to do it."

Chapter Thirty-One

Sleep on It

The moment I pulled back the covers, Commander jumped up on the bed and took his usual spot at the foot. I snuggled in and opened my book, another by Agatha Christie. Mom had read her books to me when I was a child, and now whenever I needed to decompress, I found nothing that did the trick better than Christie's intricately plotted whodunits. And boy, did I need to unwind.

When the police arrived at Cynthia's building, it had taken an hour to settle the mayhem. Burley and I were waiting for them in the lobby. Hollister had taken Cynthia (who did smell like vanilla!) up to her apartment. The woman who only Cynthia knew (her name, we later learned, was Pam) had left as soon as she figured out who we were and why we were there. Just learning that Ralphie was a dognapped Commander had drained all color from poor Pam's face.

Pam and Cynthia had met online. Pam had been smitten by Cynthia's new profile pic, which included the love of her life, her dog, Ralphie. Pam, having the fondest of memories of growing up with a bull terrier, was hooked. Hollister, Burley, and I had unwittingly stumbled into the ladies' first in-person date.

Perhaps saddest of all was that Pam wasn't out. I had a feeling it would take some time (and therapy?) before Pam was ready to wade back into the gay dating waters. As she stormed out of the lobby, I mentioned my blog and offered a card with the web address, but she didn't seem interested. *Too soon.*

Later at the police station, Hollister and I did most of the talking. Burley begrudgingly answered only questions that were directed to her—which gratefully were few. Cynthia had confessed to breaking and entering and theft. The police had taken her into custody. Hollister had argued that she should go to a treatment facility, but the cops had been clear that Cynthia's fate would be up to the lawyers and ultimately a judge.

When Hollister and I dropped off Burley at Slice, she'd said her chakras were discombobulated and that she needed "a little green therapy" followed by a "Bublé bath." When I tried to correct her, Hollister explained that Burley was a huge fan of Michael Bublé and liked nothing more than to get baked, draw a hot bath, and let the Canadian crooner transport her to a kinder, gentler world. The night of Burley's house party, I had seen the bathroom and its standard-issue shower-tub combo. Unless Burley had a roomy hot tub hidden in the basement, I found the bath the harder thing to imagine.

With Burley safely returned home, I hugged Hollister and told her to get a good night's sleep, though I knew she'd been through too much for any chance of that. For me, I was just happy to have the silly mutt, as Jerry liked to call him, back home with me.

During the recent encounter with the police, we had managed to avoid making the connection between Camilo and me. I had spent the first hour at the station looking over my shoulder, expecting either Officer Anand or Detectives Yamaguchi and Zane to show up and say, "Well, well, well, if it's not the guy with a black eye who woke up in the missing go-go boy's house, then had his home broken into and the go-go boy's dog stolen from him, and has just now stolen said dog back from a bipolar woman off her meds."

Luckily, halfway through the interview, I'd learned (while waiting and perusing a map pinned to a bulletin board) that there were five major precincts in the Seattle Police Department. The U-District was in the North Precinct, where Hollister, Burley, and I had followed the police who had taken Cynthia into custody. Camilo's house was in Columbia City, which was in the South Precinct, where I presumed the officers handling Camilo's case worked. *Whew!*

As I sank deeper beneath the covers, I wondered what progress the police had made in finding Camilo. They had yet to speak with Burley, so it was unlikely that they knew about Ryan or had made their way to Barkingham Palace and Della Rupert through Camilo's schoolmates, Tanner and Paul. Were Hollister and Burley right that because Camilo was a Dreamer who danced at a gay bar, the police weren't doing everything they could to find him? Nearly four days had passed since his disappearance. If the police had made progress, they hadn't shared that news through any update. I considered calling them but convinced myself that doing so would only call attention to myself. I could reassess the situation in the morning. Tomorrow was a new day, and Batwoman and I knew where to start: building E on Commercial Drive.

Chapter
Thirty-Two
You Were a Cheerleader?

My day started with a rare bit of good news: after a week of waiting, the replacement part for my old Fiesta had finally arrived, and my car was ready to be picked up. Hollister gave me a lift to the repair shop. Commander came along for the ride. Until I had a chance to plead my case to Ruthie, I didn't dare leave him alone in the apartment. If Sarah Lee found out that the dog had returned, she would raise holy hell. My only chance was to get to Ruthie first. I'd already decided that if she wouldn't relax the rule of no pets and Camilo didn't reappear soon, I'd have no choice but to find another place. After all I'd been through with Commander, taking him to a shelter was out of the question.

Once I'd picked up the Fiesta, Hollister followed me back to Orca Arms. She was cool with Commander in her car, as long as he sat on my lap (if not there, where?).

Out front of the warehouse complex on Commercial Drive, Hollister and I considered the challenge of getting inside building E. First, we would need to get inside the property, which required passing through the vehicle gate. Hollister had seen Ryan enter a code on the keypad at the entrance. We observed other vehicles doing the same, and in all cases, after they had driven through the opened gate, they stopped and waited for the gates to close behind them before driving on. This well-established security procedure worked as intended: to prevent unauthorized persons like us from tailgating another vehicle onto the property. We would have to find another way in.

"How high would you say the fence is?" Hollister mused.

I bunched my lips. "Hmm . . . twelve feet?"

"There's no razor wire."

"Lucky us."

"You have a better idea?"

"What's the top speed of this bucket of bolts?"

Intrigued by the question, Hollister smiled mischievously. "One-eighty. Why do you ask?"

"Should suffice for ramming speed."

Hollister spouted a laugh. "Not exactly stealthy."

"At the far end over there"—I pointed to a stretch of fencing at the eastern edge of the property—"the fence dips behind a knoll. I don't think anyone would see us, either from the street or from the gate."

"We'll still need to get into the building."

"One fence at a time. Let's see if we even get that far."

We cracked the windows, leaving Commander to guard Mo, and walked casually down the road to the spot where the fence turned and ran east. When we reached the corner, we jogged alongside the fence about thirty yards to a point where we could no longer see the road or the entrance. We gave each other a *Let's do this!* head nod and began climbing side by side up the fence.

Halfway up, I said, "You wore the right footwear," referring to her pointed-toe boots, which fit snuggly into the diamond-shaped spaces in the chain-link. My sneakers did the job well enough, but only because I wore the modest size of seven and a half.

At the top, we both paused.

"And now for the tricky part," I said, hoisting a leg over the top post. I sat up, straddling the fence as if on horseback—a very bony horse. From that vantage point, I had a good view of the grounds. Hollister matched my position, and we took a moment to survey the landscape.

"We know the building closest to the main entrance is A. So if they're numbered according to a logical sequence, that would be B, then C"—I pointed to the first three buildings in the street-facing row—"so those two smaller buildings in the second row must be D and E."

"Looks like there is a bank of windows in the back," Hollister said.

"You have something against doors?"

"If it's unlocked, I'm all for it. Just giving us an option."

We started down the fence. When I was within four feet of the ground, I pushed off and jumped. Hollister appeared more cautious in her descent. I looked up and watched her as she took care to test each toehold.

She looked down at me. "You checking out my booty, white boy?"

"Ha. It's majestic! As an owner of a typical white-boy booty, I can only marvel."

Hollister stepped down to the ground and slapped my rump. "Little, but round and firm. You got nothing to complain about."

"Thanks. I'll add that to my online profile."

Thankfully, the surrounding area was quiet, just two SUVs parked near the entrance to building D. No vehicles occupied the three spaces assigned to building E. We walked as quickly as we could, without running, to a dumpster next to a large steel door with the letters *DRE* painted on it in black block letters. I tried twisting the hefty doorknob—locked. Hollister tilted her mohawk in the direction of the rear of the building. I followed close behind.

"It didn't look so high from the top of the fence," she said, gazing up at the opaque window set high in the block wall. The window's bottom edge was about eight feet from the ground and covered by a screen.

"Tall challenge," I said.

Hollister rolled her eyes. "*Buh-dump-dump.*"

"But seriously, how do we get up there?"

"We're not. You are. Once you're in, you can find your way to the front of the building, unlock the door, and let me in."

"What?" I sputtered. "We're assuming no one's inside. No cars doesn't guarantee there will be no people. Or guards. Or attack dogs. I've met my quota of attack-dog encounters already this week, thank you very much."

"I'm surprised you didn't bring up Orcs."

"Never say never."

Hollister shook her head. "I don't think anyone is around, little dude. Really. Our timing couldn't be better."

"Yeah, but someone could come along at any moment."

209

"It's not like we have a lot of choices. Look, I understand you not wanting to go in there alone. But it's the only way."

"Speaking of which, how am I getting up there?"

Hollister grabbed my shoulders, took a deep breath, and gave me her most serious look. "I'm going to tell you something I never tell anyone."

Her sudden intensity made me uneasy. "You have my attention."

"I was on cheer squad in high school."

"Ha. That I would have liked to see, though I fail to see the relevance."

"For what happens next, little dude, we'll both need to channel our inner cheerleader."

Hollister turned, faced the wall, and squatted down so that her butt was just a foot from the ground. She braced herself by pressing her open palms against the wall.

"Gotcha," I said.

I climbed onto her back. When my sneakers were firmly planted on her shoulders, I said, "Ready? Okay!"

Hearing my signal, Hollister unfolded from her crouching position and lifted me up the face of the wall. When she reached her full height, the bottom of the window was level with my chin.

"You okay up there?" Hollister asked.

"Yeah, but I can't see anything. The windows have some privacy film on them."

"See if you can remove the screen and slide open the window."

Using one hand to grip the sill and retain my balance, I grabbed hold of the screen with my other hand and tugged. It wouldn't budge. It took me all of three seconds to determine the cause of the nonbudging: someone had sunk large screws into its four corners.

"Someone has screwed the screens into the window casing. There's no way it's coming off without some serious-ass tool or unless we cut the screen."

"All right, I'm bringing you down. Ready?"

"Okay."

I descended like a slow-moving elevator. When Hollister was crouched low to the ground, I hopped off her shoulders.

"Damn it," I said. "That wasn't a half-bad plan. But without a knife . . ."

Hollister snapped her fingers and started jogging back the way we had come. She stopped at the dumpster, lifted open the lid, and peered inside.

"Bingo," she said, reaching in and retrieving a green glass bottle.

"Nice," I said, understanding her plan. "Let's MacGyver that bad boy."

We ran back to the spot beneath the window. "Better stand back." Hollister smashed the bottle against the wall, picked up a large shard, and carefully handed it to me.

I climbed back onto Hollister's shoulders, and we repeated the process that ratcheted me up the side of the building. Holding on to the unbroken part of the bottle, I thrust the sharp edge into the mesh and sliced an opening in the screen. "Watch out below." I dropped the glass and the jagged square of screen to the ground.

"Nice work," Hollister said.

Taking hold of the window's edge, I tugged. Still stuck. It didn't feel locked, just gummed up from years of unuse.

"Will it open?" Hollister said.

"Not yet, but I think I can do it. Just needs more muscle." I flexed my free arm, showing off a hint of my bicep. "Time to bring in the big guns."

Hollister rolled her eyes. "Be careful up there, Mr. Universe."

When I tugged again, it felt close to breaking free and sliding open, but my one arm couldn't provide the strength to get the job done, so I grabbed the window with both hands.

"Wait, what are you doing? Hayden, don't do that."

"It's so close. I just need to give it a little extra force."

With both hands gripping the edge of the window, I gave it a hard yank. The window slid open, but too fast. I lost my balance.

"Oh crap," I mumbled.

Hollister jumped back and opened her arms to catch me. I fell onto her, taking her down with me.

"Oww," she groaned, looking up at the sky.

I slowly rolled off her. We lay side by side in the dirt, looking up at the open window.

"Perfect," I said. "Just as we planned it. You okay?"

"I think so. You?"

"No blood, so couldn't be better." I worked my way to all fours and stood, then reached down and helped Hollister to her feet. "No sense putting it off. Back on the horse."

"Okay, but no heroics this time."

I laughed. "We're in big trouble if that counts as heroics."

We repeated our routine a third time, and seconds later I was scrambling through the window. Inside the building, the area beneath looked to be clear for landing. I lowered myself to the point where I was clinging to the window by only my fingertips. *One, two, three.* I pushed off and landed hard on the concrete floor.

I was in.

Chapter Thirty-Three
In the Closet

Skylights. A half dozen of them illuminated an open warehouse floor roughly the size of a basketball court. The space was mostly empty, save for two large crates, several stacks of boxes, and something that required up-close examination to confirm it was in fact what it appeared to be: five bales of straw. A lighted EXIT sign marked the door. After sliding back the steel dead bolt, I cracked open the door.

"Fancy meeting you here," Hollister said.

She slipped inside. I reengaged the lock. After ascertaining that the two other doors led to a lavatory and a janitor's closet, we turned our attention to the warehouse's contents.

Hollister plucked a piece of straw from a hay bale. "What the hell is this for?"

"Scarecrow factory? World's largest manger scene?"

"Hilarious. But it was a serious question."

I shrugged. "Shipping material, I guess. This is, after all, a warehouse near the airport. Considering the large crates and that Ryan was driving a large truck, seems to make sense." Peering inside one of the already-opened boxes, I said, "This one is filled with government documents. Some sort of import and export forms." I checked another. "Moving blankets."

Hollister scanned the room. "Okay, so this is a shipping business. Shipping what?"

"Check this out," I said, opening the flaps to a sturdy cardboard box with alarming red warning labels pasted to the sides. "Medicine. Looks like several different kinds." Hollister joined me at the curious box and removed a large bottle, read from the label. "Carfentanil. Never heard of it." She selected another bottle. "Telazol. Never heard of it either. Have you?"

"Never. But all those ridiculous pharmaceutical names all sound the same to me. It's like a cat walked across a keyboard and whatever appeared on the screen, bingo! There's a name."

She lifted out a large plastic bag, and her eyes bugged. "Syringes. Goddamn syringes."

Turning to a stack of larger unopened boxes, I selected one and read aloud the white shipping label affixed to the side: "Dòngwù Exotic Nutrition, a product of China."

She looked up. "I wonder what makes nutrition exotic?"

"Marketing?"

The two large crates begged to be examined. My initial guess had been that the crates were used for shipping automobiles, as each was the size of a single garage, but at this point, nothing else we had discovered in the warehouse fit that assumption. After prying open one crate's door, I found two other containers within. One was slightly larger than the other, but otherwise they were identical. Each had a seamless outer shell of white powder-coated aluminum with an oval hatch, large enough for an average-size adult to fit through—I could slip inside, no problem, but someone as big as Burley would get only as far as her neck. The two inner containers had been designed to fit within the outer crate while taking maximum advantage of the allowable interior volume. There was nothing off-the-shelf or amateurish about the construction. Hardly. They had been crafted with a level of quality and precision equal to that of a NASA space module. I called Hollister over.

"What do you make of it?" I asked.

"Beats the hell out of me. Looks like the set of some sci-fi movie."

Being the smaller of us, I squeezed inside the crate and opened the steel hatch to one of the two interior containers. Several oxygen tanks and pipes and lines of conduit along with a sophisticated-looking battery system and mini electrical panel filled the space. I stepped out so Hollister could poke her head inside.

"Whatever it is, I don't like it," she said.

"Totally. Gives me the willies." I squeezed back inside, drew a hand across the smooth outer shell, then shimmied over to the larger container. Turning my head back to Hollister, I said, "Care to place a bet?"

"Egyptian mummy?"

"I'm going with space alien." I twisted the handle on the hatch, pulled.

What the—?

It took several seconds before I could comprehend what I was seeing. "Um, Hollister, you're not going to believe this."

She tapped my shoulder. "You may be small, but I still can't see through you."

"Oh, sorry." I stepped out of the crate.

Hollister craned her neck inside the hatch. I heard a gasp. She remained in that awkward position for nearly a minute. I understood. She was giving her senses a chance to convince her brain of what she was seeing and what it meant.

"This is seriously effed up," she said.

"I can't imagine how much it costs to make one of these. They seem soundproofed, and each one has a climate system and automatic feeders. Whatever animals get transported in these, they must be worth a fortune."

"Enough to pay for a fifty-thousand-dollar motorcycle," Hollister huffed.

"And a tricked-out bachelor pad." I stood back, looked at the crates with a perverse sense of appreciation. "By looking at the exterior crate, you'd never imagine what's inside. They're diabolical but impressive."

"No animal I know is worth that kind of investment."

I thought of dog shows on television and how much money breeders might pay for champions.

What about horses? How much was the going rate for a Triple Crown winner?

Zoos? What did a koala bear fetch these days?

Suddenly I knew the horrible truth. I wasn't one to start a fight, but had Ryan Waddell been standing there, I'd have punched him in his perfectly proportioned face. As reprehensible as his crime was, his audacity was equally shocking. Hanging on his living room wall, his nasty business was on full display. I clenched my fists, remembering the massive black-and-white photo of a black rhino—an animal so rare it was listed as an endangered species.

"Oh my God, Hollister! They're trading endangered and exotic animals." I pulled my phone from my pocket. "I'm calling the cops."

Hollister grabbed my arm. "No, don't."

I pulled free. "What are you talking about? Of course I'm calling the cops. Look around. This entire warehouse is filled with evidence. It's time to call in the professionals."

"How did we know to look here? How did we get inside? You ready to explain that to the police? I don't know about you, but there is no way I'm putting myself in a position where the cops think I have something to do with this."

"It's finished, Hollister."

"Oh no. It's not finished. Not by a long shot. You and I made a pact to find Camilo. I don't see Camilo here, do you? I see a whole lot of sketchy business but no Camilo. We don't stop until we find him. That was our deal."

Was it? I wasn't so sure. It was like Hollister and I had agreed to play a game without rules, and she was creating them as we went along. Now I had to decide whether to keep rolling the dice or call it quits. I weighed my options. There was a reasonably good chance that by staying in the game, I would get into serious trouble with the law. On the other hand was a 1,000 percent certainty that I'd piss off Hollister and probably lose her as a friend. Which worried me more?

"Okay," I said. "But we need to take pictures. We need evidence."

My hands shook so badly that it took two or three attempts before I managed to get one shot in focus. I documented the insides of the containers while Hollister photographed the exterior crates. We then moved on to capturing photos of the boxes, the medicine, syringes, food, and the bales of straw. That Ryan and Della were exploiting rare animals for profit was the most despicable crime I could think of—right up there with trafficking human beings.

Jerry was right about our too-big brains. Humans were as capable of committing hideous acts as we were noble ones. Hollister and I had stumbled upon a heinous crime. I vowed that no other animal would ever be placed in one of these crates again.

Ever since the morning Camilo went missing, my commitment to an investigation had yo-yoed. My on-again, off-again misgivings continued to gnaw at what resolve I could muster. Not anymore. There could be no backing away from this. The wrestling match in my head between old Hayden and new Hayden now seemed trivial and self-involved. The moment demanded action. *D.R. Enterprises is going down.*

Snapping a final picture, I said, "That should do it. Let's not push our luck."

"I'm with you, little dude. We've been lucky no one has shown up." Hollister hurried toward the exit. I followed a half step behind her. She opened the door, then shut it quickly. I bumped into the back of her.

"It's Ryan," she said, whirling around. "He just pulled up on his bike."

We both snapped our heads right and left, eyes darting around the room, doubtlessly sharing the same thought: where to hide?

"The window!" I raced toward the spot where I'd first landed.

"Little dude, no!" Hollister frantically waved me back. "There's no time."

She aimed a finger pistol at a crate. "In there."

"No way." I shook my head furiously. "We could end up in China, for all we know."

"The bathroom, then."

"He might need to use it."

I pointed toward the only option remaining.

Hollister scoffed. "We both can't fit in there."

"Yes, we can," I said. "We have to."

I ran to the closet. It was tight. Very tight. I stepped inside a large yellow bucket on wheels used for mopping. It began to roll. I braced myself against Hollister as she wedged herself between me and the wall-mounted sink. As she pulled the door closed, a glint of light filled the warehouse. Ryan had just opened the main door.

"Was he alone?" I whispered.

Hollister nodded.

We could hear Ryan scurrying around the warehouse, dragging boxes, fiddling with a door to a crate. At some point, my left foot fell asleep. I wanted to ask Hollister how she was holding up but didn't dare risk making a sound. I tapped her shoulder; she turned. I gave her a thumbs-up. She frowned but replied with one of her own.

A phone rang.

No, no, no!

My hand flew to my phone. I hadn't switched the ringer to silent.

"Hello?" It was Ryan's voice.

My sigh of relief came out louder than intended. It wasn't my phone—Ryan and I had the same ring tone. Hollister gave me a dirty look, pressed a finger to her lips. I thumbed my phone sound off.

Whoever had called Ryan had a lot to say. Several minutes passed before he said, "You're sure that's a good idea?" Another lengthy pause. "There are two here . . . huh? . . . No, they're both the medium size. One could be ready, I guess." A short pause. "That should work." It sounded like he'd started to pace the floor. "That doesn't give me much time." The sound of a door opening, a trickle of water. *Is he peeing?* "I need at least three hours. I can meet you here then." A flush, a door closing. "Yeah, yeah. Got it."

Another door, farther away, opened and closed—the sound of an engaged lock. I looked at my watch, let sixty seconds pass. "I think he left," I whispered.

Hollister nodded, then slowly turned the door handle, pushed it open a crack. Satisfied that Ryan had indeed left, she stepped out. I hopped out of the bucket, discovered both of my feet had fallen asleep. I stumbled.

"You all right?" Hollister grabbed my arms to steady me.

"Yeah, just need to get the blood flowing again is all." I took a few tentative steps; pain stung both feet. "So Ryan is meeting someone here in three hours."

"Della?"

"Could be," I said, "though this operation seems too sophisticated for just two people." Or for *those* two people. "We'll find out soon enough. And when we do, we'll get photos of them here at the scene. That should be more than enough evidence to put them away. The cops will arrest Ryan and Della. Then we'll hopefully find out what happened to Camilo."

"Correction. We'll *find* Camilo." Hollister raised an open hand.

"Damn straight." We high-fived. "Now let's get out of here while we still have the chance."

We slipped out the front. Would Ryan notice the unlocked door when he returned? It shouldn't matter. Once we had photos of Ryan and Della at the warehouse, it would be game over.

Inside the car, Commander jumped into my lap, gave my cheek a slobbery lick. I thought of the boxes of syringes, shook my head. "I can't wrap my head around how Camilo could have had anything to do with smuggling animals. I barely know him, but still. He's a good guy. That business with the crates, that's the other end of the spectrum. That's downright evil."

Hollister fired up Mo. "You're right, little dude. Camilo is a good guy. My guess is that he tried to put a stop to it but he got stopped instead."

The car launched out of the lot, and in seconds the speedometer read sixty-two miles an hour.

"Mysti has a kick-ass camera," Hollister said, her eyes on the road. "I'll see if I can borrow it. We may need to photograph whoever arrives from a distance. We'll want to capture their faces up close."

"Good," I said. "We can't take any chances. We need to nail these monsters."

Chapter Thirty-Four
Stay, Boy!

Before heading to Mysti's to borrow her camera, Hollister dropped me and Commander off at Orca Arms. She thought she should go alone to Mysti's. Besides, I needed to have a conversation with Ruthie about the dog.

After a quick walk around the neighborhood, I tucked Commander inside the apartment and crossed the complex to Ruthie's unit. The idea of finding a new apartment was a major bummer, but it was a definite possibility. No pets: that was the rule here—probably had been for decades. Ruthie was fair and reasonable, but as the property owner, she held the power.

Orca Arms provided tenants clean homes, a great location, and unbeatable rent. The only thing surprising about the wait list was that it wasn't longer. Ruthie had no reason to bend a rule for me. Even I found it easy to argue her case: allowing one dog even temporarily would mean opening up the entire community to pets, and there would be a negative impact on noise, the grounds, carpeting, and general wear and tear. Ruthie had nothing to gain by allowing me to keep Commander. On the other hand, I had my home to lose.

I rang her bell.

Looking more rested, Ruthie answered the door wearing denim overalls, a pink T-shirt, and Birkenstocks. She had corralled her hair beneath a black-and-white-striped cap, the type worn by train engineers. She was holding a bottle of glass cleaner.

"Hello, Hayden."

"Hi, Ruthie, you're looking well."

"*Pfft.* That's nice of you to say, son, but I haven't looked well since the nineties."

I took a deep breath and launched. "I won't beat around the bush. I found Commander. He's in my apartment. I know having him is against the rules, but I can't give him up to a shelter. And it's only temporary, just until his owner gets back. So I guess what I'm asking is for you to make an exception. I know there's no reason for you to do it, Ruthie, but still, I have to ask."

My last words came out in a garbled plea as I choked back tears. I wiped my eyes with the back of my hand.

"Thousand-dollar deposit. And you sign a lease addendum. But first I need to meet him, make sure he's as well behaved as you say. Deal?" She thrust out a bony hand.

For a moment, I couldn't breathe. I couldn't speak. I could only stare at Ruthie's extended hand. Had she really agreed? Just like that? The past several days had been one-way traffic of nothing but trouble, and I wasn't prepared for good news. I burst out crying.

I brushed past her hand, went in for a hug. "Thank you, thank you, thank you, Ruthie."

"*Pfft.* Just don't make me regret it, Hayden."

I sprinted to my apartment, leashed Commander, and ran back to Ruthie's. On the way, I impressed upon him the importance of making a good impression.

Ruthie gave Commander a quick appraisal, scratched his ears. "Interesting collar with that little barrel. It's like the ones worn by those enormous dogs in the Alps or wherever. What type of dogs are those?"

"Saint Bernards."

"That's it. They were bred to save hikers from avalanches or some such. What's supposed to be in the barrel anyway? Whiskey or brandy? Not sure that makes much sense either way. Though I do reckon the liquor would warm a person's stomach."

"Never gave it much thought," I said.

"So what's in his?" She thumbed the miniature barrel affixed to Commander's collar.

"Nothing. It's just decorative."

"Is it? I don't think so."

"Really?" I knelt.

"See here"—she pinched the two ends of the barrel, twisted—"it unscrews."

"I'll be damned." What Ruthie saw immediately, I had been blind to. And now that she'd called attention to the barrel's center seam, it was obvious that it opened.

She stood. "My fingers are too old and clumsy. Best if you do it."

I unscrewed the barrel. A small scroll of paper fell out.

"Well, what is it?" Ruthie said, peering down over my shoulder.

"No idea." I stood and unrolled the paper. A string of alphanumeric characters had been typed onto the tiny slip: *X973MTV.* "My guess is a password or code of some kind."

Ruthie examined the writing. "Odd."

"Very."

I rerolled the scroll, stuffed it back within the barrel, and screwed the ends back into place.

Ruthie wondered aloud, "What does it mean? Who put it there?"

To those questions, I mentally added others. Was it something innocent, say, a product code that had been placed there by the manufacturer? Or something more intriguing, such as the combination to a Swiss safety-deposit box? Or the access code to a stash of cryptocurrency?

Ruthie recaptured my attention by saying she'd write up the lease addendum. I had a week to come up with the thousand-dollar pet deposit. I had nearly eight hundred dollars in savings, aside from my school-sponsored retirement account. I'd need to find the other two hundred. Perhaps a loan from Aunt Sally or my grandparents?

There were still two hours before Hollister and I were to meet back at the warehouse. Until then, I could think of nothing better to do than take Commander to visit Jerry.

Chapter Thirty-Five

Wishing Hard

Talk about a mix of emotions. On the positive side, I had gotten Commander back, Ruthie had just agreed to let him stay, and Hollister and I had made crucial progress in our investigation. On the negative side, we'd discovered that D.R. Enterprises apparently stole and sold exotic animals. The whole horrible business would soon be out of Hollister's and my hands. Once we had the additional photos and took them to the police, our work would be done. *And please, please, please, let the cops find Camilo alive!*

Of course, Camilo's return would mean giving up Commander. The idea made me too sad to dwell on for long. We'd become a pair, he and I. With him, my neighbor relations were at an all-time low, my bed seemed cramped, my sleep was disrupted, my apartment and car had never been dirtier—and I didn't want it any other way.

Arriving at Jerry's townhouse, I half expected him to appear beside the car. He usually heard me pulling into the driveway (and before, I had been driving Aunt Sally's far-quieter Prius). I was excited to see his reaction when he saw that I had Commander with me.

Guessing he must be napping, I knocked loudly and gave him another minute to rouse himself and find his slippers. After what was too long of a wait, I knocked again and added the doorbell for good measure. Still no answer. Should I be worried? I was.

Aunt Sally kept a key to Jerry's front door at her place. I tied Commander's leash to the stair railing and hurried next door. Once inside my aunt's place, I kicked off my shoes—one of her many house rules never to be violated—and padded across the overlapping and mismatched area rugs that formed a crazy quilt of floor coverings. The furniture, polished with the same religious zeal she applied to her Bible study, looked as if she'd acquired each piece from a different stall at a flea market. And there were the angel figurines—her collection easily numbered into the hundreds. But nothing in Aunt Sally's modest townhome stood out as much as the large print of Jesus above the fireplace. My aunt had chosen a likeness of her lord and savior with long auburn hair, steely blue eyes, square chin, and a bit of scruff. As a child, I'd never given the portrait much thought. But now I appraised the depiction of the Galilean carpenter with greater appreciation.

I found the key to Jerry's place in a kitchen drawer. Less than a minute later, I stepped inside his home.

Jerry had none of my aunt's rules, so I let Commander run free, and together we searched for the old man. It didn't take long to discover he wasn't there.

I pulled out my phone.

"What do you mean he's not there?" Worry coated Aunt Sally's voice. "I was talking to him just this morning. He had no doctor appointments, and today isn't one of the days he goes to the senior center."

After some back-and-forth, we decided that I would stay put in case Jerry returned while my aunt phoned the local hospital. Jerry wore an alert bracelet for use in an emergency. While that was reassuring, I hoped he hadn't needed to use it.

Too anxious to sit still, I tackled the dishes in the sink and threw a load of laundry in the washer. Why hadn't my aunt called? I checked my phone. *Stupid!* I'd put the ringer on silent when hiding in the janitor's closet with Hollister and hadn't switched it back on. I'd missed five calls. The most recent two were from my aunt. One was from a local number I didn't recognize. Two had come hours earlier from Jerry's number.

I pressed call back for my aunt.

"I know, I know," I said, absorbing her irritation. She'd learned that Jerry had fallen. He was in the hospital in Ballard. I raced to the kitchen, found a bowl, filled it with water, and placed it on the floor. Commander was used to the surroundings and would be better off roaming around Jerry's place than sitting in the car in the hospital parking garage.

Channeling my inner Hollister, I drove with a speedy recklessness I didn't think myself capable of. I found a space on the second level and sprinted across the pedestrian bridge. At the information desk, a sleepy teenage girl directed me to room 512. I drummed my fingers on the wall of the elevator, willing it to go faster. I burst into Jerry's room. The bed was empty. Please, God, no.

"Relative of Jerry's?"

I spun around. A nurse was smiling back at me. His name tag read *Pete*.

"I help take care of him," I blurted. "He called me, but my phone was on silent. Is Jerry here? Is he okay?"

Nurse Pete held his smile, though the twitch at the corners of his mouth told me it took effort. "I'm afraid Jerry had a fall. He broke his hip. That would be worrisome enough, but another result of the fall is a hematoma near his stomach. Jerry's on blood-thinning medication, so internal bleeding is very concerning. He's been wheeled into surgery. You just missed him."

I squeezed my eyes shut, trying to wish this away. Jerry had phoned me. Twice. I'd not been there for him. Nurse Pete said I could wait in Jerry's room and that he'd let me know what the situation was as soon as he had news from the OR.

The room had a lovely view: in the distance, sailboats bobbed in their slips at Shilshole Bay Marina. The tranquil scene was the opposite of my thrashing brain waves. There was no way I could leave the hospital while Jerry was on the operating table. Hollister would have to get the photos at the warehouse by herself.

I called Hollister and explained the situation. She said all the right things, but I sensed her disappointment. I'd have felt the same way. We'd worked so hard as a crime-fighting duo that it was a letdown that one of us would be a no-show for the final act. I wished her luck, and she promised to keep me informed.

Next, I took a deep breath and phoned Aunt Sally. If I were to be generous and round up, I'd say the conversation went five percent as well as my talk with Hollister. I found some relief by holding the phone at arm's length during a long, rambling prayer. My aunt's heart was in the right place, but I would never understand her giving a deity equal credit for both the good and the bad that occurred in the universe.

The call would have gone on longer, but Aunt Sally had convinced herself that "God is ready to call Jerry home" and so she needed to free up the line and book a flight home to Seattle.

The quiet of the hospital room was unnerving. I walked the hallways, making sure to never stray too far from the nurses' station. After two hours, my phone vibrated, alerting me to a text: *At warehouse, waiting.*

It was killing me that I couldn't be at the warehouse with Hollister, and I was worried that somewhere within this building, Jerry was fighting for his life.

When my mom had gotten sick, I had become a champion wish maker. When she'd died, I'd had to accept that all my hopeful thoughts amounted to nothing. Cancer had won. And yet, what was life if not a long slog of hoping and wishing? I hoped that Jerry would pull through and that he'd soon be tossing a stick to Commander. I furiously wished that Ryan and that weirdo Della would get what they had coming to them: a lifetime behind bars. And I hoped more than anything that Camilo would be found alive and that he'd prove his innocence in all this.

And so I hoped. And so I wished. And so I waited.

After countless laps around the hospital corridor, I returned to Jerry's room and dropped onto the pale-green (was the color supposed to be soothing?) guest chair with a high back and long sloping arms. The chair, designed no doubt for lengthy bedside vigils, even reclined. I closed my eyes.

The buzz in my pocket woke me. How long had I been asleep? It was another text from Hollister: *A woman with Ryan. Della? Wearing a hoodie. She went inside. Ryan went around back of bldg.*

Had she gotten pictures of them? Was she still there? I texted her back: *Once you get pics, get out of there. Let me know.*

That there was no immediate reply was a relief; she must be driving home already. But twenty minutes passed, then forty. She should have been home by now. The same feeling of alarm that had hit me when Jerry hadn't answered his door slithered back. I phoned her again. The call went straight to voicemail. *Here I am, rock me like a hurricane. Beep.*

"Hollister, it's me. I'm worried. Call me."

There would be no dozing off again. I was too wound up for that. Perhaps Hollister was at Mysti's? That would explain why she hadn't picked up. Though given the circumstances, Hollister must know how desperate I'd be to hear what had happened at the warehouse.

Nurse Pete popped his head in with news from the OR. Jerry's surgery had gone about as well as expected. He'd be recovering for several more hours before being brought up to the room. I phoned Aunt Sally with the positive news on my way to the car.

Chapter Thirty-Six
Backtracking

Driving to Hollister's, I realized that for as many times as she had been by my place, I'd never been to hers. I had her address only because she had given me a Holl&Wood business card.

Hollister owned one of those live-work spaces that were popular among solo artists and small businesses. There were no lights on in any part of the building. She didn't answer when I rang the bell. I tried phoning again, but like my earlier attempts, the call went to voice mail. "Hollister, I'm here at your place. I just rang. You here?"

After walking to the end of the block and back, I rang again. I didn't think Hollister was there, but I couldn't leave without another try.

The next place to look was at Mysti's. The problem was that I didn't know where Mysti lived, nor did I know her last name. Hank or Burley might know, though.

I first tried Burley. She didn't pick up. Given our last conversation about her need for "green therapy," I'd have been surprised if she answered the phone. After leaving an urgent message, I looked up the number for Hunters, dialed. Voice mail. Had I expected anyone to answer the phone at a club during business hours?

The parking lot at Hunters was half-full. Hank was behind the bar, restocking beer in the minifridge.

"Her last name's Cho," Hank replied to my question. "Don't know Mysti's address or number. But you're in luck. She's right over there." He pointed to the same spot near the pinball machines where I'd first met her and Hollister.

Mysti had only ever conveyed dislike for me, so I approached her with reluctance. As I neared the table, I noticed she was being a little too cozy with a woman I had seen playing Twister at Burley's party. My unease turned to anger on behalf of Hollister.

"Hey, Mysti, what's up?"

Her look said she had yet to warm to me. "What do you want?"

Her companion smirked, seemingly amused by my mere presence.

Stepping closer to their table, I said, "I thought I might find you here with Hollister. You know, Hollister, your girl-friend. But I don't see Hollister here. That woman there, she's not Hollister, is she? Have you seen or heard from Hollister in the past few hours?"

As unlikely as it was that Mysti knew Sarah Lee, the look she defaulted to whenever engaging me—one whose thought bubble read *Crawl off and die*—was eerily similar to my neighbor's. The woman sitting too close to Mysti turned out to be the speak-your-mind type. She said, "Buzz off, freak."

I tamped down a snarky rebuttal. I needed an answer from Mysti. "Seriously, I have reason to be concerned about Hollister. Have you seen or heard from her recently? Like in the past hour or two?"

The word *concern* seemed to soften Mysti. Although she continued to hiss, she retracted her claws. "No. But that's par for the course these days. Why?"

One good thing about the zero rapport between Mysti and me was that I didn't feel obliged to waste any time with pleasantries. As I had my answer, I turned and hurried away. There was only one place left to look. If I didn't find Hollister at the warehouse, that was it. Final straw. I would call the police.

Soon my headlights were sweeping the warehouse parking lot, almost immediately spotlighting Mo. My stomach lurched up into my throat. I pulled up beside the empty Porsche. The door was unlocked. There was no camera, no phone, no keys. I ran toward the complex. The vehicle gate was, of course, closed. I ran down the side of the fence, beyond the knoll, and started climbing. At the top of the fence, I surveyed the area lit by industrial lamps mounted to the sides of the buildings. There wasn't a single vehicle in the lot.

Once onto the property, I sprinted to the front door of warehouse E. Locked. There was no point in going around back—without Hollister to hoist me up, I couldn't reach the window.

The dumpster. It had provided an answer before, but this time would require a lot more effort. Although on wheels, the giant metal bin wasn't designed to be pushed across a half block of pockmarked asphalt. It didn't help that it was nearly full. Impossible to pull, but as long as I had all four wheels aligned, I could push it. Slowly.

After five minutes of shoving, I stopped to assess my progress: ten feet. Ugh, this would take forever. I jogged the perimeter of the property, desperate to stumble upon some other way in. As I passed by the front entrance, my motion triggered a laser, and the gate started to open. I ran out, across the lot to the car. By the time I'd driven back to the gate, it had closed, but I had expected that. I pulled the nose of the car up close, left the motor running, and dashed back to the spot where I'd become a pro at climbing the fence. Once over, I ran back to the gate and triggered the sensor, and when the gate opened, I dashed through, hopped in the car, and drove onto the property as the gate closed behind me.

With the Fiesta parked snuggly against the wall below the windows, I climbed onto its roof. Immediately I regretted not incorporating more chin-ups into my workout routine. My first attempt was a bust. I needed to commit fully before fatigue set in. I took a deep breath, leaped. My fingers gripped the window ledge. I pulled myself up the side of the wall. As my chest reached my hands, I transitioned to a push-up, like you do when lifting yourself out of a swimming pool. The rest was straightforward.

The skylights that had illuminated the space earlier in the day were of no help. There was only darkness and shadows. Once my eyes had adjusted, the horror of what lay before me came slowly into focus. Only one crate. *Oh God.*

Fear churned in my belly. I ran to the lone crate, yanked open the door and hatch. Empty. I tried the bathroom and the janitor's closet. I hadn't needed to look. I'd known Hollister wasn't there.

An overwhelming dread flooded me. I was light-headed. I bent over, gripped my knees. My stomach heaved. I was going to be sick.

Chapter Thirty-Seven
On All Fours

As I ran to my car, a thought played over and over in my head: *You did this, Hayden. This is on you.* I had set events in motion by returning to Camilo's house when I should have walked away. Then I'd convinced myself that there was no harm in playing amateur detective and that keeping vital information from the police was somehow—absurdly—the reasonable thing to do. How would I live with myself if something horrible had happened to Hollister? I should have been there with her. I'd let her down, and now she'd been taken by Ryan. Had it been Della with him? Had there been anyone else in the truck or waiting inside the warehouse? I fell into the seat of my car, slammed the door. Two other thoughts tore at me with the ferocity of Roy Driggs's dogs: where had they taken Hollister, and was she still alive?

The situation was a code-red. I reached for my phone to call the police just as a text came in. I looked at the screen. My heart nearly stopped.

Hollister
> *A trade. Your friend for the laptop. Otherwise, we will kill her. Reply that you understand.*

I pressed a trembling finger and thumb to the phone and enlarged the screen, as if larger text would expose the message for a prank. Tears filled my eyes. I looked up and scanned the surrounding area, hoping to see Hollister jump from behind the bushes and yell, "Gotcha!" But the twist in my gut confirmed what I knew. I'd let things go too far. I'd gone along with Hollister when I should have listened to myself. Now Hollister had been taken. I typed out a reply, hit send.

Hayden
> *I understand. But I don't have the laptop.*

Hollister
> *In that case, we will kill her.*

Hayden
> *Wait. I don't have it, but I will get it.*

Hollister
> *You have one hour.*

Hayden
> *Give me 24 hours. I promise I will get it.*

Hollister
> *If you don't, we will kill your friend. Then we will find and kill you.*

Hayden
> *I will get it. I just need time.*

Hollister
1 hour.

Hayden
I need more time.

Hollister
You have till 6 a.m. Tell no one. Do not contact the police. We will know if you do. Await instructions. Reply that you understand.

Hayden
I understand.

I dropped the phone onto my lap. I was most royally and completely screwed. I didn't have the laptop. The computer was the one thing I knew for certain had been taken from Camilo's house. Plus, I was convinced it had been Ryan who had taken it. Why was he conjuring up a game he knew I couldn't possibly win? My mental state was the equivalent of a catastrophic car crash: all wreckage, bashed and smoking. I squeezed the steering wheel, beat my head against my hands.

Police or no police? I'd been warned not to go to them, but how would Ryan find out if I did? Most likely, it was nothing more than a threat. Countless television crime shows included the cliché of the villain threatening a victim not to involve the cops. And yet, could I take that chance?

"Argh!" I shouted, and punched the dashboard.

Settle down. Get a grip.

I needed to sort this out. The clock had already started running. It was 10:10 PM. There was nothing to be gained by sitting in the parking lot. I started back toward the city.

Again, I found comfort and direction in Jerry's words: *Give voice to your thoughts. Think it all out loud, poking and prodding the various possible scenarios. Keep in mind what's most probable, and follow the evidence. That is how you solve a mystery.*

How I wished I could talk to Jerry—he was wise and always calmed me down. The possibility of losing him made me realize how much he meant to me. Still, as concerned as I was about his condition, I knew that if we were sitting at his kitchen table, he'd wag a finger at me and say, "Stopping fretting about things you can do nothing about, Hayden. Focus on what needs doing."

I started by forming a foundation of assumptions from which to build a hypothesis. First, Camilo had been taken because of something he possessed. When he didn't hand over whatever it was, he was taken; then his home had been ransacked and his laptop stolen. Now I could think of only two possibilities: either Camilo still refused to give his captors what they wanted, or he couldn't because he was dead. Hollister had to be right. When Camilo had tried putting a stop to the diabolical business, he had been stopped instead.

A car horn honked. I swerved back into my lane. The image of Camilo's dead body had seized my thoughts. I gripped the wheel tighter. *Pull it together, Hayden.*

I changed lanes for the exit to Columbia City and Camilo's house. Although his home was the most obvious place to look, it was the only place I could think of. I would have to search harder than whoever had given his home a once-over the first time. The problem was, with the laptop already snatched, I didn't know what I was looking for.

Under other circumstances, I would have parked well down the block, but every second counted. I pulled up in front of the next-door neighbor's house and called it good. After waiting for a dad pushing a stroller to turn the block, I walked quickly down the sidewalk. When I got to the edge of Camilo's property, I ran across the yard and through the gate to the back. The porch light wasn't on. Only moonlight and the glow from windows of nearby homes illuminated the area. The Schwinn was right where I'd left her.

I tried the back door—locked. Kitchen window—locked. Bedroom window, surprise, surprise; it was locked. Tugging on the small opaque bathroom window, I didn't expect it to budge, but it slid open with such ease that it slammed against the opposite end of the frame with a loud smack. I dropped down to hide in the darkness. When enough time had passed, convincing me that the noise had gone unnoticed, I climbed through the opening—something of a newfound specialty of mine.

No lights could be turned on. I couldn't risk calling attention to the house. I crept into the living room, where I performed a slow 360-degree turn while surveying the rubble. Crazy as it was to think it, the house having been ransacked worked to my advantage: I could concentrate on the spots— few as they were—not already ravaged.

If I were trying to hide something, where would I put it? Heating vent? Taped to the underside of the toilet tank lid? Box of Cheerios? Litter box! Brilliant, if only Camilo had a cat. Over the decades, movies had done a stellar job of promoting the idea of a secret hatch beneath an area rug or a loose floorboard. Figuring this idea had sufficient merit, I examined the floor, but found nothing. Returning to my other ideas, I ruled out each in turn. Where else?

What was that? Voices? I froze, listened. Yes, voices. They were getting louder. Two people. More than two? They were walking up the sidewalk toward the front door. I ran on tiptoes to the bathroom, climbed onto the vanity. The screen door produced a long squeak. I pushed myself through the window. As I landed on the back patio, I heard the front door open. I ran to the back of the yard and hid behind the same tree I'd used for cover when I'd had to pee while waiting for the cops.

Lights, one by one, filled the house. Whoever was inside didn't share my worry for discretion. I watched and waited. My eyes were focused on the kitchen when the bathroom window slid shut, followed by the sound of the latch being engaged. I caught only the flash of a silhouette before the light turned off. Had it been a man? At the other end of the house, a different person passed quickly by the kitchen window. The kitchen went dark.

I turned and leaned back against the tree's trunk. *Think, think, think.* I'd wait a minute to make sure they were leaving, then sneak alongside the house and peek over the fence to see who they were.

As I counted to sixty, my gaze drifted around the surrounding area. Ah, yes, there was the large fern where someone had buried a family pet. Or was it? What else might it be? Dropping to my knees, I examined the small pyramid of stones stacked beneath the fern's fronds. After removing the topmost rock, I paused. I could do this after I saw who had been in the house.

I ran to the fence, lifted myself onto my toes, peeked over. Two people had just reached the street's sidewalk. There was no question one of them was Ryan, his build and hair unmistakable, even from behind. The other person was indeed a woman, nice body, a foot shorter than Ryan, long straight dark hair. Light from the streetlamp reflected on the surface of an object she held in her hand. Glass in a frame? The two of them walked closely together, their arms around each other's waists. They turned the corner and disappeared.

Would there ever come a time when anything going on around me made sense? So much of what I'd just witnessed cried out for answers. Was Ryan bisexual? Who was the woman? What had they been doing in Camilo's house? I gave my head a Scooby-Doo—like shake. Although the questions kept piling up, I knew of a place to start digging.

Dropping to all fours, I set aside the stones. Should I be wrong about this, I'd be disturbing a grave, but if I was right, I might prevent the necessity of a new one—a much bigger one. Thankfully, the soil was loose. Using cupped hands, I began my mini excavation. A half foot below the surface, there was something solid, flat. Digging faster, I removed the dirt around the sides of a hard-surfaced box, pried it free, and lifted it from the hole.

Holding the object up to the moon's light, I examined the several sealed plastic bags, wrapped with duct tape, protecting what looked like an internal hard drive pulled from a computer. I shoved the dirt back into the hole, haphazardly restacked the stones, and with the drive firmly in my grasp, ran to my car, got in, and locked the doors. Once I'd unwrapped it from its sheathing, there was no question that it was indeed a hard drive. My feeling of jubilation instantly flipped to despair. This was not what Ryan wanted. And yet someone had hidden the hard drive in the yard for a reason.

Racing upstairs to my apartment, I set the hard drive on the desk and stared at the black-and-silver metal case, about the size of the four-by-six-inch frame that held a picture of my mom. The hard drive, however, was thicker, about an inch in depth and fairly heavy.

I was reasonably comfortable with technology, but this was beyond me. For starters, the drive gave no indication of the type of computer it was compatible with, and even if it had, I didn't have a clue how to insert it, let alone make it work and access whatever was on it. This was a job for someone who really knew computers. This was a job for geeks.

The time: eleven thirty PM. I had six hours and thirty minutes before Hollister's time ran out. With any luck—and I was seriously due some—I knew who might help me. But first, I'd need to find the video arcade named Festers.

Chapter
Thirty-Eight
A Job for Geeks

Festers was on Pike Street on Capitol Hill. The building had
so far escaped being bulldozed for a new mixed-use mid-
rise—a development concept that had proliferated in the
neighborhood, replacing charm and character with taupe
facades, Juliet balconies, and underground parking. To enter
Festers required traveling down a long dark passageway that
ended in a narrow doorway of thick black vertical blinds. I
pushed past the flaps, sticky to the touch, and emerged into a
space the size of a classroom.

With no overhead light, the room was illuminated only
by the frenetic backlit displays of dozens of video games and
pinball machines lining the walls and bisecting the room in
a long narrow row. Random beeps and bells, explosions, and
automatic weapons fire reverberated against the black cinder-
block walls and low black ceiling. I counted eleven people,
all males, all under the age of thirty, except for one guy
who looked to be at least seventy. The strange old man was

slow-dancing with an invisible partner to music only he could hear.

As dark as it was, I had to walk the room and get up close to each group of players to see their faces, ghoulishly lit by a machine's greenish glow. At the back corner, I found Tanner and Paul engrossed in a game called Contra. Thanks to a generous application of body fragrance, there was no question it was them. Although I was on the most urgent of missions, I didn't dare risk interrupting them. The intensity with which they played the game was no less than that of an Olympic athlete participating in a final medal round. Tanner, playing a character named Lance, battled a giant alien head that spewed larvae from its mouth. Paul took over and defeated an indescribably bizarre creature, ending the game in victory. They high-fived. As they dug in their pockets for more quarters, I jumped forward.

"Hey, guys."

They turned. Paul said, "What up?"

Tanner didn't seem to recognize me, or if he did, he didn't bother to show it.

"Listen, guys. I know this will seem totally random, but I need the help of computer experts, so naturally . . ." My attempt at flattery fell flat. By the looks on their faces, you'd think I'd asked them to fetch me a beer.

"Kinda busy here, dude," Tanner said.

Believer that I was in having a plan B, I was disappointed with myself for not having one. I moved ahead on gut alone and thrust the hard drive toward them. "What do you make of this?"

Tanner's eyes narrowed. He took it off my hands, held it closer to the game console to take advantage of the light. "What is this?"

Paul took it from Tanner. "Hard drive, duh. Not commercial, nothing you can buy online."

Tanner took it back. "Not on Amazon, anyway." The guys shared a snarky giggle. I forced a smile, pretending to appreciate the humor.

"Thing is," I said, "I need to know what's on it. Do you have a compatible computer? Can you access the contents?"

The guys looked at each other warily. "Where'd you get this?" Tanner asked, looking over my shoulder. I got the feeling he thought the FBI or NSA was lurking somewhere behind me in the shadows of the arcade. So far, my gut had kept them in the conversation, so continuing with the free-flow strategy, I said, "I dug it up an hour ago from Camilo's backyard."

"Come again?" Paul said.

There could be no dicking around. I needed these guys' help. My read on them was that they'd sniff out any lies faster than they could plug another five quarters into their game, at which point I would lose them for good. I went with the truth, a very speedy overview of events that had culminated in me standing in a dark arcade holding a hard drive and getting woozy off the fumes of their body spray.

After inspecting the hard drive from all sides, Tanner picked up a backpack that had been resting on the floor next to the game, pulled out a thick laptop, and set it on top of the console. Paul reached for a second backpack and retrieved a plastic case of screwdrivers. He plucked one from the set and handed it to Tanner, who used it to open the underside of the laptop. After replacing the hard drive with the one I'd found, Tanner began tapping away on his keyboard. Paul and I stood on either side of him, watching the screen.

"What the hell?" Tanner said.

"Why won't it let you in?" Paul pointed to a spot on the screen. "Click there."

"That won't do anything; that's just—"

"Dude, just try it." Paul reached for Tanner's keyboard.

Tanner batted away his hand. "Get off, ass-wipe."

"Just try it, then."

"Shut up. I will, but it won't work. Watch." Tanner clicked where Paul had suggested. A pop-up appeared on the screen.

"See? It wants a password," Tanner said.

Paul scoffed. "Dickhead, like you knew a pop-up would appear."

Both guys turned to me. "You got the password?" Paul asked.

I skipped the part about the password being rolled up on a scrap of paper in a dog's collar and said, "It's at a friend's place. Can you come with me? It'll save precious time. Afterward, I'll give you both money for a rideshare so you can get home."

"No can do, Red," Tanner said. "School night."

As my mind scrambled for something to say, anything to make them understand the critical importance of their help, they burst out laughing.

"Your friend got any beer?" Paul asked.

Jerry, I knew, had no beer. He did, however, keep a bottle of Scotch in the cupboard that had never been opened. How long it had been gathering dust on the shelf was anybody's guess. When the guys heard this, our pact was sealed. We headed to my car.

Tanner climbed into the back. Paul sat in front and immediately started fiddling with the radio dials, found a thrasher metal rock station, turned up the volume. Both guys knew the song; they air-drummed to the beat and, when the time came, shouted the chorus, which sounded like *Hellfire death clown, Hellfire death clown* . . . I doubted this was correct, but then the song was unlikely to be based on a real biographical account, so who's to say? The only (and I do mean only) good thing about the next half hour of ear-deafening guitar squealing and screaming vocals was that it made conversation impossible.

We finally arrived at Jerry's townhome. The dashboard clock read 12:35 AM.

Commander was overjoyed to see humans. I realized at once that he was desperate to pee.

Tanner sniffed the air. "Smells old. Who'd you say lives here?"

"I didn't," I replied, wanting to avoid taking the conversation in any direction other than the code and the hard drive. They followed me into the kitchen. I flipped on the light.

"Have a seat," I said, retrieving the bottle of Scotch from the cupboard. I grabbed two tumblers and set them on the kitchen table alongside the hard drive.

"The password?" Paul lifted his laptop from his backpack. Tanner did the same.

"Right there." I pointed at Commander. Were it not for the Scotch, which Tanner was busily opening, my act of unscrewing the tiny barrel on the dog's collar and extracting a computer password would surely have earned their interest. As it was, they were fixated on the bottle's label.

"Dude, this is 1966 Glenlivet," Paul said. He poured himself a large glass as if it were milk, then passed the bottle to Tanner.

"You got any snacks?" Tanner asked.

"Biscuits." I pulled them from the cupboard and set the box on the table along with the code. "My hunch is that slip has something to do with what's on the drive. Have at it. I'll be right back. I just need to take the dog out for a few minutes." I leashed Commander, and he pulled me out the door.

"Come on, Commander, pee already, will you?" The dog casually sniffed around the yard. "Seriously, for someone's who's got to go, just do it already." An excruciatingly long few minutes passed before he selected a slat of fence to lift his leg against. "Good job, buddy!" I started to pull him toward the door. He dug in his heels. I looked up at the sky, sighed. Of all the times, he needed to poop too.

Finally, back in the kitchen, I found Tanner madly clicking away on his computer. Paul sat close beside him, his eyes fixed on Tanner's screen. They must have heard me come in, but they didn't acknowledge my presence. Their focus was impressive and, given the importance of their work, appreciated. I sat and waited. My knees jittered furiously beneath the table.

"I'm in," Tanner announced.

"Nice," Paul said.

"How?" I shouted in excitement. "How did you do it?"

"Just needed the password to access the drive."

Suddenly the expressions on the guys' faces changed from blank concentration to concerned scowls.

Paul said, "What the . . . ?"

"Unbelievable," said Tanner.

That was it. I jumped up from my chair and hurried between them, where I could see the screen over their shoulders. Had I expected elicit pictures, I'd have been disappointed. The screen showed a spreadsheet.

"Accounting data," Paul said.

"Deadly boring," Tanner said.

"Usually."

"But this isn't usual."

"Way unusual."

"What is it?" I leaned down closer to Tanner's screen so I could read the column and row headers.

Tanner said, "It's a history of sales."

"Sales of animals," Paul noted.

"Not puppies and rabbits." Tanner tapped his screen. "Check it out. Row B is labeled 'Animal Type.' "

I gasped, reading the list of animals. " 'Black Rhino,' 'C-R Gorilla,' 'Sunda Tiger,' 'Bonobo,' 'Red Panda.' " The list continued beyond the bottom of the screen.

Paul snapped his head in my direction. "What is this? These are endangered animals."

Tanner added, "Some critically endangered."

"The other columns list the origin, the date, the buyer, and the price, most of them well into six figures, several seven figures," Paul said.

Tanner shoved his laptop away, then pushed back from the table, distancing himself from what he'd just seen on the screen. "What kind of nasty business is this?"

"The worst," I said. I repeated what I'd already told them and emphasized the connection between Camilo and

Barkingham Palace. I explained that the pet store's owner, Della Rupert, also owned the business entity D.R. Enterprises, which also owned the warehouse with the animal containers. She and her accomplice, Ryan, were behind Camilo's and Hollister's disappearances.

"The information on that hard drive will send them to prison for years," I said. "Maybe even for life. Plus, it identifies the buyers. They'll all get what's coming to them. With this information, we might even save the animals."

Was this what Ryan was after? Did he have reason to believe that the record of the animal sales was on Camilo's laptop? Who, if not Ryan, had the computer? Did Ryan know about the hard drive? The password?

As maddening as the situation was, it might not matter. I now had all the evidence and leverage I needed.

"What are you going to do?" Paul asked.

"Thanks to you guys," I said, "I'm going to get my friends back."

They had emptied half the bottle of Scotch. They were hammered. I needed to get them home and out of the way. Time was ticking. After getting their address (surprise! they were roommates), I ordered them a lift. However, getting them out of Jerry's townhouse was proving difficult—they had moved to the comfort of the sofa and had switched on an episode of *South Park*.

When the app alerted me that their ride had arrived, I switched off the television, grabbed their backpacks, and dropped the Scotch bottle into one of the packs alongside the hard drive and password. I told them their packs and the Glenlivet were going home in the rideshare—with or without them. Realizing the party was over, they stumbled into the back seat of the car and were off.

The time: 1:55 AM.

In the past hour, I'd formed a five-step plan, giving myself two hours to put the pieces in place. Once done, I'd have another two hours before sunrise.

As I set out, I realized Commander must be starving. Jerry had no dog food, but a quick search of the refrigerator yielded some lunch meat. I gave it the sniff test. "Well, well, well, this is your lucky day, my friend." I tore strips of honey-cured ham onto a dinner plate. Commander gobbled down his dinner (technically breakfast). I would come back for him when this was all over. After giving his ears a light scratch, I was out the door.

Commence step one.

Chapter
Thirty-Nine
Liar, Liar

Time: 2:45 AM. Completing step one of my five-part plan proved every bit as tricky as I'd thought it might be. And yet it had come together for one and only one reason: love of family.

Time for step two. I took a deep breath and pulled out my phone.

Hayden
I have the laptop.

Hollister
Warehouse E. One hour. Don't do anything stupid.

Hayden
I must see Hollister before the trade.

Hollister
One hour.

The text exchange with Ryan had gone pretty much as expected: he continued to act the role of pretty-boy villain. Though I was surprised by the familiar location—I had expected to be summoned to a freeway underpass or an abandoned pier. Maybe Ryan was lazy or just unimaginative. I had come to suspect both.

I forwarded the texts to Burley and drove to the warehouse. With no traffic on the roads, I should be there in less than a half hour. To soothe my jangled nerves, I switched on the radio.

The voice of Stanley Kellogg filled the car. Seriously? Was this some sort of sign? Or had the entire week been a scripted play, authored by a cosmic force and this the soundtrack—*The easiest thing I've done is falling hard for you*? Too young for a bucket list, I decided that meeting the country star would be the first item on my before-turning-thirty list. I'd buy concert tickets for Hollister, Burley, Camilo, and me. We would sit in the front row and pass around a bottle of 1966 Glenlivet in a paper bag. The thought made me smile.

The warehouses on Commercial Drive were dark, the lot empty. There was no need to be secretive, so I pulled right up to the gate and shut off the engine. My knee bounced with nervous energy. What lay ahead of me was without a doubt and beyond all measure the most daring thing I'd ever done. Just a week ago, that claim would have been my attempt to tip a go-go boy. I was about to raise the bar considerably. Though hardly had I made it so far alone. I'd siphoned strength from Hollister and become a bit wiser thanks to Jerry. Next, I would need the confidence of Camilo.

I closed my eyes and returned to the night I'd walked through the doors of Hunters and seen him dancing up there on the pool table. In an instant, I'd known I was going to tip him. But not so that I could brush my fingertips against his body. It was more than that. I needed to prove to myself that I could put myself out there—live in the moment. For too long, I'd stood watching life go by from the sidelines. What had started as a symbolic act had snowballed to this: I was about to take down a dangerous criminal and save my friends and the animals listed on that spreadsheet.

Finally, a single headlight swept across my rearview mirror. I froze. The time: 2:58 AM. At the gate, Ryan punched in a code, rode through, and waved for me to do the same. I drove behind him to the back row of warehouses and stopped at the entrance to building E.

Ryan removed his helmet, set it on the seat of the Kawasaki. He shot me a quick glare before entering the warehouse. With my school book bag over my shoulder, I followed him inside. Never before had the massive ceiling lights been on. I raised a hand to shield my eyes from the harsh brightness. Ryan was standing just beyond the door. "So," he said, "let's have it."

I moved a few steps away from him. "The deal was we'd trade. I give you the laptop, and in exchange, you return Hollister. I don't see her."

He tilted his head in the direction of the one remaining animal crate. "She's in there. Safe and sound."

I shook my head. "I want to see her first."

Ryan sneered, proving even the most beautiful person can turn ugly. "Be my guest." He swept an arm toward the crate.

I walked as slowly as I could without making it obvious that I was buying time. Even so, when I'd cut the distance in half, he said, "Seriously, shrimp, could you get on with it?"

Ryan, such a charmer.

At that point, I had a pretty good idea of how he thought this was going to go. I stopped.

"I've been thinking," I said. "That large black-and-white photo in your living room, the one of the black rhino. What do you see when you look at it every day?"

Ryan gave me a cold stare. "Money."

"And what does that buy you, Ryan? Seems it cost you your soul."

"Shut up." He started toward me. *Good.*

I held my ground. "Open the crate. I want to see Hollister first."

"I told you to shut up." He lunged at me, yanked the book bag from my shoulder. He flipped back the canvas flap, looked up at me with fury in his eyes. "You're a dead man, shrimp."

His reaction to finding two large textbooks in my bag went as expected. He drew a fist back for a punch. The moment had come for step three of my plan. I shouted, loud as I could, "Liar, liar, pants on fire!"

Ryan swung, I ducked. He connected with my ear. I stumbled, and he pushed me to the ground. He screamed in my face, "Where is the laptop!" He grabbed me by the shirt collar, yelled again, "Tell me!"

"You have it," I groaned.

He grabbed a fistful of my hair and started to drag me toward the crate. I reached up and wrapped my hands around his wrists, trying to take the weight off my scalp. He kicked me hard in the side. I tried digging what fingernails I had into his flesh; another kick, this time in the small of my back. This wasn't part of my plan, and I was starting to worry. Suddenly, Burley's size-fourteen orange clog appeared a foot from my nose. Ryan let go of me and yowled in pain. Burley had lifted him by the hair. He was dangling in midair, his feet frantically kicking as he tried to touch the ground.

"You're one world-class peckerhead," she said. "Let's see how *you* like having your hair pulled." She then turned her attention to me. "You all right, Hayden?"

"Little man can take a punch, can't he?" Roy Driggs stood in the doorway. He had a rifle cradled in one arm, and the opposite hand held an enormous pair of bolt cutters.

I crawled to my feet. "You can put him down, Burley." She dropped Ryan, and he crumpled to the ground, right beside me. I was nose to nose with him.

"Where's Hollister? And Ryan, you should know before you lie to me again that wherever you say she is, Burley and I will go there. If she is not where you said she'd be, Roy over there is going to take those bolt cutters and use them to neuter you. Now, I understand you don't know Roy, but you want to trust me on this. So now that you understand your balls are at stake, I'll ask you for the first and last time. Where is Hollister?"

Ryan really could have been a telenovela heartthrob. He had a mastery of exaggerated facial expressions. In just the past five minutes, he had given me cold and calculated mastermind, menacing sociopath, furious criminal, and now his most convincing look of all: terrified douchebag.

"She's at the estate," he whined.

"Be specific," I said. "What's the address?"

"It's six-nine-six-nine Bounder Road."

"How do we get through the gate?"

Ryan was surprised, as I'd expected he would be, that I knew about the gate. "How do you know about that?"

"Just answer the question."

"You can't. The gate uses facial recognition software. If you're not already in the system, it won't open."

Burley said, "What if we took Mr. Handsome along? Smash his face against the camera? Gate opens. Bob's your uncle. Why are you smiling?"

"Because this time, I do have a plan B. And it doesn't require the face to launch a thousand ships. As it happens, in our humble case, we require only a speedboat."

I stumbled to the animal crate, pulled the door open. "He'll be safe and sound in there until I phone the police. Have him show you how to turn on the oxygen flow. We don't want him suffocating in there, not when he has so much to look forward to." I turned to Ryan. "I don't get it. You took the laptop when you busted into Camilo's house, so why this game?"

Ryan roared, "You stupid little freak, I don't have the laptop! Would I go to all this trouble if I had it?"

Ryan, champion liar that he was, was for once telling the truth.

"C'mon, chump," said Burley. She placed Ryan in the same wrestler's headlock she'd used on Cynthia and dragged him into the crate. After securing the hatch, she looked downright jolly. "Have to say, Hayden, I was more than a little teed off when you rang my phone at the pinnacle of my beauty sleep and laid this plan on me. Seemed a bit squirrely to me. Especially the part about involving Roy. But hey, it worked. And now that I'm here and got the blood flowing, got to say I'm having fun."

"Can we get the hell out of here?" Roy barked. He hadn't moved from the doorway.

"Cool your jets, big brother," Burley said. "We're going. We're going."

Outside the warehouse, before Roy climbed into his camo-painted Humvee, I said, "Thanks, Roy. I truly appreciate the help."

Roy spat tobacco juice onto the asphalt. "Let's be clear, little man. Ain't nothing I did here was for you. Was for my little sis." He gave Burley a wink and fired up the engine.

"So, what next?" Burley said. She clapped her giant hands, the smack shattering the early morning's stillness.

"Well, if you thought that was fun, just wait till we commence step four."

Chapter Forty
Elephants and Whales

Burley suggested we stop off at Slice. The bakery was midway between the airport and our next destination and served several purposes: we could use the Wi-Fi and the office computer and printer, and Burley could quickly "whip us up a couple of triple shots." Although the first three steps of my five-part plan had gone reasonably well, the unexpected violence at the warehouse had revived my concerns. I pleaded—again—for calling the police. Burley argued—again—that she and Hollister didn't particularly trust them. I pointed out that Hollister wasn't around to vote and that the seriousness of the situation tipped the scales in favor of bringing them in. Burley countered with the same decisive blow Hollister had repeatedly used and gotten me with every time.

"If we tell the cops what we know now, they'll only screw it up. Worse, they'll assume we're involved. We're a team, Hayden. You, me, and Hollister. We agreed to do whatever it takes to find Camilo. And now we need to save Hollister too. Once we get her back, safe and sound, and after we find

Camilo, *then* you can go to the cops. I'll even go with you. But first we get our friends back."

Against my better judgment, I sided with my heart. I was all in with these two ladies.

When we arrived at Slice, I was already jittery. I asked Burley to make mine a single espresso, though I wasn't sure she heard me. Against the loud hiss of steam, she whistled a tune I didn't recognize (Michael Bublé?). She really had had fun at the warehouse, which, albeit a bit disturbing, had put her in a jolly good mood.

I'd never had reason to go inside Burley's office, which was essentially a pantry. Shelving ran to the ceiling and encircled the windowless room. She had arranged the stockpile with no apparent order. French flour, exotic sugars, and hundreds of products—in brown paper cartons, multicolored bags, and copper tins with hand-painted labels—had been jammed onto every available inch of shelf space, in many places as much as four deep.

"Welcome to my laboratory," she said, sweeping a long arm across the extensive inventory.

"How on earth do you keep track of all that's here?"

"As long as no one moves anything, it should be right where I last put it."

I cocked my head, not bothering to hide my disbelief. "You can seriously remember exactly where you put every single item?"

Burley suddenly looked flustered. Calling her out on a harmless bit of exaggeration hadn't been my intent, but I wanted to know if what she said was true. Given her prolific use of weed, such an ability would refute my assumption that too much pot smoking muddled one's memory.

"Try me," she said. The twinkle in her eye was a relief; she wasn't offended by my challenge. She was eager to prove her claim.

"All right. Close your eyes."

Burley covered her face with both hands. I tiptoed around the room and identified three items at various locations on the shelves. "Okay, I'm ready," I said.

She lowered her hands, blinked her eyes.

"Bittersweet cocoa powder," I said, enunciating each word with the dramatic flair of a game show host.

Without turning around, she reached behind her and plucked a plastic jar from the shelf.

"Impressive. One for one," I said. "Next up, almond hazelnut praline paste."

She stepped around me, walked to the farthest shelf, and pulled a tin out from behind two bags of flour.

I shook my head in appreciation. "That's two for two. Last but not least, crystal glaze."

"Apricot or plain?"

"Is there a difference?"

"I'm out of the plain. The apricot is next to your elbow, there in the white carton."

"I'll be damned."

Burley beamed with pride. "Elephants and whales, Hayden. Elephants and whales."

"Sorry? I . . ."

She tapped the side of her head. "Giant heads, giant brains. It's biology. Now, what say we get back to work?"

Burley turned on the computer. I called up the website with the most recent listing for 6969 Bounder Road on

Bainbridge Island and navigated to the photos. There were two particular images that I recalled seeing that I was interested in reviewing more closely. As I scrolled through the gallery, Burley said, "Why would anyone ever want to live in a place that big? You'd never keep it clean." As I'd been to Burley's house, this concern seemed as legitimate as a nudist worrying about their dry-cleaning bill, but I let it pass.

"There," I said, pointing to image 24/32. "I've always found drones creepy, but man-oh-man do they provide sweet aerial footage."

Image twenty-four depicted the waterfront portion of the property from a height that clearly showed the dock, the grounds, the tennis court, and the terrace. I tapped the dock on the screen. "We tie up there." Tracing a finger across the grounds, past the tennis court, and to the terrace, I said, "We cross the lawn, find a way into the house from the back."

"Won't they hear the boat?"

"We'll have to cut the engine when we get close, paddle the rest of the way to shore. The sun's just coming up, so we won't have darkness in our favor, but hopefully Della and whoever else might be in the house will still be asleep."

"And then what? That house is huge. They could have Hollister anywhere. How will we know where to look?"

I waved a finger in the air. "That, my good lady, requires"— I continued scrolling images until I got to 31/32—"a floor plan. I'll print two copies. One for each of us."

"Once inside, we split up?" Burley gave my shoulder a gentle squeeze. "Don't take this the wrong way, Hayden, but you didn't match up so well against pretty boy. You sure you want to go snooping around that house all by your lonesome?"

That was a fair point. In hearing it, I realized I'd made a sexist assumption: that if it came down to it, I could take Della. But what did I know? She could have her black belt in jujitsu or be an expert at throwing ninja stars. Or she might own a gun and have the marksmanship to shoot the freckles off an intruder's nose. But all that was fear talking. I wasn't deaf to it, but I couldn't allow it to drown out rational thought. The house was too big. Burley and I could cover twice the territory if we searched separately.

"We'll chart our paths through the house now, and while we're there, we'll maintain constant contact by text. That way, each of us will know where the other has been and where they're going next." With a finger, I circled the master suite on the second floor. "That must be Della's bedroom. We'll avoid it to begin with and start in the coach house, lower level, and first floor. With any luck, we won't even have to go upstairs. Once one of us finds Hollister or Camilo, we huddle wherever that is, then go out the way we went in." I brushed my hands as if wiping crumbs from my fingers. "Easy peasy."

"I'd feel a whole lot better about this if I had a gun," Burley said. "I should have borrowed one from Roy." She reached for her phone. "I'll have him meet us in Magnolia."

"Please, no, Burley. No guns." Ugh, Americans and guns. We were a nation of trigger-happy nitwits, and I was adamant that we not join their ranks.

"No guns? What if this Della chick has one? How does that work with your no-guns policy?"

"We don't know if she has one or not. Put it this way: if she isn't armed, no one can get shot. If she does, at least there is one less gun in the equation. The fewer guns, the less shooting."

"Sounds just dandy, unless you're the one being shot at."

Raising my hands in surrender, I said, "Okay, okay. How about this argument? Regardless of how stinking guilty Della is, we're still breaking into her house while she's at home. From a legal standpoint, it's far worse to do it with a gun. There's no reason to make our crime more crime-y."

Burley sucked her cheeks. "Fine, you win. But I'm taking my nunchucks, no two ways about it."

After printing out two copies of the floor plan, we charted our paths through the mansion. I mapped Burley's route in blue ballpoint pen and mine in red marker. She'd start on the lower level. I would take the coach house, then move on to the ground floor.

Burley poured a second espresso in a to-go cup, grabbed a hunk of pound cake for each of us from the pastry case, and we were off to commence part four of the plan.

Chapter Forty-One

All Aboard

Mysti lived in a condo, bought for her by her parents, in the swanky Magnolia neighborhood only blocks from their house. Mysti had made it clear from the start that she didn't like me, so it was decided that Burley would do the sweet-talking—or Burley's best version of it.

No one likes to be awoken by a knock on the door at 4:25 AM, and Mysti didn't prove the exception.

"Well, howdy," Burley said cheerfully.

"You do know what time it is?" Mysti said through a crack in the open doorway. "Are you stoned?"

Not one to take offense easily, Burley replied, "Never before nine. Can we come in?"

"Huh? Who?"

I was standing behind Burley, so we had taken Mysti off guard. There was no putting off the inevitable. I stepped out. "Top of the morning." I tipped my invisible cap.

Mysti rolled her eyes. "Oh my God, you're like a bad penny."

Unfamiliar with the reference, though assuming it wasn't favorable, I decided to pretend she was delighted to see me. "A pleasure to see you too."

"We need a favor," Burley said. "It's urgent."

This coming from Burley seemed to crack Mysti's armor, if not her scowl. "You can come in, but make it quick."

Mysti's home's interior was lovely. Although put together as painstakingly as her outfits, it was nothing like her: it was warm, inviting, and colorful. She didn't ask us to sit. The three of us stood just inside the door on the slightly raised landing.

"Well . . ." Mysti huffed, crossing her slender arms across her pink silk robe.

"It's Hollister," Burley said, starting the story of what had brought us to her door about an hour before sunrise. She concluded with, "And so we need to borrow your speedboat."

Mysti scoffed. "My boat? You can't be serious?"

I clenched, unclenched my fists in an attempt to relax and fight back my compulsion to scream, *Yes, we're serious! We're trying to rescue your girlfriend from a ring of international criminals!* Instead, I let out a quick breath and said, "Yes, Mysti, we are serious."

Another scoff. Mysti addressed her next question to Burley. "Are you familiar with boating rules? Do you even know how to operate a boat? It's not some dinghy, you know. It's a seven hundred and seventy horsepower Sleekcraft."

"Sounds like a blast," I said. I couldn't help myself.

"Why don't you come along?" Burley suggested. "That way, you won't have to worry."

"Some of us have to go to work," she said.

Mysti made it sound as if Burley and I planned a frolic in the sea. She was being difficult and wasting time. Burley stood taller, shoulders back. I sensed she shared my impatience.

"We need that boat, Mysti," Burley said, her voice suddenly firm.

A moment passed during which Mysti just stared coolly at Burley. Suddenly she whirled around, marched from the room, and disappeared into what must be the kitchen. She returned a minute later with a gold key chain in the shape of what I guessed must be a Korean symbol. Two keys hung on the chain. She dropped the keys into Burley's open hand, which closed around them like a fielder's mitt catching a ping-pong ball.

"There," Mysti said. "The round one is for the gate leading to the dock. Slip eighty-eight. The square one is for the boat's ignition. I hope I don't live to regret this."

Now that we had the keys, I felt freer to speak my mind. I opened my mouth, but Burley was faster. "We promise not to spill too much beer." She turned to me and winked.

Elliott Bay Marina sat below hilly Magnolia just west of downtown. It was a spectacular location and, because of that, catered to high-end yacht owners, who were already members of the upper class—meaning the place was *fan-cee*. There were hundreds of boats; their towering masts swayed like leafless trees in the moonlight. Gates lined the water's edge, each with a set of numbers denoting the slips that lay beyond on the dock.

After finding the right gate, we used the round key and began trudging down the rocking wooden walkway, searching for slip 88.

There is something primal about larger people projecting an air of capability, so when Burley, the most massive person I'd ever known, stopped at slip 88 and said, "I don't know, Hayden, you sure about this?" her misgivings packed an extra punch. The Sleekcraft was true to its name, long and narrow with a bow tapered to a sharp point. The boat's shell was glossy smooth, painted a vibrant orange. The name *Wild Child* was painted on the stern in chubby white letters. Considering what I knew of Mysti and her conservative parents, the boat's name seemed wildly inappropriate.

During the short drive to the marina, Burley and I confirmed that neither of us had ever operated a speedboat. Her experience of having once rented a Green Lake row boat was only slightly bested by my having twice worked a small skiff outfitted with a gutless outboard motor.

Aboard the speedboat, we stood for a long moment in silence. I was summoning the confidence to take the seat behind the wheel while also hoping Burley might beat me to it. But this was my plan. I needed to cowboy up.

I fell into the white padded seat. Above the wheel on the dashboard were twelve smaller round gauges and three large gauges. To my right sat two large shifters. The one nearest my body was thankfully marked *D-N-R*. *Drive, neutral, reverse. Got it.* The other had to be the throttle, controlling the speed. Burley squeezed into the bucket seat beside me.

"We need to untie the lines," I said. "Would you please?"

"Aye-aye, skipper." She dislodged herself and wobbled to the first of four points on the Sleekcraft where someone had wound lines from the dock around cleats affixed to the boat. She removed each in turn and tossed them onto the dock, then returned to her seat.

"All right, let's see what this water rocket can do!" I said, willing myself to get swept up in my own forced enthusiasm. I turned the square key in the ignition. The engine roared to life, reminding me of the sound of Harley Davidson motorcycles that passed me on the freeway. With a trembling hand, I tried shifting the nearest lever from neutral to reverse; it wouldn't budge. I pulled harder—nothing. We hadn't left the slip, and already I was in panic mode.

Burley tapped my leg to get my attention. "Squeeze the underside of the handle. That releases the lever."

I did as she instructed. The lever slid back. I glanced over at her. She was watching a YouTube instructional video on her phone.

"The boat will go in the direction you steer, whether it's forward or reverse," she added helpfully.

"Got it," I said. Not wanting to launch the boat out of the slip, I ever so slowly shifted the throttle backward in tiny increments.

"Reverse speed is limited," Burley said, "though you're right not to push it."

I nodded. At that moment, even speaking risked distracting me from the tricky task of easing the boat out of the slip and then turning without colliding with a giant three-level yacht named *Daddy's Boy.*

"You're doing great," Burley said.

Again, I chanced only a nod.

For all the ferocity the Sleekcraft conveyed, its quality came through in controlled movement. I maneuvered the boat out of the slip and into the harbor's main channel.

Game on.

Like an airline pilot in movies, I gripped the large handle on the throttle and began to thrust it steadily forward. The engine roared louder, and the boat glided effortlessly ahead. Feeling comfortable if not yet confident, I allowed myself to take in the beauty of the morning. A faint arc of orange was creeping over the horizon, casting a pale golden light across the bow of the boat. The water glimmered. The mountains soared majestically. The skyscrapers of the city shimmered in the distance.

Burley, also appreciating the scenery, said, "Who needs heaven?"

"Heck yeah," I replied.

As we emerged into the open water of the sound, the boat rocked in the light chop. After identifying a compass on the dashboard, I steered the boat northwest toward Bainbridge Island.

"Once we cross the bay, we can motor up the coastline and use the GPS on our phones to zero in on Della's estate."

Burley replied with two thumbs-ups.

Fortunately, the ferry ran south of our location, but Elliott Bay was still a major shipping lane, so I asked Burley to help keep watch for freighters as well as other vessels. Should the Sleekcraft need to get out of the way fast, it had ample horses to do the job.

Perhaps it was the early hour, but few other vessels were out on the water, just a few fishing boats chugging farther north toward Whidbey Island. After five minutes of steadily ramping speed, I had the boat skittering across the surface at fifty knots. Burley made the conversion with an app on her phone.

"Nearly sixty miles per hour!" she shouted gleefully over the wind and engine noise.

For fifteen minutes we bounced along, closing in on the coast. I reduced speed to seventeen knots.

"We're going twenty," she announced.

"Should be getting close. We don't want to miss Della's house. Match the pictures on the printout with the houses on the shore."

Burley gave me another thumbs-up. The waterfront homes were ridiculous; each seemed designed with one singular purpose: upstage thy neighbor.

"How do people get so much money?" Burley said.

"Inherit or make it, I suppose."

Burley said, "Yeah, well, I don't care who you are. Nobody gets that rich without stealing from the cookie jar."

"Problem with wealthy people?"

"I have a problem with dishonest people. Seems to me the wealthier you are, the harder it is to tell the difference."

"Hey, Burley, is that it?" I pointed to a two-story glass-and-timber structure that looked more like a ski lodge on steroids than a residence.

Burley looked back and forth between the photo and the real-life image. "Even bigger than in the picture." She gave me a devious look. "Can you use that line in your blog?"

I just shook my head, downshifted, and crept the boat up to the dock. Fortunately, there was no need to paddle; the Sleekcraft's engine, once warmed up, purred softly at low speed. Burley moved to the port side of the boat to reach out and grab the lines. The significant weight shift splashed a wave of water onto my lap. I shut off the engine. Burley tightened the lines and knotted them onto the cleats. We'd arrived. The time: 5:55 AM.

Step five of my five-step plan was about to commence: The Rescue.

Chapter Forty-Two
Blaze to the Rescue

Burley had made good on her promise to bring along her nunchucks; they protruded from a back pocket of her baggy jeans like two silver sticks of dynamite. For the actual rescue part of my plan, Burley had opted for a simple, single long ponytail, explaining that she could channel the earth force with her hair pointed downward, which would lead us to her spirit sister. I presumed she meant Hollister and not Della.

The massive house looked quiet, but given the hour, that was expected. Burley and I dashed across a deep-green lawn trimmed with the precision of a golf course fairway. As we passed the tennis court and neared the terrace, we stopped to exchange a fist bump.

"Be careful," I whispered.

"Where's the fun in that?" she whispered back.

I lifted my phone, confirming our plan to stay in constant communication via text. Burley repeated the gesture. She crouched down, achieving a height still taller than my own, and jogged toward a back corner of the house in search of an open window. Most basement windows would have been a nonstarter, but as every aspect of the house was grotesquely oversized, Burley stood a fighting chance of finding one she could fit through.

I ran toward the coach house located above the garage—though this garage could easily accommodate a half dozen cars. Listening for creaks or squeaks, I began my creep up the staircase. There was a wraparound deck at the top with views every bit as spectacular as the main house would offer. A floor-to-ceiling glass double slider faced the water. It was open. The room was quiet. I stepped inside.

The scent of gardenia filled a room exploding with color: pink-and-white-striped walls, overstuffed periwinkle-blue sofa and chair, and giant red throw pillows. A chandelier resembling an upside-down circus tent hung in the high-domed ceiling.

Yip.

By the sound of the bark, the dog was small. While relieved there would be no experience like that with the hellhounds at Roy's compound, any size dog could rat me out.

"Hell's bells, Peekaboo. You went out not thirty minutes ago. Mama's putting her face on."

There was no mistaking the singsongy voice coming from the adjacent room. What was Della doing here and not in the main house?

Yip.

"Oh, for the love of cream cheese."

I heard a rustling. Della was approaching the living room. I leaped behind the sofa. A door opened.

"Now you be quick about it, Peekaboo. Mama means it."

A white ball of fluff the size of a house cat scampered around the end of the sofa, saw me crouched there, and stopped. I stared back at Peekaboo. Slowly I reached out an open hand for her to give me the sniff test. The dog backed up, whined. *Please don't bark, please don't bark.* Miraculously, Peekaboo took another step back, whined again, then turned and ran around the sofa and out through the sliding glass doors. I started to stand.

"Blaze?"

I jerked, looked up. Della Rupert peered down at me from over the back of the sofa.

She blinked her eyes as if tuning an antenna. "What the . . ."

"I came for Hollister and Camilo." I stood tall (as much as possible). Given how painstakingly well put together Della had been when I'd first met her at the store, I was taken aback at seeing her in a floral housecoat and hair curlers. She was, however, wearing a full mask of makeup.

"Now, Blaze darlin', you know better than this. You can't just show up unannounced in a woman's home. Shame on you. You could have given me the most awful fright. Now I want you to walk right on out of here, you hear me? Scoot."

Della might have been surprised to find me lurking behind her sofa, but she didn't seem particularly surprised to see me.

"Where are they, Della? Where are Hollister and Camilo?"

Della's eyes darted around the room. Checking to see if I was alone? Looking for Peekaboo? In the next instant, she ran back into the bedroom and locked the door behind her.

"Della!" I followed and jiggled the handle, pounded on the door. "It's over, Della. Just tell me where they are before this gets any worse."

She spoke through the door. "Now I told you to skedaddle, Blaze. This is far from over. You seem like a sweet boy, so go on home now. Go on home before anyone gets hurt."

With a stalemate on my hands, I texted Burley: *Della is holed up in a locked room in the coach house.*

A moment later there came a reply: *Found an open door. In basement. Nothing so far.*

Della wasn't going anywhere, so I checked the rest of the coach house. There was a second bedroom, half bathroom, and galley kitchen, along with a few closets. At the far back of the house was a small den. I did a double take. There on the edge of a desk sat a laptop. Thanks to the college decal, there was no mistaking that it belonged to Camilo. I found an enormous faux-leopard-print handbag. After tucking the laptop inside, I came to my senses. Taking the computer with me would slow me down. I shoved the handbag under the desk. I no longer needed the laptop. All the leverage I needed was on the hard drive, which—along with the password—was safe with Tanner and Paul.

Back at the door to Della's bedroom, still locked, I was wondering what to do next when Peekaboo pranced in from outdoors. The tiny dog blinked at me with large brown eyes as if to say, *Pick me, please, pick me.*

At first I had not liked the dog, but she had suddenly grown on me. I said loudly through the door, "Della, I have Peekaboo. Now, where are Hollister and Camilo?"

"Now, Blaze, you just calm down out there." Her voice had changed, the singsonginess replaced with agitation. "Don't you go and do something you'll regret."

I scooped up Peekaboo. She produced a startled yelp.

"Blaze!" Della threw open the door. "Don't you dare harm my Peekaboo!"

With the dog in my grasp, I ran outside to the edge of the deck. I held Peekaboo over the railing, making sure I was in view of Della.

Della gasped—she was hyperventilating. "No, no, no. Okay, okay, okay. That woman's in the main house. Now please give me back my Peekaboo."

"Where in the house?"

"Now darn it all, Blaze—"

I gave the dog a pretend shake.

"The wine cellar! Now give me back my dog!"

"What about Camilo?"

Della looked genuinely baffled. "Camilo? Why, Blaze darlin', Camilo's long gone."

Long gone. The words knocked me against the railing. Peekaboo yipped, nearly squirming free of my grip.

"Peekaboo!" Della screamed.

I regained a firm grip on the dog and fought to hold it together, keep a clear mind. "What do you *mean*, Camilo's gone?"

"I'm no Merriam-Webster, but I do believe gone means gone. As in, not here."

"Where, Della? Gone where?"

Her anger was palpable. "Shouting really isn't necessary. I'm standing right here."

"How did you get Camilo's laptop?"

"The way one attains things, love bug. One takes."

"Yeah, that I figured out all by myself. But who did you take it from?"

"From whom would be inaccurate. More to the point would be from where. I took it from Camilo's kitchen table. Now, I'll thank you to give me back my dog."

My brain was somersaulting. "You? You tore up Camilo's house?" As crazy as Della was, I couldn't picture this oddball woman in curlers ransacking a house. The number done on Camilo's home had been a violent, undisciplined, testosterone-fueled act. It had to have been the handiwork of Ryan.

"Certainly not." Della looked stung. "I won't tolerate a mess. And that goes for my own home as well as others'. Once I saw you ride off on that cute-as-can-be girl's bicycle, I dashed in, snatched the laptop, and dashed out, quick as you please."

The sequence of events snapped into place. Ryan had kidnapped Camilo, then Della had slipped into Camilo's home and taken the computer before Ryan had had a chance to search for it himself. Ryan had turned the place upside down, looking for a laptop that wasn't there. Even now, Ryan didn't know where the laptop was.

But wait, weren't Ryan and Della working together?

The phone vibrated in my pocket, notifying me of a text from Burley. I needed to cut this chitchat short, but I had to know: "Why are you living here and not in the main house?"

Della raised her chin. Her composure had returned. "If you must know, sweet pea, I'm remodeling. The previous owners had the most pedestrian taste. Whoever knew there were so many shades of dull?"

I set Peekaboo down on the deck, and the dog ran inside. Della followed, slid the door closed, and engaged the latch. She glared at me from the other side of the glass. For a moment, I imagined the glass as prison bars. Her time would come soon enough.

My phone displayed Burley's latest text: *Nothing yet.* I texted her back: *Hollister is in the wine cellar! Meet you there.* I raced down the staircase of the coach house and across the lawn.

From the terrace, I could see into the kitchen; it looked empty. The door was unlocked. Odd. If this room was undergoing renovation, there were no signs of it. I ran into the dining room. Here, as with the kitchen, nothing was out of place. The furniture was neatly arranged, art on the walls, luxurious rugs on the floor. Perhaps Della's remodeling efforts had been confined to the second level? Pulling the mansion's floor plan from my pocket, I confirmed the location of the wine cellar. The elevator was straight ahead, through a library and down a short corridor.

I ran through the doorway into a sumptuous library with a wraparound balcony filled with bookshelves. As my eyes registered what was before me, I skittered to a stop. Burley sat squeezed into a leather wingback chair in the center of the room. Someone had bound her legs together and tied her hands, which rested in her lap. A dishcloth had been stuffed into her mouth.

"Burley?" I whispered.

A click sounded from behind me. I whipped around, look up. A woman standing on the mezzanine held a gun pointed in my direction.

"Hello, Hayden," she said.

Chapter Forty-Three
Where Do We Go From Here?

She was beautiful. Latina. About thirty years old, long black hair, emerald-green eyes.

"Who are you?" I said.

"Really? That's disappointing. For all you've figured out, for all the inconvenience you've caused, I'd think you'd know who I am."

And in that instant, I did. Camilo had the word *Familia* inked across his rib cage. He also had a tattoo of a beautiful Latina with long dark hair on his bicep. That woman had come to life, and she was pointing a gun at me.

"Where is your brother?"

"Camilo is at home."

Home? I had been at Camilo's house the night before; so had Ryan and Daniela.

"But he's not. You know he's not."

I glanced at Burley. She looked frightened and uncomfortable but unharmed.

"Home," Daniela said. "I sent my brother back home."

Sent. Back.

"How could you!" My body trembled with fury.

Daniela scoffed. "What do you know about it? Do you have any idea how much money I send home to my family? To my community? Camilo was going to ruin everything. Everything. He got it into his stupid head that we needed to stop. Stop? I've barely started. When he wouldn't listen to reason, I had no choice. He had to leave."

"But Camilo is a Dreamer. He has DACA protection—"

"His protection will expire in a few weeks. Camilo is outside the country. He has no ID, no papers. He will find it difficult to return. And if he tries, I will know about it."

I now had a picture of what had happened to Camilo that morning. After receiving an urgent text from his sister, he had raced off to meet her. When he arrived at the parking lot, he'd been kidnapped and transported across the border. He had no way to get back home, back here—to his real home.

"But he's your brother."

"Which is the only thing that kept me from killing him. It cost me a small fortune to get him out of the country without a trace."

I glanced at Burley, tied to the chair. Were Roy around, he'd tear this place to the ground with his bare hands to free her. I had no doubt Burley would do the same for him. The Rodriguez siblings were a different story. Camilo must love his sister—or once had. What else explained the tattoo? But Daniela? What had happened to her? How did a person become so heartless that they turned on their own family?

"And Ryan? What's his role in all this?"

"Ryan . . ." Daniela chuckled. "Ryan, Ryan, Ryan. He's good-looking, yes? He keeps me entertained. He does work for me. He is loyal."

"But he's gay. He dated Camilo."

Daniela laughed, not an evil laugh, a genuine full-throated laugh. "No. No, Ryan is not gay. Ryan is gay-for-pay. Ryan is anything-for-pay. He danced at the club because I paid him to. He became friends with Camilo because I paid him to. He suggested Camilo get a job at Barkingham Palace because—"

"Yeah, yeah, because you paid him to. But why?"

"Because I wanted my brother to join me in this business. Finding people to trust is not easy. If I had come right out and told Camilo what I was doing, he'd have said no. He would never have agreed to my business plan. He was always too sensitive. But once he got a taste, once he started making so much money, he'd find it harder and harder to say no."

"But he did say no, didn't he?"

Daniela nodded. "Which was very disappointing."

"Why did you and Ryan go to Camilo's house the other night?"

"My brother had a family photo. I couldn't have a picture of me lying around."

"And Della? How does she and the pet store figure into all this?"

"I needed a legitimate business. A place I could use to buy and sell supplies, make and receive shipments. As everything in my business involves animals, what could be better than a pet store? When I approached Della, she was about to declare bankruptcy. She had one sad little store with a leaking roof and no customers. I offered Della her dream store and more money than she could ever imagine making."

"In return, she had to let you use the business as a front for your illegal trade in rare animals."

"Everyone has their price. Della's was Barkingham Palace. Now, where is my brother's computer? You can't imagine my displeasure in seeing you arrive without it."

Daniela read the look of surprise on my face.

"If you hadn't noticed, which you are not meant to, there are hidden security cameras everywhere on the estate. I watched you get out of that boat you came in on. Quite impressive, by the way. I might have to get one for myself."

Daniela, like Ryan, didn't know it had been Della who had taken Camilo's computer.

Della had stolen the laptop, then lied to both of them, throwing the blame on me and endangering my life and the lives of my friends. Whatever Della's reason, it was high time that Daniela be set straight on the facts.

"I never had the computer. Della took it before Ryan got to Camilo's house. She has had it all along."

Daniela scoffed. "Della? No, I don't believe that for a second. Della is not that stupid. When I didn't hear from Ryan, I knew he'd screwed up somehow. And then you came along. You've shown yourself to be quite formidable. Unexpected. I know you can't help your appearance, but—and no disrespect when I say this—you don't look like you'd be much trouble to anyone."

The slight would have bothered the old me, but the new me delighted in being underestimated. I had proven I was stronger than I looked.

"Della has the laptop, I'm telling you."

Again, Daniela dismissed my claim, this time with a toss of her hair. "Della wouldn't. I have given her everything she has ever wanted. Why betray me? Where would she go? What would she do?"

"This has been an interesting chat, Daniela, but where do we go from here? Believe me or not, I don't have the computer. It's sitting right now under a desk in the coach house."

"Enough. I prefer to deal in facts. I have not one but two of your friends. You have two hours to go and get the computer and return it to me."

Two hours? I needed only five minutes to dash back to the coach house, grab it, and return it to Daniela. Or I could save us all time.

"You prefer facts? How about this one: you sold a Sumatran tiger to an Oklahoma businessman last spring for five hundred thousand dollars."

Suddenly Daniela's expression changed; her posture shifted.

I had arrived at the final step of my plan. Up to this point, I had channeled Hollister's strength, the wisdom of Jerry, and the confidence of Camilo. Now I needed only one thing more: the courage of my mother.

I walked over to where Burley sat bound and gagged.

"Stop," Daniela commanded.

I kept walking. When I reached Burley, I removed the towel from her mouth. "Are you all right?" I patted her mountainous shoulder.

"Word to the wise: don't ever get hog-tied to a chair with nunchucks in your back pocket."

"I said stop!" Daniela waved her gun in my direction.

After untying Burley's hands, I freed her feet. Only then did I turn and face Daniela.

"You've lost, Daniela. It's over. I have the evidence to convict you and everyone you did your dirty business with."

"Impossible," she scoffed. "The laptop is nothing without the password."

"You sold a mountain gorilla to a Russian oligarch last April for a quarter million dollars."

"You know nothing!" She pushed back her shoulders, but her voice had lost its swagger. "You don't know what you're talking about."

"Two different people have copies of the accounting records. They have the names Barkingham Palace and D.R. Enterprises, along with the address of your mansion and warehouse, where, by the way, your boyfriend is cooling his heels in an animal crate." I checked my watch. "If Burley and Hollister and I don't show by eight AM, they will take everything they have to the police. So your move. What's it going to be?"

Daniela remained defiant. "If what you say is true, I will shoot you all."

Burley whispered, "Hayden, you sure you know what you're doing?"

I whispered back, "We're about to find out."

"You're right," I said to Daniela, "I'm no tough guy. I'm terrified, to tell you the truth. I don't have a plan for this part. I just know I'm not leaving here without my friends. Maybe you're a bit scared too. Maybe you don't know what to do either. Maybe at this moment, we have that in common.

You'll do what you do. But right now, I'm taking Burley, and we're going to the wine cellar to get Hollister."

Burley gave me the strangest look, then worked herself up and out of the chair. As many times as I'd stood next to this crazy wonderful woman, her massive size never failed to demand a moment of awe. Heading toward the corridor for the elevator, I took every step wondering if it would be the one where I'd hear the bang and feel what it was like to be shot. But as we made it safely out of the library and the shot never came, I realized I'd been right: Daniela was unsure of what her next move should be. But killing us wasn't it.

The elevator had only one button. The doors parted immediately. Funny the things you think about even in the most stressful of situations. Hollister was hardly petite; how would the three of us ever fit in this tiny compartment on the way back up?

Like curtains parting at the start of a show, the doors slid open, revealing a dazzling scene. Dazzling if wine is your thing. Thousands of bottles filled wooden racks that surrounded the oval subterranean cellar. At the room's center was a tasting table of glass with four barrels for legs. A small army cot sat against the far wall. Hollister was lying on the canvas, a leg shackled by a chain, which was looped through a large eye hook bolted into the wall.

"This must be hell on earth for you," Burley said to her. "You love wine but don't get to taste a drop."

Hollister sat up. "I'm taking as much as I can carry with me. I've had plenty of time to pick out the bottles I want."

We both ran to her and smothered her—well, Burley did—in a hug.

"I need to go back upstairs, find something to break you free," I said.

Burley grabbed and held my shoulder. "Sometimes, Hayden, you have to make do with what you've got." She reached behind her and pulled out her stainless-steel nunchucks. "Stand back." She didn't have to say it twice.

Hollister raised a hand. "Burl, baby, I appreciate what you've got in mind, but—"

Burley hooted an earsplitting laugh. "My aim's good, but not *that* good." She bent down to where the chain met the wall, grabbed the hook with both hands, and yanked. The hook, along with the bolts and a chunk of cedar paneling, pulled free. She coiled up the chain and the rest of the mess and handed it to Hollister. "Hold this."

"Let's get the hell out of Dodge," Hollister said.

I hadn't been wrong about the elevator ascent worry. While we managed to squeeze inside, we exceeded the weight limit. As I was last in, I hopped out. Although I was the most minimal contributor, the reduction of my 125 pounds did the trick. "See you in a few," I said as the doors closed on them.

Seconds later, I heard a chime, followed by a rumble of feet, then the elevator descending. When the doors opened to let me out on the first floor, I expected to see Hollister and Burley standing there. But they weren't. It had been less than a minute since they'd gone up ahead of me, and in that short time they'd vanished.

Chapter Forty-Four
PULL!

I ran down the corridor. I ran through the library, through the dining room, and into the kitchen. No sign of Hollister and Burley. They couldn't have gone far, and yet the house was enormous, so many doors and hallways, so many possibilities. Movement on the lawn caught my eye. Marching toward the dock were three figures: Burley and Hollister, followed by Daniela, who presumably still had a gun.

Daniela! She might not have had a plan before, but she had developed one, and I didn't like it one bit. The dock began to rock as Burley stepped onto the long wooden walkway leading to *Wild Child*. This was a problem—one that Daniela and I would see quite differently. For my part, I would need to talk her out of making a cluster of epic proportions even worse. For Daniela, she was about to discover I had the key to the boat.

Running across the grounds, I watched as Burley jumped aboard and nearly tipped the boat over. She lost her balance, toppled to the opposite side. The weight now on the starboard side, Hollister, still encumbered by the chain, jumped awkwardly onto the port side. Her attempt to balance the weight only increased the momentum of the boat's pitching.

A loud *pop!*

I froze. Had Daniela fired her gun? Burley tumbled overboard and into the water.

"No!" I screamed, and sprinted toward the boat.

Pop!

Daniela turned, but not in my direction. She was looking toward the coach house. As I kept running, I looked over my shoulder. Della was standing on the elevated deck, her arms outstretched, both hands grasping a pistol, pointed toward the dock. Who was she trying to shoot?

A third *pop!* Daniela fell into the water.

As I leaped onto the dock, Hollister was in the boat, leaning over the side, frantically trying to pull waterlogged Burley into the boat. I spun around to where Daniela had fallen into the bay, ready to jump in after her.

"Hayden, help!" Hollister screamed. "Burley can't swim!"

I pulled my eyes away from the air bubbles marking the spot where Daniela had gone under. I lunged for a rope and threw it to Hollister, who tossed it into the geyser of water Burley was creating with her desperate flailing.

"Grab the rope, Burley!" Hollister screamed. "Grab the rope!"

I jumped onto the boat beside Hollister. Immediately I could see that Burley was in full-on panic mode. Although the line was bobbing on the surface just a foot from her, she couldn't register Hollister's instruction.

"You'll have to pull us both in!" I said.

Hollister turned, shouted in my ear, "What?"

"When Burley grabs a hold of me, *pull!*"

I dove into the water. I'd read somewhere that a drowning person's desperation can cause them to drown their would-be savior, so I assumed Burley would grab me and pull me under. As long as I held on to my end of the rope, when Hollister reeled it in, she'd pull both Burley and me to the dock.

The instant I came within Burley's reach, I was shoved under, trapped beneath a three-hundred-pound mass of torso and limbs. I tightened my grip on the rope. *C'mon, Hollister, pull!* The rope jerked. Then again. We were inching our way back to the dock. Suddenly the thrashing above me stopped. I kicked to the surface. Burley draped her arms over the side of the boat. She gasped for air and wept. Where was Hollister? I hoisted myself onto the dock—not easy with water-heavy clothes—and collapsed in a shivering heap. I rolled onto my side and coughed. Salty water gurgled from my mouth and nose.

"Hayden!" The plea came from the other side of the dock. Hollister, her mohawk looking like a shark's fin cutting the surface, was fighting to keep her head above water while holding on to Daniela, who appeared unconscious. It didn't help that Hollister was also weighed down by the chain still clamped around her ankle. With Hollister pushing and me pulling, we got Daniela onto the dock.

It was only then that I saw the bullet wound. A reddish mixture of blood and water oozed from a hole in Daniela's shoulder. Hollister started CPR.

Daniela didn't have much time; I needed to call 911, but everyone's phone had just been submerged in the bay. Thank heavens some homes still had landlines.

Della was no longer standing on the coach house's deck, which was somewhat reassuring. I could only hope the lunatic didn't reappear before I made it across the lawn—where I'd be easy pickings—and safely inside the main house.

Chapter
Forty-Five
Three-Dollar Words

It couldn't be every day that a 911 operator got a call with so much to offer: a kidnapping, an armed animal smuggler shot by her employee, and a near drowning (times two). And for good measure, the would-be assassin was still on the loose somewhere at the scene, which was a multi-million-dollar waterfront island estate. I skipped the part about Burley's and my water aerobics; no reason to make the story more complicated than it already was.

My nose sniffed. Sweet, floral: *gardenia*.

I spun around.

"Now gall-darn it, Blaze, if you aren't a pesky little pest."

While I'd been calling for the police and EMTs, Della had stealthily entered the kitchen. She appeared dressed for a night out at the local steak house. She'd replaced the curlers and housecoat with a meticulously coiffed updo and a navy-blue jacket with a poodle lapel pin made of tiny crystal gemstones. She took a seat on one of the eight chrome-and-taupe leather barstools that fronted an island the length of my entire studio apartment. Peekaboo sat in her lap; the dog's front paws rested on the marble countertop next to the gun.

"Are you going to shoot me too?"

"Why, that's just silly, sweat pea. Why on earth would I want to go and do something like that?"

"You appear to be in a shooting mood."

"Goodness me, you make it sound like I was just popping off rounds willy-nilly."

"Okay, so what was your reason, then? Why try and kill Daniela?"

"Try? You mean she's still alive?" Della blinked, only the second occasion I'd seen her do so.

"I see you're disappointed."

"Hmm, am I?" She tapped a finger against her red-painted lips.

"I don't get it. Daniela was your fairy godmother. She made all your dreams come true. Fancy store, nice car, sweet setup here. Why do you live in the coach house, anyway? Who lives with their boss?"

"Servants, love bug. Servants live with their master." Della spoke in her telltale singsongy way, but I detected a hard edge in her voice that I'd never heard before. "Ms. Rodriquez isn't naturally trusting of others. Ms. Rodriguez prefers essential staff to reside nearby so she can monitor their movements and associations."

"Sounds like a cozy setup." I might expect a sarcastic smile with anyone else, but with Della, I got no reply.

"Why did you shoot Daniela?"

"A person can be expected to put up with only so much. Don't you agree?"

"Um, no. For the simple reason that I have no idea what you're talking about."

"No? I suppose you don't. First, it was that boy—"

"Camilo?"

Della repositioned the squirming Peekaboo on her lap. "No, no. Ryan. The moment I laid eyes on him, I knew he was trouble. A gold digger, we called them in my day. Mind you, I figured he wouldn't last long. Ms. Rodriguez may have been charmed by his appearance, but she wasn't one to tolerate slipshod work." Della paused, smoothed the lapels of her blazer. "That fancy boy prancing about the main house in his tighty-whities did fray my nerves something awful. He was even allowed to use Ms. Rodriguez's first name. Shameful. The last straw was when that three-legged gigolo had the unmitigated gall to start ordering me about. He simply had to go. No ifs, ands, or buts."

"Wait, wait, wait. Is that why you stole Camilo's laptop? So Ryan couldn't? You tried to, what? Get him in trouble with Daniela?"

"Ms. Rodriguez had concluded—all on her own, I might add—that Ryan had been sloppy. Under his watch, he had allowed Camilo to make copies of certain files. An utterly forbidden act. Ms. Rodriguez then tasked Ryan with retrieving the stolen property. I saw to it that he would fail in that task."

"Okay, let me get this straight. Ryan shows up. He's good-looking. He runs around the hallways of the mansion in his skivvies. He's doing the boss. I can see why that might be annoying, aggravating even, but why go to such lengths to get rid of him?"

"I have my pride. I created Barkingham Palace—no one else. When I sought to modify the business arrangement with Ms. Rodriguez, she refused to even consider my proposal. I wasn't raised to play second fiddle to anyone." Della gave Peekaboo a few strokes.

"Was it worth it? Selling out to the devil?"

Della lifted her padded shoulders, let them fall. "Some people quite naturally do what society might consider wrong. Pishposh. Who's to say? Good, bad, right, wrong. You can get stuck as a fur ball trying to guess what you ought to do, or you can simply do what is in your nature. That's what I do."

"That's like a textbook definition of a sociopath."

Della blinked furiously, as if static had blocked out her thoughts. After a few moments, she appeared to find a clear channel.

"Now don't you go and try to confuse me with your three-dollar words. It's a simple fact that doing the opposite of right isn't necessarily wrong. So many people all in a dither about political correctness—"

"You just tried to kill someone!"

Della gave me an annoyed look, though I got the sense it was for interrupting her and not because of what I'd said. She stared at me with those unblinking eyes, magnified by the thick lenses of her large, gold-rimmed frames. After a moment had passed, Della slid off the stool, tucked Peekaboo under an arm, and plucked the gun off the counter. "You take good care now."

She walked out of the kitchen as sirens sounded in the distance.

Chapter Forty-Six
Devil's Chew Toy

Jerry was sitting up in bed, a plastic breakfast tray in front of him. Cheerful banter from a morning television talk show filled the room.

"That looks good," I said, referring to his plate of bacon and eggs.

"Looks can be deceiving." With a bent finger, he pointed to the chair I had napped in during my last visit to the hospital. "Take a load off." He turned the volume down on the television.

"How are you feeling? They say the surgery went well."

"Oh, I won't be chasing Commander around the yard anytime soon, but all things considered, I will live to tell the tale."

"Speaking of tales . . ."

I spent the next hour telling Jerry a whopper of a story. Nurse Pete was on duty and on two separate occasions entered the room to check various monitors. On the first visit, he walked in just as I was saying, ". . . then Burley arrives and picks Ryan clean off the ground by his hair, drags him to the animal crate." On the second, I had progressed to the part where "Della fired in the direction of the boat. I wasn't sure who she was shooting at . . ."

When I had first met Nurse Pete, I had wondered if there might not be a spark between us. Overhearing the story I was telling Jerry, he refused even to make eye contact.

"So Commander is back where he belongs," Jerry said.

"At least until we get Camilo home. I'll be seriously bummed to give him up, though."

"But it's the right thing to do," Jerry said.

Slumping in the chair, I sighed. "Doing the right thing can be emotionally exhausting."

"Can be at that"—Jerry shifted his weight, sat taller in the bed—"but what's the alternative, Hayden? Doing wrong when you know better will chew you up, hollow you out."

"You think so?"

"I'll answer that with some surprisingly wise words I heard once. Surprising because of the source: my grandfather. Name was Archibald. The man was an ass. I was only a child, mind you, but still, I had his number. Archibald was a preacher in the Midwest and traveled from town to town with a circus tent and my grandmother in tow. A 'revival preacher,' they were called in those days. Whenever my grandparents were within driving distance, my father would pack up us kids and we'd go listen to old Archibald. The sermons were your garden-variety fire and brimstone. Trapped under that hot tent for hours was hell on earth for us kids. If you're paying attention, that is what you call irony."

"Why just your father?"

Jerry slipped a grin. "My mother didn't cotton to old Archibald. Let's just say he had antiquated notions of a woman's role in the world, and my mother wasn't buying it." He gave a dismissive wave of his hand. "Story for another day. Anyway, on one particularly miserable day when I was stuck on a wooden chair beneath that infernal tent, Archibald surprised the hell out of me by saying something that rang true. So much so that it's stuck with me to this day. He said there are three kinds of people in this world: those that do their best to do right, those that do wrong because they don't know any better, and then some do wrong despite knowing what's right. That last type of person was bound for hell, of course. But until then, life on earth wouldn't be much better. That person would live each day as the devil's chew toy."

"What kind of a name is Archibald, anyway?"

Jerry frowned. "Is that all you took away from my story?"

I laughed. "I'm just joking. It's a good story. I might have to borrow it."

"Public domain. Enjoy." He looked down at his tray, grimaced. "Want any eggs?"

"They look awful; besides, they're cold." I pulled the backgammon board from my book bag. "Now, you prepared to get your ass whipped, old man?"

Jerry smiled. "Big words, little man. Care to make a wager?"

"Hmm." I stroked my chin. "Last slice of bacon. Unless that's too rich for your blood."

"Ha. Cholesterol medicine is just one of many potions coursing through my veins. I accept your challenge."

I cleared the breakfast tray and dragged the guest chair closer to Jerry's bed. With the board set up, I handed him the dice. "Best of three?"

"How about best of five? I'm not going anywhere."

Chapter Forty-Seven

Mates on Dates, Post No. 24

MATES ON DATES: Wishful Thinking

Recently I met a guy I like. Oddly, I learned what I know about him mostly through a crazy series of events that I won't begin to get into here. That could be the subject of a book. Who knows? Someday! For now, I'll concentrate this post on my feelings about meeting him again. After all, this is a gay dating blog, so I'll try my best to stick to the theme and make this relevant.

Again, it's important to understand that I've spent little time with this guy. Let's call him Blaze for now (perhaps if it works out, I'll reveal his real name). The truth of the matter is, Blaze and I spent only one night together. But it was terrific—and no! not just because of the cuddling (which was ☺), but because he was nice (see my former post, no. 22, on this topic).

"Connection" is something I'm increasingly seeing guys looking for. I think this is a positive sign. Perhaps

the ease with which apps allow us to find sexual part-
ners has made us all less horny but a lot more lonely.
I know I'm seeking a connection. I want someone to
argue with about what we'll have for dinner and what
show we'll watch afterward. I want to end a day by
saying, "Nightie night, babe." I want to wake up to
the sound of the shower, thinking, *Blaze had better
hurry it up, or I'll be late for work.*

You see, guys, I've got a severe case of wishful
thinking. And I'm finding it both exhilarating and ter-
rifying. But isn't that what we should be striving for?
Of course, I recognize that not all dates can promise
such excitement. Too many dates end in disappointment, some even in disaster. But here's the question:
why do we keep at it?

I believe it's because we are alive with wishful
thinking. We all want the same thing. We want to
find that one other person who is reading this and
nodding his head. That one other person who is meant
for us.

Is Blaze the one for me? I'll find out soon enough.
But if he's not, I'll keep looking. I hope you do too.

Till next time, I'm Hayden.

And remember, if you can't be good, be safe!

Chapter Forty-Eight

Five Days Later

"Pecan sticky buns," Burley announced. "New recipe, Madagascar sugar. Tell me what you think." Wielding a long set of aluminum tongs, she placed a caramelized mound of decadence onto a saucer, slid it across the counter. "I'll give a holler when you and Queen B's espressos are ready."

"Thanks. By the way, how's the new baker working out?"

Burley turned back toward the kitchen. Sarah Lee was busily kneading dough with the focused determination of Commander chasing a stick. "She's a cubic zirconia in the rough. Reminds me of most karaoke singers at Hunters. More enthusiasm than talent. Though she does what needs doing well enough. Knows the basics. Sweet girl."

Semisweet was as far I was willing to round up, and only in the past few days. When Sarah Lee had phoned the police for me after Commander had been taken, she'd said that I owed her. She was right. I'd not have gone out of my way to issue any payback, but when Burley had asked if I might know of anyone who would be interested in "getting up to their ears in batter," I had remembered my neighbor's claim of being a half-decent home baker.

Inexplicably, Burley and Sarah Lee had hit it off. The upside for me had been an about-face in neighbor relations, or as Burley had put it, "dealing with the chick next door went from frosty to frosting."

Burley waved off my attempt to pay. I carried the sticky bun to what had become Hollister's and my regular table. Hollister busily tapped the keyboard of her laptop with unwavering concentration. I appreciated her focus. We were on a new mission.

"What's the latest?" I asked, taking my chair.

Hollister glanced up, smiled. "Six thousand. More is bound to come in, but I say we don't wait. Book our tickets now."

"Yeah, I only have two more weeks before the start of school. We need to get going so I'm back in time."

Daniela had just been released from the hospital and transferred to the county jail, where she—along with Ryan— awaited arraignment. In her attempt to reduce her future sentence, she'd provided information on her operation in addition to the accounting records Camilo had copied to the hard drive. The FBI was tight-lipped about their investigation, but through Detective Zane, I'd learned they were confident that most, if not all, of the stolen animals would be found and relocated to protected environments.

No longer needing to safeguard her business, Daniela had also been forthcoming about her parents' address in Onoto, a town of twelve thousand in the eastern Venezuelan state of Anzoátegui. Our GoFundMe campaign to pay for a lawyer and the other expenses involved with bringing Camilo home had raised enough money for Hollister and me to fly to Caracas to find him and begin the process. Having never been outside the country, I was nervous but stoked to be traveling with Hollister. We made a good team.

Of course, the idea of seeing Camilo made me stupid with excitement. For a while there, I'd thought he was involved in some criminal activity. Then as the days passed and there still had been no sign of him, I'd feared he was dead. We'd soon be face-to-face.

Checking my expectations, I understood that we hadn't shared a long-smoldering attraction or even a glance back after passing each other on the street. We'd shared one single night—and only because of a freak accident. Was I deluding myself? Was I setting myself up for a fall? As protection from disappointment, I told myself to expect only friendship, as if that would be equally satisfying.

Besides working on the fund-raising effort, I hadn't seen Hollister much since her rescue from the estate. She'd been spending her evenings with Mysti. "Commit or split," was how she'd put it. I had doubts about their partnership, but what did I know about making a relationship work? I was still just trying to get one started. On the upside for Hollister, she had won a prestigious commission to design dining room tables and chairs for some high-end retailer, the type of store I could never afford to shop in. Perhaps living on a school teacher's paltry salary would one day get me down, but for the moment, I was happily hanging out with friends, playing backgammon with Jerry, running in the park with Commander, and working on a blog post for *Mates on Dates*. I'd also made an effort to spend more time with Aunt Sally—who had returned home after getting news of Jerry's hospitalization—though with the constant praying and references to "God's plan," I was already backtracking on that commitment.

Burley's near-death experience had made her "reflect on the mortalitude (she insisted this was a real word) of life." She was entrusting the bakery to Sarah Lee for a month and traveling to Tibet. When asked why Tibet, the only explanation she would give was, "When you spell it backward, it's Tebit." After a while, Hollister and I had stopped asking. We were planning a bon voyage party for her this coming weekend. The event was trending on Twitter. Even Tanner and Paul had RSVP'd, though how they'd gotten the invite, I didn't know. They'd texted me to ask if there'd be a lot of hot babes at the party. I'd answered truthfully, figuring they wouldn't be too disappointed when they saw all the free booze.

The oddest thing to have happened was something that hadn't: the reappearance of Della Rupert. It seemed I was the last person to have seen her that day when she'd walked out of the kitchen with Peekaboo and a gun. As soon as I'd heard sirens, I'd raced to the front of the mansion to direct the EMTs to the boat dock. The large gate with the letters *D* and *R*, which I'd come to realize were for Camilo's sister and not the proprietress of Barkingham Palace, had been left open. I'd not seen Della drive away in the Cadillac, but later, when the police searched the property, they'd found neither Della nor the car. Her whereabouts remained unknown.

"Order up!" Burley shouted from the bakery side of the counter. I went to collect our espressos.

"That's your single"—she pointed to the cup on the right—"and that there is Hollister's double." She slid me a wink.

I returned a two-fingered salute. Her secret was safe with me.

Acknowledgments

Part 1—Good Fortune Smiles
I believe that a stroke of luck—right place, right time sort of thing—is an ingredient in most success. My good fortune arrived when Ben LeRoy and Sara J. Henry read *Devil's Chew Toy*, argued for its acquisition, and Matt Martz agreed to take it on. That's how writers get published, of course, but I suspect few authors enjoy the double luck of landing in the hands of someone as remarkably supportive as Sara J. Henry. I am profoundly grateful for not only her skillful editing but for championing this novel in more ways than I can recount. Ben LeRoy deserves my hearty thanks for his wisdom, kindness, and being a positive force on the planet. My thanks also go to Matt Martz and the Crooked Lane team of Rebecca Nelson, Melissa Rechter, Rema Badwan, and Meghan Deist. A special two-scoops shout-out goes to Madeline Rathle for her partnership in all things marketing and publicity.

Part 2—Head Down, Spirits Up
Anyone who has written something as long as a novel knows it is chiefly a matter of keeping at it. As Jerry might say, "You'll

never reach 75,000 words if you keep getting up to play with the cat." (Sidenote: our cat, Mr. Chomps, is a mighty powerful distraction!) But commitment alone doesn't cut it; one needs time and space. And so, immeasurable thanks go to my super trooper partner, Brian Custer, for giving me the support and room to *tap, tap, tap* away.

Encouragement to a writer is as gratifying as a vigorous belly scratch is to Commander. Along this journey, Brett Goldston, Tanya Egan Gibson, and Matt Hope provided valuable reviews and appreciated attaboys. If you haven't yet visited me at robosler.com, you must! There you will witness the stellar design of my good pal Jennifer Bartlett, who also created a delightful bounty of promotional materials to support this book. Also, a big thanks to Stephanie Krimmel for her web-tech wizardry.

Part 3—Better With a Rainbow
In closing, another belief: this world is WAY more colorful and vibrant thanks to each of you who identify as lesbian, gay, bisexual, trans, queer, or other gendered or oriented. I did my best—inspired by the iconic novels of Amistead Maupin (I tip my hat, sir!)—to create within these pages a world reflective of the friendships and big-heartedness I see every day in your—*in our*—community. This story is for you, our allies, and anyone with a soft spot for pocket gays, Black girls with Mohawks, and gentle giants.